MW01264556

HIS WILL

as told by Buddy Olsen

A CHRISTIAN NOVEL

Written by
Kent L. Larson

INFINITY
PUBLISHING

Copyright © 2011 by Kent L. Larson

ISBN 0-7414-6419-5

Printed in the United States of America

This is a work of fiction. Names, characters, places, and incidents either are the product of the author's imagination or are used fictitiously. Any resemblance to actual events or locales or persons, living or dead, is entirely coincidental.

Published March 2011

INFINITY PUBLISHING
1094 New DeHaven Street, Suite 100
West Conshohocken, PA 19428-2713
Toll-free (877) BUY BOOK
Local Phone (610) 941-9999
Fax (610) 941-9959
Info@buybooksontheweb.com
www.buybooksontheweb.com

To the Honor of my Lord
Jesus Christ

Fulfilling the Dream

1957

"You're a southpaw!" Uncle Harry coughed in disbelief as he fell forward. Sounding like a crashing hickory, he likewise bounced off the rich black soil. From a short distance, my family and I gawked in amazement before our astonishment quickly changed to concern. I could hear Uncle Harry gasping for air as we ran to his side. Only the whites of his eyes were visible; his irises had floated back into their sockets. Slowly bringing him to an upright position, Dad let him catch his breath. "Where," sputtered Uncle Harry, "did that come from?"

Rapidly analyzing her brother's condition, Mom exclaimed, "I'll run and grab a cup of water from the pump!" After drinking several cupfuls, Uncle Harry caught his breath enough to announce, "We're going to name that throw Buddy's Blazer!"

Today was different. This return rocketed squarely into his chest. Uncle Harry's initial throw had flung the oversized, hand-me-down glove off of my left hand and onto the ground. This time I grabbed the dirtied red stitched hardball with my unencumbered left hand and *naturally* threw it back to him. For the first time ever, I too had thrown my own fast ball! He and the others suddenly discovered I had been throwing with the wrong arm all along.

As they did typically each Sunday, Uncle Harry and Aunt Amanda had come to the farm for dinner that sunny Easter Day.

During previous Sunday afternoon games, Uncle Harry was regularly disheartened when I would pick up the

1

dropped ball resting between my feet and return it wildly. Nothing was out of range, even Mom's chicken pen.

Standing by his car door before he and Aunt Amanda headed home to Chicago, Uncle Harry commented, "You know Buddy, if you are as stubborn as your mom was as a kid, I'll bet you can overcome this obstacle too – even in a world dominated by right-handers."

"I will!" Then, wrapping my short arms around his hips, I said, "Uncle Harry, when I grow up, I want to be just like you… and a catcher too!" Recalling her older brother's past all too well, Mom visibly cringed at my innocence.

Waving goodbye, I vowed in my mind that next weekend I'd show him this was not just a fluke.

Indeed, I continued where I left off the following Sunday, and every Sunday thereafter, progressing to where I actually caught the ball in my right-handers glove, now worn incorrectly on my right-hand. Smoothly transferring the ball to my left hand, I accurately threw the "Blazer" back to Uncle Harry. Being the former baseball professional that he was, Uncle Harry easily handled all my throws.

Over the summer Uncle Harry was never hit in the chest again; however, spells of wheezing and shortness of breath became frequent as the baseball action intensified. Sometimes he asked to take a break, his raspy coughs coming from deep within his chest.

To my young eyes, Uncle Harry was the greatest! Everything – every end or coffee table, knick knack shelf, and even the big RCA tube radio in Grandpa and Grandma Carson's living room – was covered with his photos. With natural athleticism, he had been able to succeed at any sport; the call of the diamond was his passion. As a youth, he excelled in the sport. He became a local legend with his hard throwing, accurate arm and ferocious hitting. But now, with Little League, Pony League, Babe Ruth, Legion Ball, and semi-pro ball all in the past, it was just he and I in our little fantasy games: "Catcher to second base, the runner slides, he's *out!* What a great play by Olsen! This lefty catcher's accuracy is something else!" Later, "Looking for Olsen's sign, Carson winds, he fires ... SSSTERIKE three! Olsen has called a perfect game!" Uncle Harry's imagination was as wild as my right-handed throws had been.

⌂

This Easter Sunday morning had begun like all other Sundays. Today's "good clothes" wardrobe started with a well-starched shirt, loose-fitting wool "church" pants, brightly polished shoes, and of course the obligatory clip-on tie. The old, musty smelling, blue Dodge sedan was promptly loaded at 8:45 a.m. for the short drive into town, where the red brick church stood as a mighty fortress on the corner of Cherry and Church Streets. Grandpa and Grandma Carson always arrived ahead of us, patiently waiting on the curb to look us over before we entered God's House. Grandma's strong perfume, however, lingered with me the rest of the day, frequently setting off a brief sneezing spell.

Sunday School classes were held in the church basement before worship. The small cast iron bell tolled three times at precisely 10:00 a.m. – one for each day Jesus lay in the tomb. When Sunday School was dismissed, all families congregated quietly in the Sanctuary. The larger bronze bell tolled loudly as the opening hymn began. Pulling the large, coarse rope, the bell ringer knew exactly how many times the clapper was to strike the sound bow – one for each day of the month.

There were always several "choice" pews for the worship service. When the choir was singing, it was the short hardwood pew to the right of Aunt Ella, Mom's older sister. She was the church organist. There was also the corner seat in the balcony if you wanted to see all of the ritual. But to get permission from Dad to sit in any of the choice pews, you had to have shown exemplary behavior during the past week and completed all your daily chores – without being asked even once. Sunday School was the final test for the week. Even if I made it through the week, if I slipped up during Sunday School, Dad sat on my left, Mom on my right – same pew, different week.

Aunt Ella proudly displayed her talents on her new Wurlitzer pipe organ on this Easter Sunday. No longer did her thighs strain from pumping the pedals of the old reed organ or its short-lived successor, the Hammond electric. Aunt Ella herself had successfully spearheaded St. Bartholomew's Organ Replacement Project, with its rumored $25,000 price tag.

Heavenly notes escaped out the slightly opened, stained glass windows. This Easter morning's hymns, "The Strife is O'er, the Battle Done," "Christ the Lord is Risen Today," and "Beneath the Cross of Jesus" were easily heard as far as a block away. Sadly, Aunt Ella's natural talent at the keyboard didn't move the stoic congregation to the thundering applause I thought she deserved. Unlike southern congregations, Pastor Buchanan's flock displayed no emotion – almost as if some of them couldn't hear! Tradition meant there were no shouts of praise, hand waving, speaking out, or laughter. Of course, that included children's behavior. No turning around, fussing, snickering and no water or bathroom breaks unless you appeared close to passing out.

From his carved wood pulpit high above the pews, Pastor Buchanan bellowed: "Christ is alive in the Spirit! Congregation, do you hear His voice?" His taut, weathered face never relaxed. His satin black cloak was always the same. Only his vestment and the altar parament colors were changed with the church season – Easter Sunday they were white.

Even on this warm Sunday morning, Pastor Buchanan, a large man of great endurance, did not take a glass of water to the pulpit. However, he did allow the congregation to discretely cool themselves with hand fans provided by Mattson Funeral Home. An Easter tradition, there in the pews' hymn book racks were new fans, with a picture of the resurrected Jesus with an empty tomb in the background. On the backside, a Psalm verse was printed along with the funeral home's logo and phone number. The flat wooden handle reminded me of a doctor's tongue depressor.

Week after week it became evident to Dad and Mom that the congregation was becoming uninspired and lifeless. It became evident to me, in later years, that Pastor Buchanan's strong biblical teaching had indeed provided the cornerstone for many a solid foundation.

⌂

Traditionally, on the Saturday before Palm Sunday, Mom went out to the chicken coop to begin the task of killing the young chickens culled for slaughter. Only her best laying hens and prime roosters survived the butchery. The horrible smell of water soaked feathers permeated the air as the headless bodies were dunked into and pulled back out of the barrel of boiling water. The smell of burning chicken skin and feathers was only slightly masked by the odor of Dad's cigar. Dad normally smoked cigarettes, but on this occasion, he cleverly used the burning stogie to singe off the small remaining pinfeathers.

Dad and Mom were usually busy completing these and other spring chores during Holy week. However, they always completed their work so as to honor the Day of Rest and enjoy the homemade food and fellowship of our frequent Sunday guests. It seemed Uncle Harry and Aunt Amanda made the hour and a half drive from Chicago just so they could smell the fresh country air and drink our ice-cold well water pumped deep from the aquifer below. Mom's baking appeared to be a secondary draw.

With Grandpa and Grandma Carson no longer living on their own farm, and renters occupying the farmhouse, Uncle Harry's retreat was now our place. Curiously, however, Uncle Harry and Aunt Amanda's visits never coincided with culling the flock and plucking the headless chickens. They preferred to enjoy the food and bypass the work it took to prepare it. In retrospect, who could blame them for not wanting to view those bloody, headless bodies flopping around the barnyard – especially before sitting down to eat! Finding Mom alone in the kitchen I asked her once, "Why, even on Easter Sunday, does Uncle Harry get here after church?" She didn't answer the question and quickly asked me to grab some napkins for the table.

Mom served her perfectly baked spring chicken, mashed potatoes, beets, and carrots. She hung her red-checked apron on the kitchen door knob; her hair was slightly mussed as she sat exhausted in the chair nearest the kitchen.

"Sis, you really out did yourself," Uncle Harry announced. Taking a gulp from his large water glass, he declared, "I have traveled many a mile for your good well water! Now that the food's finally ready, let's eat this grub!"

Dad tersely interjected, "Let us pray!" I saw a tear running down Mom's cheek – she had given it her all. Curious as to whether Uncle Harry prayed or not during the blessing, I peeked at him and saw that he indeed had his eyes closed... *but...* Dad hadn't! This meant I could forget about the choice seats in the balcony next week.

⌂

After we were all in bed one early summer Sunday night, the phone began to ring. After several rings, I could hear Mom from their bedroom below stumbling to safely make her way toward the tall table by the kitchen wall. "Did you make it back home?" she asked. I knew it was Uncle Harry; he always called just after they returned home. With that assurance, I slowly drifted off to sleep.

From the kitchen the next morning I overheard: "Leif, when Harry called last night, he told me why it would be virtually impossible for us to find a left-handed catcher's mitt. He said there were very few left-handed catchers because it is believed they cannot throw around right-handed batters. I asked him what difference that made. He explained the sport was dominated by right-handed batters and it is believed by most experts, a left-handed catcher would need extra time to step out of the box to throw out a first base runner heading for second. He also said that a play at the plate would be to a left-hander's disadvantage because his mitt containing the ball could be away from an opponent sliding into home. I told Harry that we'd either train him to use his right arm, or if he wants to play baseball as a lefty, he'll just have to play some other position."

Dad shook his head, laughing at Mom's optimism, and said, "Anna, I don't think we can train him. I've seen too many of his balls end up in the chicken coop!"

There were no hand-me-down gloves for left-handers at all, much less a left-handed catcher's mitt. But, lucky for me, September and my sixth birthday would arrive in a few months. My birthday present was somewhat predictable. The nearby Sears store had only one left-handed glove in stock. The golden leather fielder's mitt was branded with Yankee shortstop Phil Rizzuto's signature. To make it even more unusual, it only had three fingers plus the thumb. The J.C. Higgins model number 4231 felt like catching a ball with a waffle. More importantly however, it fit neatly over my right hand.

September also meant that leisurely kindergarten half-days were replaced by the full days of First Grade. My class doubled in size as both the morning and afternoon kindergarten classes were combined into one. Ours was a large, low-ceilinged, first floor corner classroom in the old, turn-of-the-century brick schoolhouse. The steel frame desks, with their attached wood swivel chairs and lift top writing surfaces, all neatly faced the long, three-paneled blackboard. Fall also brought the distinctive smell of the school's sooty coal furnace. Chalk dust and coal fumes began to make breathing more difficult.

○

In retrospect, I remember this as a time when locals smiled and waved at each other as they passed on the road – a traditional greeting of their rural forefathers as they drove their wagons along the furrowed earth. Our county was blessed with rich black topsoil and plentiful rains. There was no need for irrigation even in the driest of years. Large tracts of land could be farmed especially by families where sons had inherited and continued to work alongside their fathers. Families without sons, or where the sons had no interest in continuing the occupational tradition, leased their acreage to those who made the choice to continue farming from one generation to the next. This was Grandpa and Grandma Carson's circumstance, since Uncle Harry had no desire to be a farmer. World War II veterans, now reaching their mid-thirties, were expanding their families. More mouths to feed meant more land was needed to produce an income.

Modern diesel engines replaced steam locomotives. Bright steel Zephyr trains zoomed by the foraging, range-raised cattle. In turn, the cattle responded wildly to the whistles and resulting wind draft. However, fewer and fewer open slat railroad boxcars could be seen standing along the backside of the feed lot pens on the outskirts of town. Crops were quickly replacing cattle.

Cash crop acreage, such as corn and oats, was expanding as pastureland was plowed under for this new trend in farming. The risks of price fluctuations were acceptable because cash crop farming took less time and physical effort. Brightly colored machinery, distinguishing competing manufacturers, became more popular as each of these new inventions allowed the farmer to work long hours during the peak times of planting and harvesting. It did however have a drawback; new machinery would not tire like its predecessor, the draft horse. Many farmers lost limbs – or lives – to accidents that were the result of becoming exhausted after working long hours. Now with more time on their hands, some farmers began to seek more social activities. Work became more seasonal with the introduction of modern farming methods. Despite the annual predictable pessimism of naysayers, the harvest of 1957 was plentiful.

◌

About three inches shorter than Aunt Ella, Uncle Marvin was a well-to-do businessman who owned the feed lot as well as the meat locker and market. Just before Christmas he purchased Providence State Bank from the founder's family. He was the only one around who wore a cowboy hat wherever he went. It made him look taller. "Do you wear that cowboy hat to bed?" I joked with him as I snuggled beneath his wide brim. He laughed, "I'll tell you if you tell me – do you always wear that old ball cap to bed?" Turning red, because I did, I was embarrassed to tell him the truth.

Having no children of their own, Uncle Marvin and Aunt Ella spoiled us at Christmastime. Uncle Marvin's wealth was apparent when we exchanged presents. Aunt Ella made sure their presents were always neatly wrapped in multi-colored paper, wound with matching ribbon and topped with a fancy bow. Dad and Mom were noticeably disappointed when I opened Uncle Marvin's gift. Inside the box was a Ford replica Tonka truck – much fancier than the pale green International model I had received from Dad and Mom early that Christmas morning. The Tonka model pulled a horse trailer containing two miniature Palominos. The pickup bed was covered with a removable topper camper complete with a rear door and removable tailgate – all painted with high gloss beige enamel. "Buddy, both Harry and I looked to find a left-handed catcher's mitt for you. Yesterday, after I left the Stockyards, I looked on Chicago's south side. Earlier this week, I looked in Peoria as well. The two I found were for righties; I guess they don't make them for southpaws." Pausing, Uncle Marvin then laughingly added, "I hope you like your truck." I later overheard him say to Dad, "Sorry for getting him a toy truck too, it was about the only thing left on the shelf."

Once we got home, I played with the International much more. Although very plain compared to the Tonka truck, the International, using two small axle springs, had front wheels that actually steered. More importantly, its simplicity was a reflection of my parents' sacrificial love for me.

$$\bigcirc$$

Although the life of a tenant farmer did have its ups and downs, Dad and Mom always seemed to have the right provisions at the right time. Our clothes were clean and crisply ironed thanks to Mom's prized, and one-of-a-kind, mangle. Food was plentiful and our house was warm in winter. We soon learned that not everyone led such a sheltered life.

1958

"You won't be coming out today?" I heard Mom say. I could see the lights in the barn; Dad was already milking. Her tone turned exuberant, "Yippee!! Of course! We'll be on our way shortly after Sunday School. We need to hurry and get everyone ready. No, don't tell me how you got them. I don't want to know! Goodbye!" I sensed her excitement; however, I hadn't seen her act like this before. Through the bedroom floor grill I could see directly to the kitchen below. She was jumping up and down, excitedly dancing back and forth across the kitchen floor. Mom truly loved baseball as much as Uncle Harry.

Seeing her quickly making snacks for the trip to Chicago, Mom stopped long enough to yell up the dark stairway, "Kids, it's time to get up! We'll need to leave church early. You'll go to Sunday School but we'll take off for Chicago directly after that. We won't be going to the worship service. Uncle Harry has tickets for the Cubs' afternoon game." I guess she didn't realize her excitement had already awakened us. Maybe she was practicing for the game!

The Pittsburgh Pirates were in town, hoping to build on their early spring successes. With fair weather predicted, the Sunday game was expected to be a sellout. As I recall, the Cubs were struggling to improve their record during this early season match-up. Today's game was to be the series' rubber match.

The brick stadium seats were bustling with excited fans. We had seats on the third base side, just two rows up from the dugout. The cheering and jeering were as I had heard on

11

the radio except now I was a part of it. It was my first professional game; this Sunday, June 8th, the Cubs sealed the 4–0 shut out by holding the Pirates to just one hit – a broken bat single. The victory put the Cubs just one game below their immediate goal of .500 ball. We strolled to the car with renewed excitement and optimism.

Our return from Chicago's Wrigley Field took several unexpected turns. Uncle Harry had given Dad clear and precise directions for getting back to the main highway heading westward. For some reason we were taking an alternate route. Rather than driving straight west from the ballpark, Mom gave verbal directions to Dad, who methodically drove us in a southerly direction along Chicago's Miracle Mile toward the Loop. The drive along Lake Michigan's shoreline was spectacular. Towering above nearby buildings, the Prudential Building was easily recognizable with its bold red lettering and television antenna spike. Buckingham Fountain was foaming to full capacity. A cooling northerly breeze puffed the sails of the sleek yachts that dotted the clear blue water. Large numbers of couples, some pushing baby strollers, appeared to be enjoying their afternoon of rest.

Dad headed west just south of the Loop. Within a short distance, we came upon sprawling Cook County Hospital. Mom had completed her nurse's training there; she knew the area well. Just beyond the glitz of the Loop, real poverty had choked the surrounding area. Dad purposely drove at a snail's pace between stoplights. With our faces plastered against the back seat window glass, we were indeed viewing another world, one we were not familiar with at all. Several men stood at entrances to missions, some were sleeping on bus stop benches. A couple of flashily dressed men, along with what I later learned were prostitutes, walked down the sidewalks, laughing and whooping it up, holding tightly to their telltale, brown paper bags. Several times, brightly colored doors opened almost automatically as these couples swiftly moved indoors.

It was only after several more trips to Wrigley Field and other Chicago attractions that I understood what was going on and Dad and Mom's real purpose for these detours. They were subtly teaching us one of life's important lessons.

⌂

Sunday worship always revived Dad and Mom. Leaving church, walking down the concrete steps, Mom glowed as brightly as the harvest moon as she walked toward the car. Dad's outward expressions were much more subtle, but we could tell that he received as much inspiration from his brotherhood of men and Pastor Buchanan's preaching as Mom did from Aunt Ella's organ playing and the choral singing. Dad was much more inspired by the Word than the chanted liturgy. His favorite expression was: "The answer is the Word!"

Uncle Harry and Aunt Amanda's visits became briefer and more sporadic. Our hurried Sunday mornings gave way to lazy, restful afternoons. The entire family enjoyed an afternoon nap.

⌂

In retrospect, at about this time, I remember several local churches were making significant changes. Gone were the traditional black robes as new white or colorful cloaks were introduced. Local Catholics were hoping the Vatican would replace the traditional Latin Mass with English. Some churches began to hold more than one service, both Contemporary and Traditional, so families could spend leisure time together. Summer services were sometimes held informally out-of-doors.

Golf was introduced to the area with the newly formed Providence Country Club now occupying former pastures. On Sunday mornings, some fathers drifted towards the clubhouse rather than the church house.

⌂

The summer of 1958 was the first year my brother George was eligible for Little League baseball. George was born in December 1949, making him 8½ when the season began. He towered over all but a few of the other boys.

Recognizing his range and body strength, Orioles Coach Fox positioned right-handed George at third base. George could easily propel the ball to any base, even in the air, from any part of the diamond. He had the catlike reflexes required of a good third baseman. The left side of the diamond proved to be great positioning for his strong arm.

One Saturday morning in mid-August, before a large crowd of spectators, George completed one of baseball's rarest plays. The challenging Braves had loaded the bases in the bottom of the final inning. Although George's team had a comfortable three run lead, with bases loaded, the Braves now had a chance to deliver the Orioles a heartbreaking loss and take the league championship with it.

Ten year old Bill Schmidt was the Braves' most powerful batter. He was strong for his age and his upper body muscles were becoming clearly defined. Bill could easily power the ball over the corn cribbing fence located 120 feet from home plate; he had done it many times.

From my position behind the backstop, I could clearly see Bill rotate the bat's trademark toward me. I stared straight at the Hillerich and Bradsby "Louisville Slugger" brand. Knowing wooden bats required the trademark centered up, I yelled out, "Schmidty, turn your trademark up!" Whirling around on his rubber spikes, he yelled, "Shut up kid! You aren't old enough to know anything about baseball!"

With no one out, Orioles pitcher Larry Dreger threw a watermelon right into Bill's strength. Smack...crack! The sound of the shattering bat was as deafening as the hit ball itself. To a few, the two sounds were different. From his previous hits, the runners knew Bill had belted the game winner. George knew otherwise, the ball weakly fluttered over the third base bag. I heard him confidently say, "I've got it."

Then, like a jack-in-the-box, he leapt to his right and caught the harmless Texas leaguer. While putting a tag on the aggressive runner from second base, he lightly brushed the third base bag with his left foot and sauntered toward the dugout.

It took several seconds before the spectators realized that they may have just witnessed the only unassisted triple play they'd ever see. And it all seemed to happen in the blink of an eye. Even Umpire Fitzgerald paused a brief moment before waving both arms and announcing, "Game over!"

Bill Schmidt returned to the Braves' dugout with two slivers of broken ash. In an instant he hurled them toward the far corner of the dugout. His accompanying expletive shocked everyone within ear shot of his young and still high-pitched voice. Timidly, I continued to watch from behind the backstop. Having had a good chance to look at the broken handle that landed near my feet, it took me just a few seconds to discover that Bill had carelessly taped his already slightly splintered bat handle, upwards from the knob, with white medical tape. Dad's advice to George and me was: "Always wrap the shaft with glossy black electrical tape. And never try to reuse a splintered bat, even if it's your favorite. We'll buy a new one." Evidently, Bill had not received the same guidance from his father.

⌂

Throughout the dog days of summer, I continued to play catch with Uncle Harry; however, his and Aunt Amanda's visits became even more irregular. More and more, what had once been lively, talkative sessions between Mom and Uncle Harry became awkward for both. She continued to needle him about his loose living, nonexistent church attendance, and persistent coughing spells. Despite her encouraging him to attend church with us, Uncle Harry continued to arrive afterward. And, her intuition told her Uncle Harry's cough was a symptom of something worse.

Around the same time she started hearing wheezing from me. "I can taste the ragweed!" I would tell her. I frequently sneezed, sniffled, coughed, and scratched at my watery eyes. Sometimes, the periodic coughing lapsed into spells. Bending over for relief, on two occasions my face turned blue as the sea. Seeing my deteriorating condition, Mom tried several home remedies including hot, steaming lemonade and menthol vapor rub. The home remedies seemed to make me sluggish. If I had been laughing, a tightening in my chest was followed shortly by severe wheezing. Dr. Fitzgerald prescribed a thick, sour, grape-flavored cough medicine that tasted bad and made me nauseous!

Mom asked Dad to no longer smoke in the basement; however, she agreed he could still have his own smoking area in the machine shed. After milking, Dad entered the basement directly through the outside cellar doors. In the basement, he showered immediately. Finished, he changed into clean, house clothes, throwing the smoke and manure smelling clothes into the ringer washer tub she had readied. As episodes became more frequent, George went out of his way to make sure I did not over exert myself while doing chores. Mom eventually stopped all of my unnecessary outdoor activities as it became more and more difficult for me to inhale the hot humid air of late summer. Both Dad and Mom were puzzled by what was becoming a recurring event.

At twilight one evening, Mom joined Dad in the milk house just as he finished his twice daily milking chore. The small whitewashed building adjacent to the barn contained the cream separator and stainless steel cooler. Peering through my bedroom window facing the barn, the single incandescent light projected eerie silhouettes back through the flyspecked milk house window. I was only able to view what appeared to be an emotional conversation. I finally gave in to drowsiness and laid my head on my soft feather pillow and fell asleep quickly.

⌂

Mom's intuition and training as a nurse led her to believe it was time to take immediate measures. She announced one evening some weeks later after the killing frost and the harvest was in full swing, "I'm not going to see that kid suffer anymore! I'm going to take him to see a specialist." Dad and Mom had no employer paid medical insurance. The harvest would bring in much needed cash. They knew they would be footing the doctor's bill out of their own pockets. Dad confirmed his suspicion. "I wondered why you'd been visiting the town library so frequently." We later learned she had reviewed the symptoms associated with various respiratory ailments – including tuberculosis. Later, she confirmed she had made an appointment with a specialist in Chicago for Wednesday, September 24th.

Mom and I made the trek alone. Grandpa Carson told Mom to drive his new Dodge the two hours it would take from our farm. Mom knew there wouldn't be a moldy smell in his cars – he bought new cars so often the mold never had a chance to grow! Even though she was not accustomed to the busy streets, she showed no signs of being nervous.

Dr. Moeller's office was located on Winnetka Road in a well-to-do part of the City. Once inside the large edifice, and after walking by a richly appointed drug store and an adjacent corridor, we proceeded up the moving stairs. Mom, sensing my anxiety over my first escalator ride, gently grasped my right hand and helped me onto the rapidly moving tread. A wood placard directed us toward Dr. Moeller's office, at the end of a long, well lit, white plastered hallway. Only Mom could pronounce the various medical specialties written on the frosted glass of each office door we passed.

Suite 344, set apart from the others, read: Dr. Abram I. Moeller, M.D., clearly stenciled, just like the others before it. We soon realized Suite 344 was likely chosen by Dr. Moeller because it was removed from the other suites. After walking through the first door, just off to the right, we entered a second door leading to the Waiting Room. At first the room was deathly quiet. The silence was soon broken by loud wailing and crying. Somewhat unnerved, Mom and I proceeded to the receptionist's window, at the far end of a line of chairs. Mom's warm handhold provided comfort for both of us.

The stiff-backed, mahogany chairs added to the stark, sterile atmosphere of the office. My hands remained clammy, my mouth was parched. The large white room felt as cold as snow. Anxiety engulfed my thoughts. After a brief waiting period, at precisely 9:00 a.m., a door opened and a nurse called out, "Mrs. Olsen." Motioning us through the door, she escorted us down the hallway to Patient Room 8. The room contained a padded exam table, stiff backed chair, desk, and a frosted glass fronted instrument cabinet. After a few opening questions, the nurse asked me to remove my shirt; she then dressed me in an open-backed smock. The smock was as cold as the exam room. Why it was open backed soon became evident. Just then the wailing and crying in the adjacent room abruptly stopped…little did I know it was soon to begin in Room 8!

I was then ordered by the stern nurse to lie on my stomach on the exam table. Even the vinyl cover was cold! Once again, Mom's comforting hand assured me everything was going to be all right.

Positioned so I was looking away from the door, I heard his accented voice as he entered the room. After a brief conversation with the nurse, Dr. Moeller put his large warm hand on top of Mom's and mine. In a gentle tone, he described the tests as a series of skin pricks. With each prick, an irritant would be injected under the skin. He told us the most significant irritants would cause a reaction that could be identified, measured, and catalogued. After receiving twenty-four small needle pricks on my back, although they felt to me more like large piercing spikes, my crying and wailing slowly came to an end when Dr. Moeller's nurse began rubbing a soothing ointment onto my skin. My back no longer felt as if it was on fire. She then gave me a refreshing drink of cold water.

It seemed like an eternity, but after I settled down the nurse told Mom we could leave the room. Dr. Moeller stopped us in the hallway and said, "The preliminary results will be mailed to Dr. Fitzgerald in about two days." His final statement, however, appeared to be most upsetting to Mom: "We'll see you again next week." Mom hoped it would only take one trip to Chicago. She knew the second trip and appointment would be an unexpected expense.

Walking down the hall, we ran into Nurse Dora who said, "It's so good to see you, Anna. I'm sorry I wasn't able to meet with you and Buddy first. I was tied up longer than I expected. Hopefully, next time we can spend time talking about the good old days rather than your son's health. I really miss your parents' farm. After you wrote to me, Dr.

Moeller informed me that he will not charge you for the follow-up visits. Don't forget to stop in to see Dad!"

Composing herself, Mom could only say, "Oh, thank you!" With that, Nurse Dora said goodbye to her loyal friend and former college roommate.

Prior to going into the doctor's office, Mom and I had jointly agreed upon the reward for our visit to the specialist. Mom took my quivering hand as we walked out of Suite 344 and directly to the moving stairs and the soda fountain awaiting us at the bottom of the two-story ride.

"Hi, Mr. Balbach." Turning around, the tall golden-haired man in a bright white jacket beamed as he said, "Well, Anna! Good to see you! What'll you have – the usual?"

"Of course, one large banana split with double hot fudge on the chocolate scoop! Buddy is feeling rather nauseous; a few spoonfuls of strawberry ice cream will probably be enough for him." Mr. Balbach echoed the orders to his soda jerk.

Just as we finished, pharmacist Balbach returned to the soda fountain remarking, "It seems like so long ago when you and Dora would come in to get an ice cream treat. You know she's worked for Dr. Moeller since he emigrated from Germany 15 years ago." Tearfully he told us, "She has taken good care of me since her mother died. I am so proud of her. I'm sure your parents are proud of you, too! Say hi to them for me. Don't make it so long between visits next time. As usual, these are on me!"

Once home, Mom quickly announced she needed a good sleep after the day's drive. "Leif, I'll fill you in in the morning," Mom said as the bedroom door closed. When I crawled into bed that night, I noticed the bed clothes had been freshly laundered and a plastic covering had been fitted over both the mattress and feather pillow. The large braided rug had been removed. Two small rugs remained, both strategically placed alongside the bedrails to support knees during bedtime prayers.

Before hearing our nightly prayers, Dad addressed my brother and then me: "George, you are under strict orders not to speak, laugh, or make extraneous noises once we are done. Buddy, give me that old smelly baseball cap Uncle Harry gave you. I don't think you need to wear it to bed anymore." With that, we all knew this was a serious situation.

The serum Dr. Moeller formulated to diminish the reaction to irritants was initially administered at his office in Chicago twice a week on Mondays and Thursdays. Our reward, stopping at Balbach's Soda Fountain, remained as negotiated. To be truthful, I think Mom sort of enjoyed the indulgence as much as I did.

⌂

Something was afoot as Dad and the Grandpas Olsen and Carson along with Dad's two brothers busily rearranged farm implements for no readily apparent reason. The harvest was complete; the early killing frost had ripened the crops sooner than anticipated. With darkness now coming earlier, we children were all in bed the night we heard Dad and Mom slaughter the remaining chickens. Some of the cows had been sold to Uncle Marvin and the chicken coop was knocked down and torched the following afternoon. Uncle Marvin drove the fire department water truck out from town to make sure the fire did not spread. Roasting marshmallows was out of the question; the pungent odor was overwhelming.

Late that evening, we gathered in George's and my upstairs bedroom. Dad announced: "Kids, we're going to auction off all the remaining cows except Maybelle, two steers, a few implements, one tractor, and the grain. I will be quitting fulltime farming and I will find a job, hopefully not too far away." Using his large red kerchief, Dad stopped to wipe a continuous avalanche of tears from Mom's face. "Buddy has developed asthma and is allergic to many things here on the farm. In addition to animal dander, pollen, and feathers, he is severely allergic to household dust and likely cigarette smoke. We will need to make some significant changes to make him more comfortable, and frankly to save his life. He will continue receiving allergy shots twice a week from Dr. Fitzgerald. On Mondays and Thursdays, Buddy will walk to Grandma Carson's after school. George, you and I will need to do most of the remaining chores." Mom added, "Yes Buddy, she's thrown out her French perfume and she will not powder her face when you are there." Straining hard to keep her composure, she explained, "Grandma will drive Buddy to Dr. Fitzgerald's office to get his shot, wait for him, and then bring him home. Susanna, you and George will ride the bus as usual. We hope and pray that the shots will help his immune system not be so sensitive. Over time, his shots should become less frequent."

With that Dad and Mom bowed their heads as Dad began, "Our Father, who art in heaven…" We all joined in. I could see their shadows as Dad pulled Mom close as they walked down the hall to the stairway. Reaching the bottom tread, Dad shut off the stair and hall lights. Just before they closed the stairway door, Mom called up tenderly, "Kids, go to sleep; we love you."

⌂

Following the hard freeze, journeys out of doors became more comfortable. The old gravity furnace was not replaced, since it did not blow the warmed air as violently as the newer forced air models. The cold winter air however felt like a tourniquet on my chest. Whenever I went outdoors, Mom insisted I cover my mouth with one of Dad's kerchiefs. Vigorous outdoor activities were restricted.

⌂

Cars parked along County Road 23 as far as the eye could see on Saturday, November 22, 1958, just after Armistice Day. The auctioneer was a longtime family friend. Hay wagons were loaded with various tools and household goods. Several farmers helped clerk and the St. Bartholomew's Ladies Aid Lunch Wagon did a booming business. The first snowflakes of winter appeared.

From behind his machine shed I could hear Dad trying to convince Auctioneer Hanson that Grandpa Carson's horse-drawn, four wheel manure spreader was an "antique."

It was apparent Dad was becoming weary as the day wore on. "I can't believe you don't think it is an antique! Come on, Karl, you know it should fetch a high dollar."

Dad had a big surprise awaiting him when it came time to settle up at the end of the auction. I had mimicked bidders throughout the afternoon with my arm raised ever so slightly in the air, and then at the most inopportune time, George jabbed me squarely in my ribs. Never missing a sale, Auctioneer Hanson quickly spotted my, by then, fully extended arm and cried out, "Sold! for twenty-five dollars, to Buddy Olsen!" The crowd laughed heartily at my "wise" purchase of the old and worthless manure spreader. George's and my horseplay cost Dad twenty-five hard earned dollars.

⌂

We continued to play catch each Sunday during the early part of fall, but the second weekend in December, Uncle Harry and Aunt Amanda didn't come out to the country. Mom must have known more than she let on. While at the breakfast table on Tuesday morning, Susanna asked, "Who called last night? We didn't hear you say much."

Mom's cheeks were red, "Uncle Harry died in his sleep last night after finishing supper and telling Aunt Amanda he was ready for a good night's rest. His lungs finally gave out." Starting to cry again, she moaned, "He never came back to the Church and now he's gone!"

Wednesday was unusually somber. After the school bus ride home, I spent my remaining evening hours in my room; I lay in bed remembering the good times I had with Uncle Harry, realizing we would never again play our fantasy games of catch. I began to sob uncontrollably.

Thursday morning, Mom called up the stairway, "Put on your church clothes; we've decided you won't be going to school today or tomorrow after all." I could see deep sorrow in Mom's eyes. "All of us will be going to Uncle Harry's visitation this afternoon and stay with Aunt Amanda until after the funeral tomorrow." Loading the old Dodge with three mismatched suitcases, we headed toward the rising sun and Chicago.

Entering the large wooden doors of the ornate Catholic cathedral on Friday morning for Uncle Harry's funeral, I realized it was the first time I'd ever seen Uncle Harry in church. After the service, the hearse made the long drive to Providence for the burial. When the last visitor left the burial plot, Aunt Amanda began sobbing loudly. The priest drove her and her car back to Chicago. It had been two long days of mourning. As the sun began to set, everyone, except Dad who was driving, quickly fell asleep in their seats for the short drive home. Arriving home, someone still had to feed and bed Maybelle, the Ayrshire cow and the two steers. Dad told George, "I'll get them. You go on to bed." We kids headed straight upstairs. No coercing was needed that night.

"Why?" I again asked Mom. On Saturday afternoon, she finally told me. "In 1938," she said, "Pastor Buchanan, recognizing some of the untapped wealth of the congregation, gave his yearly 'giving' sermon based on Paul's Second

Letter to the Corinthians 9:6–10. He quoted verse 7, reading, 'Every man according as he purposeth in his heart, so let him give; not grudgingly, or of necessity: for God loveth a cheerful giver.' Harry thought the sermon was directed specifically at him. Apparently feeling guilt from Pastor Buchanan's forthrightness, Harry stormed noisily out of the side church door, slamming it with all his might. Foregoing his normal sermon benediction, Pastor Buchanan abruptly closed by reminding us that: To whom much is given, much is expected.

"As you know," Mom continued, now with George and Susanna joining us, "Harry never returned to St. Bartholomew's, or any other church for that matter, until yesterday. Just after his tantrum, he moved to Chicago and started a wholesale distribution business on the south side. Uncle Harry became blind to his many blessings. He believed what was his was his, and not God's. No tithing and no giving to the church, Harry believed St. Bartholomew's, and any other church for that matter, could make it financially by cutting back the pastor's salary."

Uncle Harry had been raised in the same Christian home as Mom and Aunt Ella. Local traditions had not changed much from those early years. And, as the first born son of Grandpa and Grandma Carson, he was to become the sole heir to the 640 acre Carson homestead. He was not obligated to share any of the inheritance with Mom or Aunt Ella and Mom never brought up the subject. Uncle Harry had had a relatively free and easy lifestyle during the Depression. That same lifestyle continued even during World War II. Born in 1908, he was too old for World War II, thus he was deferred from service. Essentially, he became a war opportunist, primarily distributing sugar, tires, and chemicals throughout the Midwest from a modern South Chicago warehouse.

As Mom continued to tell the whole story, I thought: How quickly he is gone – forever.

As Mom told it, his invincible attitude was also reflected in his spiritual life. It seemed Uncle Harry always had an excuse for not following in the religious footsteps of his parents and ancestors – footsteps they had crossed an ocean to preserve. Infant baptism and confirmation were just speed bumps along his life's roadway.

I recall Mom's candor. She believed Uncle Harry could do nothing wrong in the eyes of Grandpa and Grandma Carson. If he needed financial help or if he got himself into a bind, Grandpa and Grandma's soft hearts and financial good-standing were always there to help.

Susanna inquired, "So why didn't Uncle Harry just find a different church?"

Mom resumed the monologue: "The secular world offered all he desired: money, friends, and fame. He selfishly believed if he couldn't buy them, then he could just run over them all with his perceived power – and he believed he didn't need the church for that. You probably didn't understand our many discussions about Aunt Ella's organ fund drive. I have since discovered Uncle Harry made a big donation to the church on New Year's Eve last year. Cleverly, he timed the contribution so he would receive a tax deduction in 1957. His deed paid for the entire project – in cash! "

⌂

On the coldest Sundays, church attendance became less important for a large part of the congregation. Pastor Buchanan continued his sheepherding, oops, I mean shepherding, only to a smaller flock. There was never a doubt about our family routine on Sunday mornings. The pastor's sermons were always biblically based. Ears were tuned to hear. However, family traditions changed ever so slightly. After Uncle Harry's death, Sunday dinners were now at the local restaurant.

As we sat down at the restaurant table, Mom reminded me, "Buddy, did you hear Pastor Buchanan's sermon today? Remember what we talked about after Uncle Harry died? Even though this world offers money, friends and fame, it's impossible to buy eternal life. Jesus purchased that for you."

Although some churches broke with tradition, St. Bartholomew's continued its traditional Christmas program. For the annual Sunday School program, boys were required to wear white shirts, navy blue jackets and blue ties; girls were required to wear red velvet dresses. The program consisted of reading the Christmas story as it is written in Luke, Chapter 2. Each grade level was required to memorize individual verses. Since the classes were small, each class contributed to the manger scene as shepherds, wise men, or angels. One additional boy and girl from the eighth grade played the parts of Joseph and Mary. When the final verse was spoken, Pastor Buchanan stood boldly alongside the newly created manger scene as he sang "Silent Night" in his native German.

It was a charming program but over the years it had become too predictable for this change-seeking congregation. In fact, some longtime St. Bartholomew's members left for other congregations. As the newly elected church president, Dad had to face new congregational challenges. Having served St. Bartholomew's for over forty years, Dad knew the church council would need to present Pastor Buchanan with retirement options in order to gain new vitality the congregation so desperately needed. It would be hard to speak with the shepherd who had, to date, baptized, confirmed, married – including them – and buried all of his and Mom's families, except Uncle Harry. Since Pastor Buchanan was a Protestant and not a recognized member of the clergy by the Catholic Church, he had not been allowed

28

to participate in the funeral service in any capacity – Uncle Harry would not have wanted him to participate anyway.

⌂

Dad and Mom elected to have a quiet, family Christmas dinner alone, without the fanfare of relatives or reunions. The weather had turned unusually cold and blustery. The winter sunshine made a short appearance in the south facing windows. It was a beautiful day to enjoy games and listen to Christmas music from Dad's 45 rpm record player playing through his new Hi-Fi radio. Always ones for Cat's Cradle, cribbage and cards, Dad and Mom also brought out Chinese checkers and Parcheesi for the afternoon's entertainment. After exhausting ourselves with games, Mom served hot chocolate, candy cane cookies and date balls. We still had time for our afternoon naps.

That season, winter on the prairie was colder than usual. Although in later years I began to more fully understand the life of a displaced tenant farmer, at the time, everything still seemed routine and rosy. We kept Maybelle for milking and butchered the calves when they weighed between 600–700 pounds. Replacing it with a newly born calf, Dad continued to feed out and butcher one feeder every nine months. Mom pasteurized the rich milk and separated the cream, trading cream for eggs with our neighbor, Darlene Davis.

1959

The old farm house was structurally sound but its 50 years were beginning to show. Catching the landlord in one of his better moods, Dad was able to trade monthly rent payments for hard work and sweat. With the help of his brothers, Dad salvaged lumber and wood lath from an old farm house just down the road. Dad added a structural header and removed the partition wall between the living and dining room. He dramatically increased the size of the farm house by building a family room addition that included indoor plumbing and a combination tub/shower. Dad and his laborers also built a free standing two-car garage with two overhead doors and a side service door. He connected the house and garage with a screened in porch, something Mom had always wanted. Dad and Mom replaced Mom's ringer washer with a Speed Queen washing machine and matching electric dryer.

Mom's new income as a fulltime nurse helped offset the low wages Dad was being paid as a hired man. Dad dug ditches and laid field tile for Uncle Marvin's newest company, Marv's Tiling. However, the laborious work appeared to be wearing him down. Dad lost almost 20 pounds – too much for his already lean frame.

⌂

Since winter came early, springtime in turn made an early entrance. As the ground thawed, warmed and dried, more outdoor activities began. In those days, boys who would turn eight that calendar year were old enough for organized baseball; I was ready for the diamond. I joined George as an Oriole. Our league consisted of four teams with 12 players on each roster. We played on two fields. Thus, on each game day, each team would play. All of the town boys and most of the farm boys played in the twice weekly games. There were tall ones, short ones, and even some overweight ones. All sported new caps representing their individual teams. Those whose head was smaller than their hat simply flipped up the brim – just one way they could get it to not push out their ears. The smartly styled uniforms were to be worn only on game days, never at practice. Most of the uniforms were oversized. All were made of warm flannel cotton, duplicating the colors of the professional team they were named after.

Several dads and a few older men were responsible for organizing and coaching. Like last summer, one of the older boy's father, Coach Pete Fox, led the Orioles. Local professionals and businessmen volunteered as umpires. Although my dad never participated in athletics, he was always there to help. Mom helped by donating homemade cookies, date pinwheels and snickerdoodles, and other desserts to the food stand.

Coach Fox had difficulty finding a suitable position for me. With a keen baseball mind, Coach Fox knew I was limited to the right side of the diamond, more commonly known as right field. Not much action there, he thought. He figured he could use me when the game had already been decided. Oh how I dreamed of the games with Uncle Harry! I just wanted to be the catcher. Without any other southpaws on the team, I came to consider myself an oddity.

During one game I actually got to play the ball. We were short players that Wednesday evening; Coach Fox needed all the players he could muster. Camped out in my right field cavern, the ball at first looked short. As I quickly corrected my misjudgment, I heard it swoosh over my head only to see it roll all the way to the corn cribbing which had been stretched to make the outfield fence. Coach Fox had taught me: on a single, always throw towards second base. Someone will be there.

I picked up the ball, now resting on the blade of a tall dandelion. Envisioning Uncle Harry in his usual erect location, about 80 feet away, I let it blaze.

To me it was just like another game of catch with Uncle Harry. Hitting him squarely, shortstop Buster Mazzocco never saw it coming. When all the dads had moved away, I could see Buster, just like I had Uncle Harry, lying flat on his back seeing every star in the heavens. Buster had unfortunately been visited at the same time by my blazer – and Bill Schmidt. Coach Fox was right about one thing, someone would be there, but he didn't mention there could be a train wreck at the crossing.

Buster appeared very stiff and sore as we slowly picked him up. His right eye was turning purple and his left eye was swollen shut. He caught my throw and luckily tagged out Big Bill just in time for the third out in the bottom of the fifth. No runs scored and we beat the number one Braves by the slimmest of margins. Buster had two walnut size bumps on his head – one from Bill's out-of-control elbow and one from his own glove. Buster's glove stayed on only because the free-sailing ball lodged deeply into the glove's web, which stopped moving at his forehead! Coach Fox frequently reminded us to tightly tie our glove around a baseball. Buster's perfectly formed pocket proved the importance of that daily ritual!

Except for Coach Fox, no one else acknowledged the throw. As we piled into the old Dodge I heard Coach Fox call back to Dad: "It was that blistering throw again. From now on, in this league, it will be unofficially known as Buddy's Blazer!"

△

Dad didn't say anything about the game that night. On our way home however he did announce to the family that he bought a new car. Fewer livestock meant hired man jobs were unpredictable. The only farm offers Dad could muster required moving away from Providence or out of Itasca County, something neither he nor Mom cared to undertake.

When things appeared to be at their lowest, Dad found full time work at the new plastic extrusion factory, 30 miles away. Several other men in the area had found work at that same plant. With fixed steady hours, they shared driving and its escalating expenses. Dad now had both steady hours and a steady income – something he had not seen since he returned from the war. Even though he would be on his feet all day, he didn't believe his war wound would be aggravated. The large piece out of his calf was healing oh so slowly. He was unable to squat since most of his calf went out with the shrapnel. For this reason, he never wore shorts, a new custom for farmers turned golfers.

The new job also meant he would receive yearly vacation time.

△

Buster Mazzocco was still sporting his blackened eyes and forehead bumps when he arrived for Sunday School four days later. Buster became unusually religious that morning. He told me he wanted to go to both Sunday School and worship. Buster told his parents to pick him up an hour and a quarter later than usual. Fear had now become a four letter word in his eight-year-old vocabulary.

Dad was anxious to show off his new car to his brotherhood of men at church. A strong sense of fellowship was evident among these men; all had served their country well. Some fellow soldiers, however, were gone. This remaining militia was restarting their lives on the prairie. Girlfriends had become wives, and empty nests were being filled with additional mouths and hands. Each Sunday these men would meet during Sunday School. They always carried their own large black Bible. From their meeting room, it was a short distance up the mezzanine stairs to the sanctuary.

The summer season began with Pastor Chuck Davidson's sermon on the Apostle Paul's conversion on the road to Damascus. Pastor Davidson was now deep into Paul's writings – the smaller epistles.

I pondered, "Who was this man Paul?" I guessed his ministry started when he changed his name. I had always been "Buddy". Would changing my name to "Bud" make a big difference in me? Is that what new Pastor Davidson was talking about?

⌂

In 1959, life's troubles began to appear for Dad's younger brother Theodore. Younger than Dad by six years, Theodore had served in WWII as an infantryman, seeing his first continental action on D-Day plus two. A natural fighter, yet small in stature, his red, curly hair soon became part of his proud uniform.

As a young man, Theodore had entered several Saturday night bouts held weekly at the Hog Pen Tavern. I remember Uncle Theodore's face was always puffy and scarred. It was said that each fighter was paid $25 per fight, with $75 additional prize money to the nightly winner of the three-bout bracket. Frequently Poles and Irishmen from Chicago would join the competition. As the months went by, the cash pots and the popularity of the events increased.

In late 1958, however, the fights were abruptly cancelled when state and county health, vice, and taxation authorities made an unannounced visit. The operators were charged with several violations, resulting in both the fight events and tavern being immediately shut down.

During the subsequent trial, it was discovered that the Chicago imports were not just innocent participants but younger, paid professionals climbing the ladder at the expense of the hard-working farm hands, most of whom had returned with both internal and external scars from the European or Pacific theaters. In exchange for cooperating with the investigation, the county judge was more lenient with the local hands, ordering them only to perform civil service for a year.

Suspiciously, just a week after the end of the trial, Uncle Theodore's barn burned to the ground one early summer night. Although "spontaneous combustion of newly cut hay" was the County Sheriff's official cause, the investigating deputy could never explain the discovery of several partially empty, five-gallon gasoline cans found in the ditch just north of Uncle Theodore's farm. The County Sheriff reconsidered the cause when several other amateur boxers reported suspicious visits and occurrences around their farm buildings; however, the county's records were never changed.

Our new black dial phone rang one Saturday afternoon in August, just before supper and our usual trip to Grandpa and Grandma Carson's for our weekly Saturday night television date with the Lawrence Welk Show. At that time, only a few people in town had televisions. Dad answered. The caller identified himself as Vaughn Dreger.

Even though the two of them were unacquainted, Dad had anticipated his call for some time. Frequently, Dad had seen Uncle Theodore's car parked behind Providence's Town Square Tavern, especially on Saturday afternoons. This became the first of many trips to town in order to drive his drunken brother home. It now became a problem well beyond Aunt Millie's control. At 36, she had all she could handle with four young children and herself suffering from the early stages of what was later diagnosed as Lou Gehrig's disease.

⌂

The harvest was completed by mid-November. Ears of corn, colorful tree leaves, and brown cat tail were transformed into beautiful dinner table centerpieces. An air of joy, blessing, and relief was on the face of every adult. The Lord truly blessed the land with another bountiful harvest. Corn cribs were bursting. Large piles of ear corn looked like giant yellow glaciers. This abundance was never attacked by a plague of rodents or great flocks of birds. It appeared that a blanket of protection was draped over the bounty. As cold became frigid, the invigorating north wind provided enough chill to bring out an ingrained tough-it-out spirit.

The joy of Thanksgiving quickly turned to gloom when both Grandpa and Grandma Carson passed away, just one week apart, shortly before Christmas. They had always seemed old to me. Their house was always stale smelling, but toasty warm. Never was an item out of place. Even the whitewall tires on Grandpa's car were as white as snow. Their in-town home now became just another "house" as the yard's *For Sale* sign was quickly topped with a *Sold* sign. Mom knew only that it had been sold to the bank's trust. Mom worked hard to bring the large estate to a close. Treasures were shared amongst the family.

One such treasure was discovered in a wooden chest in the attic. Although most of the other pictures in the chest were water stained, one picture remained without blemish. I knew the smile immediately. I had seen that same smile many times through the fingers of my old JC Higgins mitt. With his bat in a slightly cocked position and his bill slightly rolled and tilted, Uncle Harry looked to be rather tall even at this early age. I recognized his ball cap as the one hanging from my dresser mirror frame. His large biceps and forearms were clearly evident in the old black and white photograph. The EAGLES name and number "08" were the only appliqués. Mom said the team owner had allowed him to use the zero prefix. She thought it was a great find and she said I was welcome to put it on my dresser. "Do you remember how superstitious Uncle Harry was about that number?" Mom asked. "Since it was the year he was born, he considered 08 to be his lucky number." Mom always loved her brother, despite his religious and narcissistic attitudes.

⌂

My Christmas packages included a new ball and bat. It seemed Grandpa and Grandma had prospered more than they showed outwardly. With Uncle Harry's passing, Aunt Ella and Mom were now farm owners, each receiving a half section of land. Mom received the proceeds from the sale of the in-town house, Aunt Ella received the 320 acres bordering the paved road, including the out buildings and house. Only Mom received a cash inheritance; that blessed her and Dad with enough money to purchase our farm house, buildings, and its 120 acre land parcel. This meant Dad and Mom no longer rented from an antagonistic, short-sighted landlord. Mom continued her nursing career full time; with her servant's heart, it was something she thoroughly enjoyed. Strongly believing first fruits belonged to the Lord, both Mom and Aunt Ella bequeathed a large endowment to St. Bartholomew's.

Grandpa and Grandma Carson had always been faithful church goers. The days of their respective funerals were unusually warm and radiant – not unlike the Birth of the Season.

1960

Frantically running in the back door I cried, "She's laying on her side with her feet straight out! She's stiff as a board! She looks like Humpty Dumpty!" Slipping on his boots, Dad quickly went to see what had happened to his lowly Ayrshire cow.

Dad readily saw that sometime during the night, Maybelle slipped through an open gate into neighbor Davis' early spring, alfalfa field. Uncontrollably enjoying the dew laden leaves, Maybelle simply ate until she bloated. Returning to the house Dad angrily scolded, "Next time I ask you to be sure all the livestock are in and the gates are locked, Buddy, I expect you to follow through! I don't care if *Gunsmoke* was on the radio!" With that he demanded, "Now go get the belt!"

Having to go into the basement stairway to retrieve the antique razor belt was as painful as the punishment it inflicted. I shook and sweated as the judge determined the sentence. Dad, slow to anger, effectively let me stew before he painfully scolded, "Turn around... bend over." I don't recall the severity of the belts or the number of times. That is unimportant. However, I learned to keep my mouth shut; excuses and back talking would only lengthen the duration. Following the punishment, I was sent to my room. After what seemed to be an interminable amount of time, he called me back to the living room.

Calmer with the passage of time, he said sternly, "At 10, I guess she had given us more milk than most cows. Buddy, I am going to take $15 out of your savings account to pay the rendering works. I probably could have gotten $50 for her at the packing plant! I guess it's too late now, she's dead!"

Remorsefully, I offered, "I'm sorry, Dad. I'll try harder not to let you down."

Mom saw an opening, "We don't need all that cream anyway. I'll phone Darlene and let her know we won't be trading cream for eggs anymore. I can pick up milk at Myrt's Market when I do the other grocery shopping. No...better yet! Buddy, from now on you are in charge of making sure we never run out of fresh milk and eggs! Do you understand?" Pointing toward the stairway door she commanded, "Now, you may go."

◯

Decoration Day, May 30, 1960, was a sunny, warm day. For fifteen years, America had seen unprecedented growth, prosperity, and vigor. The veterans attempted to contain themselves emotionally as the springtime anniversary had now become a time of parades, picnics and horseshoes. Marching lines wavered as the makeshift battalion moved slowly up Main Street. For veterans like Dad, war wounds made the march much more difficult. For some, their youthful uniforms fit very snuggly; for others, there wasn't a chance of fitting into them. Valor and service medals were neatly pinned on the hats, jackets, or shirts. Since most local veterans were active members of the Providence American Legion, white shirts, yellow ties and crisply folded blue hats, with the simple American Legion logo and the state embroidered on both sides, were the dress of this day's activities. Mom let out the pants' seams as far as she could in order to fit over Dad's spare tire – he loved his beef. After a sharp cleaning and pressing, it looked as good as new.

Proceeding from the high school parking lot, down Cherry Street to where it intersected with Main, the early morning parade of bands, red, white and blue decorated cars, and floats four abreast, ended just short of City Hall. As the Legion's brass band played the *National Anthem*, three former commanders proudly raised the American flag on City Hall's pole. Removing all hats, the gathered crowd became deathly silent as the Post Chaplin read the invocation followed by the reading of the names of those who had lost their lives in battle. The slightly off key brass band then played *The Battle Hymn of the Republic* and *America the Beautiful.* Dressed in his aging Army uniform, the mayor then addressed the crowd and praised the successes of his fellow heroes. Following closing remarks, the mayor called for a moment of reflection. Out of immediate eyesight, the crowd's silence was dramatically pierced as a group of veterans volleyed a 21 shot salute. *Taps* reverberated off the brick buildings. Children instinctively muffed their ears as the telltale rifle smoke hovered above and the odor of spent gunpowder permeated the crowd.

A closing prayer was given for the WWI veterans who were still alive, WWII veterans, Korean Conflict veterans, and soldiers currently serving. The troops were then dismissed and the crowd walked to the high school gymnasium where a potluck supper was readied by the Auxiliary. Once the troops were dismissed, like their older siblings had done, the youngest children scrambled along the pavement in order to retrieve one of the spent shell casings as a souvenir.

Even the holiday was predestined for change. The Federal government sometime later decided that it would be better called "Memorial Day" and be celebrated each year on the last Monday of the month of May, regardless of the actual date. Rather than a specific date to remember those who died in our nation's service, some thought it could now be summer's first three day weekend – individual recreation gained a new foothold as attendance at patriotic events began to decline. Later, fed up with our country's disrespect of traditions, Dad tersely remarked: "Next thing you know they'll have just one day to honor all of the Presidents, or for that matter, change the Fourth to the first Monday in July!"

⌂

With Dad's steady income, he was confident the family could afford the cost of a used television. Part of Dad's justification was the upcoming national election and the introduction of the new fall shows. Dad and Mom were able to entertain just as Grandma Carson had done for so many years.

The anticipation was high as Dad and Mr. DeHaven carried our "new" pecan stained television cabinet into the living room. The southeast corner of the living room seemed the most appropriate. Attaching a clothespin-like fastener to two screws on the backside of the TV cabinet, Mr. DeHaven then snaked the flat antennae wire under the double hung sash to the outside. Dad had earlier mounted an antenna wire to a bracket and antenna mounted high on the barnyard light pole. At first the reception was very cloudy. Mr. DeHaven quickly recognized Dad had mistakenly severed several pieces of copper while pulling the wire from the pole towards the window. Restringing only took a matter of minutes since Dad had strategically installed a junction box at the bottom of the pole.

The large RCA cabinet radio, originally bought by Grandpa and Grandma Carson in 1938, was moved to another area of the house. It soon became apparent the six cubic foot video cabinet would methodically begin to dominate the lives of its viewers. Recognizing its power, Dad and Mom quickly added new rules to the household including restricting the time and what programs could be watched. The rules were to be: No television during meals, however, suppertime was suddenly changed so it could be completed before the Huntley Brinkley Report; All homework was to be completed before other evening television programs were turned on; Regular programming was limited to Saturday afternoons and evenings, and only until 7:00 p.m. on Sunday nights.

In earlier years, while watching television at Grandpa and Grandma Carson's, we had never been allowed to watch *The Honeymooners*. It had been considered off limits; arguing between husband and wife was strictly taboo. However, the long standing shows *To Tell the Truth*, *Lassie*, and *Gunsmoke* were acceptable.

○

George and I continued playing for the Orioles. Since competition was limited to the three other teams, winning the league championship, as we did, was not front page news in the *Providence Purveyor*. George and his peers led the team throughout the summer. Our sole loss was the last week in July, against the cellar dwelling Phillies. George and I began to play catch more frequently in our side yard bullpen. We installed a wood board for the pitching rubber and a peck sized, woven basket cover as the makeshift home plate. With my health improving, I was able to play daily except on the most hot and humid of days.

Following the 1960 Decoration Day parade, it became even more apparent and important to Dad that he reconcile and renew some of his WWII experiences and friendships.

Mid-summer was also the first time Dad used his yearly vacation time – paid, and one week at that. Seeking to take full advantage of the time off, Dad had originally wanted to leave on Friday night after he came home from work. Ed Davis agreed to watch over the house. Mom won out – we left at 5:00 a.m. sharp on that Saturday morning in late July. She filled a picnic basket with sandwiches, several snacks and cookies, and juices. Even a new Road Bingo game was included, along with several books and scratch pads. Playing cards and board games were not forgotten.

42

You see, this was the first time Mom could also enjoy paid time off. Piling into the pink, white, and black 1955 Dodge Royal Lancer, we headed due south for the Smokey Mountains of Tennessee. Dad had fabricated special wood benches so that we could easily peer over the car's high window sills. Dad's army buddy, Barney Collins, lived just outside the small town of Maryville, Tennessee.

Late that day, we arrived at the freshly painted Valley View Motel in Maryville. It was a grueling fourteen-hour drive. These were the days before automobile or motel air conditioners. The best ventilation our room could offer was the breeze from the side flankers of a picture window facing the street and a small venting bathroom window facing a forested area behind. The front window was a mere 20 feet from the highway. After a late supper, Dad phoned Barney from the nearby restaurant, because there were no phones or television in the modestly furnished motel rooms.

Barney's wife Colleen answered and eagerly confirmed her invitation for church and Sunday dinner. Dad agreed; we would meet the Collins family in time for Sunday School and Worship at Maryville's Fundamental Evangelical Baptist Church. With the comfort of a full meal in our bellies, we were in bed by 8:00 p.m. – sleeping soundly despite the traffic that literally sounded like it was coming through the front door. Before dozing off however, we agreed the return trip would be divided between the following Saturday and Sunday.

Mom had brought several breakfast fruits. Her famous coffee cake was sliced and served by 8:00 a.m. sharp. In the car a quick 30 minutes later, Dad carefully followed Barney's directions. With George claiming to be nauseous, more likely anxious, Susanna and I were appointed to attend Sunday School with the two Collins children. I joined Beth and Susanna went with Brenda.

"Are you saved? I am! I went up two weeks ago. I felt it in my heart!" So went my introductory conversation with Beth Collins.

I thought, "What was this girl talking about?" Beth's Sunday School teacher continued the barrage as she lectured each student about the wrongs of this world. We were told to dress modestly, not play cards, nor dance – ever! The teacher told us it was very important to not stray from this teaching. The Sunday School literature reinforced these rules with illustrations and questions – multiple choice and true/false with only true statements. Each student had their own Bible, except me! With open Bibles always at the ready, I could see I was amongst a group of students who quickly moved from one supporting verse to another.

As soon as the car doors were closed and we were on our way up the winding roads from the church to the Collins' farmhouse, we children quickly began asking Dad and Mom many questions. I began, "Why doesn't the pastor wear a black robe and colored whatchamacallit?"

"I think you mean vestment Buddy," Susanna corrected me.

"Where were the acolytes? Why don't they have a liturgy? There was no chanting. Beth even wrote in her Bible!"

Susanna chimed in, "How come those people wave and clap their hands, saying 'Amen' to everything? They even talk back to the preacher. If that preacher yelled any louder, wouldn't those light fixtures have fallen down? Why do they baptize in a large bathtub? I have never heard some of those hymns! Why don't they use the same blue hymnal we do? And, what do they talk about when they walk to the front after the sermon?"

In a calming way, Dad said, "Take a breath Susanna! We'll tell you about it on the way home. Now sit back and relax; I think we'll be at their house shortly."

It was just after twelve noon when our troop of five descended on the small farm of former Staff Sergeant Collins. Barney too had married and started a family when he returned home from WWII. Like Dad, Barney went back to the land, where he raised a few head of cattle along with 80 acres of tobacco on a farm homesteaded by Colleen's grandparents. Without siblings, Colleen was destined to become the sole heiress.

After eating a hearty meal of redeye ham, boiled potatoes, and Jell-O, I was ready for my usual afternoon nap. That didn't appear to be part of the Collins family routine. "Do you want to go for a ride?" young Beth Collins asked, with a twinkle in her eye and a tomboy way about her. Peering out the window I could see that it would be awfully hard to turn down a 10-year-old girl who had two paint horses already bridled and standing at the fence gate.

However, I had many questions before I would commit. "Oh yeah, I always ride with a saddle. Is there one in the barn?" I tried to bluff my way in order to gain some fortitude, since I had never ridden before in my almost 9 years. I was determined not to let some 75-pound girl from the hills show me up. Uncle Harry wouldn't have it!

"You won't need one. Just get on!"

My stomach was still churning from the hearty meal. How, I thought. I had seen cowboys use the saddle's stirrup on television. The Indians seemed to be able to even jump on a moving horse, but this was different. This was reality – a girl was telling *me* to "just get on" her horse.

With that said I walked through an open gate just as Beth catapulted off a strategically placed stump, landing perfectly upon the gelding's back. Thankfully, I thought, the mare was slightly shorter. Sensing my quandary, Beth pulled the dapple colored American Saddlebred alongside the fence. I was then able to climb the closed gate and swing my leg over the wide body. Both instructor and horse knew they had a rookie, or at best a greenhorn on board.

Traversing rich green pastures, Beth began to release more control of my mare's reins. I was gaining confidence as she opened each pasture's gates. I remember thinking, "I am not going to get bucked off and embarrass myself trying to get back on!"

The slow, leisurely pace along the narrow worn trail gave me a chance to further perfect the art of riding and reining. Following slowly behind, Beth turned back to me and said, "Speed up a little. Just tap her on the neck every once and a while to give her a little encouragement."

The low hills were shrinking as we climbed toward a beautiful overlook. From our perch we viewed the surrounding valleys and farms. Allowing the horses to lightly graze, Beth used her bent leg as a step to help me remount. Herself, remounting this time like a high flying trapeze artist, she quickly turned her horse toward home.

"Whoa!" "Stop!" "Halt!" I believed the horse was deaf! None of my commands worked!

I soon learned the first rule of riding. An uncontrolled horse will run for the barn when it knows it's on its way home. I can still hear Beth's laughter as the mare sped by her at what seemed to me to be breakneck speed. "I've lost my reins!" All the way down the mountain, the loose reins swatted the mare's side, making her spur ahead even faster! I grasped the only fixed object I could – the mare's long mane.

Beth's loudest laugh, however, occurred when the mare stopped so suddenly at the watering tank that I slid straight down her neck and into the water! The moss covered walls were treacherous as I reached for the rim to pull myself out. Watching from the back doorway, both families roared with laughter.

When I walked into the farm house breezeway, where Beth was standing perfectly dry, I observed several show horse trophies and ribbons covering the entire breezeway wall–each engraved with the name *Bethany Collins*. Only then did I realize I had met someone who knew a whole lot more than she let on.

△

The highly contested election of 1960 was destined to bring about subtle changes to the American political scene. Richard Nixon, Vice President under World War II hero General Dwight Eisenhower, appeared to be distinctly different from the young savvy demeanor of the flamboyant son of Joseph Kennedy. "Jack" was frequently portrayed as the ideal family man standing alongside his young, beautiful bride and their two perfect children.

After seeing the country sharply divided in what was perceived as the past versus the future, I awakened to discover the country had elected John Fitzgerald Kennedy as its new leader. Ike looked like Grandpa Carson. I knew I could trust him; I didn't know about this new man. I had been taught that Catholics were different than Protestants.

This time proved later to be the beginning of a shift in attitude regarding respect for authority, when a confrontation with Communism in Cuba expanded to become a full fledged war in the remote jungles of Southeast Asia.

△

Late one November afternoon, Dad had just left town to take Uncle Theodore home when our phone rang.

"I can't find him! He's been lost for almost three hours!" Aunt Millie was hysterical as she described the disappearance of their youngest son, Ted. Mom used her well trained manner and calmness as she busily organized a search party of neighbors, friends, and relatives. Ed Davis drove Mom to Uncle Theodore's farm just as Dad and Uncle Theodore arrived from town. Theodore had passed out in the car on the way home from the tavern. Like so many other times before, Dad immediately put him to bed. Unbeknownst to Uncle Theodore, his problems were soon to become much greater.

Theodore's long, two-wheel lane ran between corn fields, coming to an apex directly in front of the large square two-story farmhouse. Well past the summer solstice, dusk was rapidly approaching as the search parties arrived. "When the child is found, use your rifles as a signal. Fire one shot for each degree of trouble with one shot meaning 'all is OK'". Like the sergeant he had been, Dad ordered the searchers, now numbering forty, to disperse in all directions. Each group was equipped with flashlights and rifles. Farm dogs were unleashed in hopes they would sense the urgency and lead the searchers to the boy.

As the minutes became hours and as the sun set, dog howls and shots rang out from the drainage ditch near the end of the driveway. One, two, three, four, five shots; everyone knew it signaled the worst. Rushing to the location, we could see Ted's small body lying face down in a steel culvert. Ted had a large bump on the back of his head. Several large cobbles had been loosened near the mark of a slipping sole. Knees buckling, Dad suddenly collapsed under a heavy conscience as he remembered digging that ditch just a few short years earlier.

Doctor Fitzgerald arrived as Venus began to twinkle in the eastern sky. After completing some paperwork, the hearse left the farm to take the small body to Mattson's Funeral Home. Retired Pastor Buchanan began a mourning and grieving vigil that went well into the night.

Except for Pastor Buchanan, an empty house greeted Uncle Theodore the next morning. Aunt Millie and the remaining three children were given warm beds in the parsonage for what became a very short, sleepless night.

They came from far and wide to attend the funeral of little Ted. School was dismissed early; his second grade class of 12 was seated in the front pew of a very solemn St. Bartholomew's. The family could not financially afford this tragic loss, all funeral costs were miraculously paid from memorials. Healing would need to come with time.

⌂

A new vaccine had become readily available for polio – the debilitating childhood disease of the '60s. The vaccine was first administered under the skin; however, in later years a sugar pill contained the needed protection. Tuberculosis, Uncle Harry's killer, was also on the decline following dramatic quarantine efforts.

John Kennedy brought an enterprising vision to the country. His bold plan to enter the space race and his passion for his country were just two of his many attributes. He challenged Americans to look at what we could do for our country, not what our country could do for us. This proclamation will never be forgotten by those whom he led. Tragically, his hopes and legacy were left to this world.

1961

"Go ahead, Dad, open it!" Since George was becoming a good pitcher, in jest and with Mom's cooperation, George and I combined our money to purchase a Remco Industries catcher's mitt as Dad's Father's Day gift. At first he was dumbfounded; then, after realizing he had become part of the well-meaning joke, his sense of humor came out as he laughed heartily with the rest of the family.

Outwardly, Dad was thrilled with his gift, but truthfully, his heart remained on the land. In *his* mind, baseball was just a game to keep boys occupied. During many games of catch with George, I awkwardly wore the catcher's mitt that was intended for right-handed players.

With more houses being built near the farm, the boy population significantly increased. Pick-up games became frequent. With the minor addition of a few wood blocks, a clover pasture quickly became the new spring baseball field.

After Easter, Dad unveiled his springtime surprise. Over the winter, he secretly fabricated *The Contraption* in his OFF LIMITS portion of the machine shed. With the final installation of a couple of bolts, it was ready to go. Set squarely at four corners, having two with wheels and two with posts, "Connie", as she was affectionately called, was easily moved from place to place. Rolling out on what had been the manure spreader's front axles, Connie's frame and backstop had been constructed from the different parts of the aging manure spreader.

Cleverly, dad had engineered a strike zone opening that was easily adjusted by moving a lever; the opening could be sized for batters from four feet to six and a half feet tall. The operator secured the desired opening by locking the lever's position.

Balls not in the strike zone hit the remnants of a soft leather horse collar and dropped harmlessly into a small egg basket below. Those in the strike zone, after passing through the opening, were stopped by a chicken cage which had been mounted onto the backside of the wooden backstop. The cage door remained and the opening pointed downward.

Enlarging the strike zone opening to its maximum size, both baskets and the rear cage could be removed if I elected to catch George's pitches. Sometimes, though rarely, we traded positions. The enlarged opening forced both pitcher and catcher to accurately throw within the opening's perimeter. I wondered why Dad had eagerly purchased baseballs during the past few months. Old ones, new ones, it didn't matter.

Dad's ingenuity was even more evident by the fact that "Connie" could simulate different batters. Dad painted batter silhouettes on both sides of two panels. Quickly exchanging a painted panel with a blank, both right- and left- handed, small and large, four different situations could be simulated.

About the same time, that spring, Dad began work on a new ball field, including a real batter's box complete with a manufactured home plate. Using his tractor and remaining implements, nightly he disked, hauled, and leveled soil until he believed it was just right. Utilizing each implement in one operation or another, he maneuvered them with the precision of a well-trained surgeon. Laughingly Mom said to him, "We are going to call you the 'Diamond Doctor' if you keep this up. Later that summer, Dad re-built the pitcher's mound, adding a regulation pitching rubber.

We didn't need a baseball camp – we had our own.

◠

In an effort to balance teams, both George and I were placed on a mediocre team – the Phillies. Our potential for winning was severely hampered; several boys were not allowed to play or practice on Wednesday nights.

Vaughn Dreger managed our team until business conflicts forced him to turn the team over to his eldest son Ron. Age-wise, according to town rules, Ron was eligible to coach. However, Ron did not have the mentoring skills of a well-seasoned coach. Much to his father's frustration, Ron turned a good portion of his attention to blossoming 13 year old, Monica Finch. Having just turned 18 years old, Ron believed wooing girls was more important than helping teach young boys the fundamentals of baseball... and life in general.

During one of Ron's vulnerable moments, Dad somehow convinced the younger Dreger to let me play catcher instead of right field. My natural ability to stretch for and scoop up bad throws caught the eye of the other coaches, including veteran Coach Pete Fox.

Dad believed neither Vaughn Dreger nor his son were a role model for his boys. In his own tolerating way, Dad respected the league's decision to appoint Vaughn and his son, but, Dad made sure he attended every practice and game. When it came time for our family's vacation, Dad let his real position be known. "We're taking a two-week vacation to California the last two weeks in July. I have seen enough baseball this spring and summer. You've learned what you needed to."

With that we knew there was no room for negotiation. With fewer farming chores, had Dad and Mom suddenly become California beach bums?

"Anna, Ed said that Mae Lynne has agreed to do the chores while we are gone. For such a young girl, she is a very hard worker." Pausing, Dad added, "She's in your class, isn't she, Buddy?"

Not missing the opportunity, Mom jumped in, "Buddy, you'll need to turn it up a notch if you ever expect to keep up with her." With that she put her arms around me, kissed me on the forehead and said, "Just remember, I love you no matter who you become."

The two week trip likely cost Dad and Mom a sizable amount of money. I think they were both determined to build strong, long lasting memories for their children. I can remember Alcatraz, Disneyland, Dodger Stadium, and Huntington Beach. Frankly, I don't remember my Little League baseball games that year – other than it was the first time I actually played catcher in a league game.

⌂

That fall brought new challenges as I entered the fifth grade. Two elementary school sections of ten year olds were combined in the newly built junior high school. The building contained locker rooms and a gymnasium, something the old 1920s elementary school lacked. All of my elementary teachers had been lifelong residents of Providence. That would no longer be the norm.

It was also time to begin taking showers after a new class – Physical Education. PE, as it was called, included wearing proper clothing: a school monogrammed tee shirt and shorts, socks, shoes, and yes, a supporter. At the time I wasn't sure why.

The Boy's PE teacher was a former Army sergeant who had just returned from service in the Korean peninsula. In charge of grades 5–8, he believed it was important to train both the body and mind at this early age. Our activities were held outdoors as much as possible, weather permitting, which he determined of course!

Ultimately and reluctantly resigning to indoor activities in late fall, Mr. Roberts decided it was a good time to take some excess body fat off his fifth grade boys. Both boys and girls classes were combined to play indoor field hockey. Mr. Roberts didn't use the lightweight plastic puck supplied – he used the optional tennis ball. With two more boys than girls, it was decided that one boy would be the goalie of each team. I was selected as goalie for the Blue team.

Mr. Roberts decided that the Monday, Tuesday and Wednesday before Thanksgiving would be perfect for a three game, total goal tournament. The winners would be awarded priority seating in the cafeteria and a special bonus in addition to the turkey dinner – ice cream novelties, compliments of Mr. Roberts. Mr. Roberts knew he had a severe team balance problem late Tuesday morning following the second Blue team victory in as many days. The Green team had been shut out 7–0 and 8–0 on Monday and Tuesday respectively.

Tuesday, during lunch hour, Mr. Roberts pulled me aside and said, "Well Buddy, I see you are pretty quick with that glove hand, even though you are wearing it backwards. You use your blocker and stick as much as you catch the ball. Those were some good shots by the Green team. What do you say we make a deal? If you let them win the third game by more than 3 goals, I'll give you an automatic 'A' for the course. It will make them feel better about themselves."

I couldn't keep the scheme from him that evening. Dad sensed I had a dilemma when he asked, "What are you going to do? Let the other team score on you so you get the automatic 'A', or play honestly to the best of your ability? Tell me how it comes out."

Pressure was at its peak as the 8:45 a.m. bell rang for the class change. The first hour of the day had been unbearable. I had not focused during Miss Severson's English lesson. This new challenge was tugging at me from several different ways.

△

Running off the bus and in the back screen door, I ran into Dad who immediately asked, "Well how did it go?"

"Even though you didn't tell me what to do, Dad, I knew what was right. The pressure was even greater after I lost my concentration and let the first shot get through the five hole. But then I got to thinking, 'What is wrong with what he said? Can good grades be bought or do they come with hard work?' It got real easy then. We beat the Green team 7–1. I even had two assists!"

"Dad, after the game Mr. Roberts came up to me and said, 'Buddy, I really wanted to see what you were made of. You didn't surprise me.' Then he patted me on the back and told me to 'hit the showers'."

△

My end of semester report card surprisingly contained an "A" in Physical Education. My biggest surprise however were the marks Miss Severson included in the *Honesty, Integrity, Ethics* and *Works Well with Others* columns. All four contained exemplary marks. When I thanked her for the marks, Miss Severson reminded me that doing right when *everyone* is looking, is not what counts, rather, it is doing right when *nobody* is looking.

As I was leaving the classroom later that afternoon, Miss Severson remarked: "Buddy, be sure you tell Mr. Roberts 'Thank you and have a nice Christmas', just as you have to me. He would appreciate it. After all, he did influence my marks."

At Christmastime, it was a family tradition to cut down a coniferous tree the first weekend in December. This ritual was followed by decorating, seasonal baking, and hot chocolate. Frequently my parents' good friends, the Lundgrens and the Bensons, would come over that evening and join the festivities. If the weather cooperated, ice skating was also part of the fun. Sledding and a hayride were part of the fun during especially snowy winters. Mom believed one of the reasons Dad specifically kept his implements was that he enjoyed pulling the hay wagon with his brightly decorated tractor as much as the riders enjoyed the ride.

Mom did not seem the same this Christmas. Although she said she felt fine, overcoming the reality of being in her early forties seemed to draw away some of her festive spirit. We could only guess why she had not talked to the Lundgrens or Bensons about getting together as she had done in the past.

"Buddy, give me a hand unloading those boxes from the car." After she returned home that first Friday night in December, I found large boxes crammed tightly into the rear seat while two smaller boxes and a large box had been forced into the oversized trunk. I found a third small box and several paper bags on the front seat. I could tell Mom was on a mission. "I think I'll stay home tomorrow and decorate here instead of going to the church." This was very unusual for a servant like Mom.

⌂

"Kids, its 8:45; it's time to go with your dad."

"Are you sure you are going to be all right?" Dad asked Mom on Saturday morning as he made one last attempt at changing her mind. I could see the unopened boxes remained in the garage where she had asked me to stack them. Unusual, still dressed in her bath robe, Mom assured Dad, "Run along, I'll see you tonight."

Mom knew we would be putting up decorations all day at church. We returned home to find what Mom had so meticulously planned for this Christmas. There, in front of the picture window, complete with its own tri-color revolving light and base, was our own eight foot tall, aluminum Christmas tree! No more tinsel, popcorn strings, or homemade ornaments. We were entering this decade in style – at least Mom's style. The tree only had one color of ornaments – red – all the same size, each having the exact same wire hanger. There was only a star on top! Gone was her gold, antique angel – a gift from her father.

There may have been other reasons why this Christmas was different; after all, it was an upside down year. It may have been Mom's way of adjusting to the end of another year and 15 years of marriage. Maybe she was just letting her hair down. Mom had worked several hours of overtime between September and December. She looked a bit gaunt.

1962

Over the all school intercom, Miss Severson announced, "As you know, I taught most of your parents. I am so proud that you have become their prodigies and not their prodigals. Yes students, those are your two words of the day." Without missing a beat, each student hurriedly attempted to write "prodigies" and "prodigals" on anything they could find. The wise, anticipating her actions, had had pencil and paper at the ready. Like every other day, Miss Severson sprung her "Words O' the Day" at the most unsuspecting time. Her chosen words were always similar in pronunciation but different in meaning. Miss Severson awarded a special gift to the student who best wrote each word's definition and used it properly in a sentence. Special recognition went to a student who successfully used both words in the same sentence. Each entry was time stamped before it was placed in her specially marked entry box. Her deadline was always 12 noon. A tie was broken by awarding the gift to the earliest, successful entry. Today was to be no different – except for one thing.

June 1, 1962 had been designated by the Providence Independent School District as "Miss Severson Day". This Friday was designated as her special day because it was her retirement day.

An early morning assembly had been called. Pausing to reposition herself in front of the massive public address console, she leaned into the microphone, tears smearing her trademark rouge; softly, almost prayer like, she closed with the regal style she was known for, "May God protect you as you seek Him." Gaining new strength in her own words, she

58

carried on, "Once again, my humble thanks to each and every one of you. You have been such a blessing to me! Now let's start the day!"

Decorations and congratulatory banners were placed everywhere. The dress code was relaxed; students were allowed to dress casually for this day only. Precisely at 12:55 p.m., Miss Severson announced, "And the winner is… Mae Lynne Davis! Mae Lynne, you may pick up your gift at Hendricks's Drug Store. Her sentence…"

After 45 years of teaching life's lessons, everyone recognized this was also the end of an era. At day's end, the entire school followed her down the wide hallways to the front entrance where she was cheered, applauded, and wished good luck as she drove off that afternoon in her shiny, new, beige Plymouth Valiant. Only 4'11" tall, she could barely be seen; her car was loaded with suitcases and boxes as she headed north to her retirement cottage on Minnesota's Lake Bemidji. I personally saw at least four fishing poles.

However, later that year, all of Providence was shocked as we sadly learned she died within two months of her retirement. Although she was not a Providence native, her will's executer carried out her request to be buried in the town she loved and adopted. It was a mutual adoption. She truly had given her all.

⌂

"Oops!" I was chagrined as glass shattered into the garage and fell to the floor.

George didn't need to remind me, but he did anyway: "Now you're in trouble Buddy! I told you we shouldn't use the garage door as a backstop."

It didn't take much to realize that a baseball and garage door window were not compatible; I had insisted we play on the gravel driveway. After all, the pasture had too many early spring thistles, mole holes, and cow pies. Anxious as ever for drying spring air, my eleventh year began with unusually wet conditions. Many of the local farmers spoke of relentless rains and of their inability to work the fields. Although not the same degree of impact as on farming activities, the spring "catch" season was significantly delayed. "Connie" was too heavy to pull over the saturated ground. The winter's Wiffle Ball Garage League was just not the same. Dad recounted his many warnings, "See, that plastic ball and bat did hurt your hand/eye coordination. Its light weight gives you power, but it is severely limited."

Returning to the Orioles in the spring and with my catching and batting ability once again under the constant eye of veteran Coach Fox, I knew something would need to improve or the bench could be very hard.

One thing did change. What I believe was a result of all of the winter activities, I was now 15 pounds heavier and three inches taller – a whopping 100 pounds and four foot six inches! None of the other boys had grown as much. The core players were now mid-age for Little League. Coach Fox thought this reorganized group had a good chance of improving on last year's performance. If we didn't, at least we would be in the league's best physical shape; he was going to see to that.

Coach Fox continued to look with concern at his lone southpaw. My right fielding was improved but I clearly wasn't batting as well as he had hoped. What was he to do? He believed Mark Farmer and Larry Dreger made up our best battery. Kenny Stahl, David Fox, and George had all moved on to Pony League.

Early season practices seemed to be going well, however, the team was doggedly short staffed because several boys had mid-week church. "Why do they have to go to church during the middle of the week?" I asked Dad when he picked me up after Wednesday night practice."

"Maybe we should start going more often ourselves; it wouldn't hurt us, would it?"

This absenteeism, however, gave Coach Fox an opportunity to try the remaining players at different positions; some even unconventional. About mid year, he relegated me to play pitch and catch behind the dugout with his son David. Later, checking my progress, he must have thought that with enough games of catch, he could make me either a pitcher... or a catcher?"

David Fox found all the equipment a catcher needed: mitt, mask, chest protector and knee pads, in the extra equipment bag. From time to time, we traded off use of the equipment, except for the mitt. I always brought ours, or rather Dad's Father's Day present.

"Buddy, we need to help you harness that thing. I'm tired of coming over here to give David smelling salts and ice packs if he unfortunately catches your 'Blazer' in the wrong place."

I too began to learn the significance of a supporter, especially one outfitted with a protective cup. Although not as swift and accurate as my throw, David pitched a very good fastball. However, frequently throwing wildly, I began to handle his short hops well; I now remembered and understood Uncle Harry's frustration.

As he put on additional weight, Larry Dreger had not developed a muscular build. Larry had always been able to intimidate batters by his sheer size and presence on the mound.

"Time out!" Coach Fox yelled to the umpire as he looked behind the dugout. With Don Longly at church and the roster already lean, Coach Fox made an important decision. We held a precarious 3–0 lead over our archrivals, the Cubs. A win would assure us of at least a tie for the league crown. Coach was visibly anxious as he indicated a player switch. I awoke from disbelief when Coach Fox yelled, "Buddy, come on in!" Several emotions were suddenly cooped up in my body. Was I was getting a chance at my dream?

Stopping by the dugout, I threw the practice ball into the equipment box. Lucky for me, I thought, I'm already wearing David's catcher's equipment.

Coach Fox instructed me, "You had better go back and take off the equipment. I want you to come in for Larry not Mark."

Grudgingly, I returned to the dugout – this time to take off the catcher's equipment and to grab my four fingered glove.

As we crossed paths, Larry offered some much appreciated words of encouragement. Mark Farmer was a good catcher. He too was the properly equipped soldier. Only slightly larger than me, we had never played catch up until now. After many hours of playing catch with David, and throwing pitches to "Connie", my accuracy and speed had become highly defined. But that was all I had, no other types of throws. During warm-ups, suddenly Coach realized there was one other problem; Mark was unable to catch Buddy's Blazer. Any "pass ball", when the catcher fails to catch, block, or stop the ball, had the secondary result of advancing runners.

With just two innings to go, Coach Fox only said it once, "No one can get on base, got it? Mark, set your target right in the center of your chest." Did Coach really know what he was saying?

Poor Mark suffered the same fate as the others but he had a chest protector on; they hadn't. Fortunately, he was able to keep Buddy's Blazer in front of him. He repeated the process the 18 required times.

Coach Fox was noticeably relieved. Each ball had been thrown to the same place, at the same speed, with the same result. We walked off the field that August evening with the possibility of becoming sole league champions. "Ol' Connie kind of helped, didn't she?" Confidently, Dad knew his contraption had made a difference.

Coach Fox had a large smile on his face when we ran onto the field three days later for our last game of the season. He believed we had built up enough of a lead to seal the victory. We had.

Besides being the end of the season, it was a time to say goodbye. You see Coach Fox, although a brilliant baseball coach, could not overcome his addictions to alcohol and cigarettes.

In late summer, a tall, thin visitor watched each of us with intensity and the keen eye of an eagle. Just as predictable as his attendance, he always wore a soiled, golden baseball cap with an embroidered emblem. Though they never spoke in public, Coach Fox assured us that the stranger was looking after our best interests.

⌂

"Did you meet the new bank vice president?" I heard Mom ask Dad that early fall, Friday afternoon. "She has as many freckles as I do! With our auburn hair, she could almost pass as my younger sister – if I had one." Dad always drove the carpool on Fridays. After dropping off his co-workers, Dad would head straight to the bank in order to deposit his weekly payroll check. Mom suggested, "Maybe she can answer some of our questions on a more personal basis. Ed Davis has already spoken well of her. I know she's married but I don't know what her husband does. Ed says she is from somewhere downstate. Maybe we should find out what all the excitement is about. Frankly, she can't do anything but help that ramshackle institution. They sure could use a woman in there to brighten things up! I was beginning to think Marvin's idea of progress peaked the day he convinced his fellow board members they should spend money to install electric lights – that was twenty years ago!"

⌂

I didn't like the change. Every Thursday, because of Mom's new fall work schedule, we would ride the school bus up Main Street to its intersection with Cherry. Mom had given the bus driver permission to drop Susanna, George, and me off at the corner for our short walk to the church and Youth Choir practice.

I began to miss the bus frequently. Walking alone, I began to arrive precisely fifteen minutes late. Mom sympathized with my lack of interest, but she would not tolerate my method of resistance. Not only was she angry with my tardiness, she was disgusted when Aunt Ella told her that I sang grossly off key, sang some other tune, or some other words, as my subtle means of protest. Head-strong, she knew I got it naturally.

Mom agreed it was probably time for me to pursue new interests, but she was also one to make her point clear. Working in collusion with Aunt Ella, they agreed to set a trap.

One afternoon, at the beginning of choir practice, Aunt Ella repeatedly stopped the choral singing at one particular point in the song. It seemed she always had something to correct, even if it had been sung perfectly. Knowing the precise time I could be expected, she repeated this same exercise several times. The choir was unaware of her motive. She knew she could hedge on my tardiness.

"Late again Buddy? Quickly, slip into your chair. Choir, let's try it one more time."

Disruptively slipping into my back row chair, the choir again followed her direction and abruptly stopped at the same point – mid-verse. Not following Aunt Ella's directing, I continued singing – by myself. However, the rest of the choir had not been singing "Zippity Do Da"! Without saying a word or cracking a smile, Aunt Ella started the verse once again; this time I carefully watched her every direction.

Coming up after practice, I remorsefully said, "Aunt Ella, I want to quit choir."

"Quit? What is that? Did something happen that made you decide choir wasn't for you?"

"I've thought it over. Like Dad, music isn't for me."

"Well, what other service for the church are you going to pursue?"

"I would like to help Mr. Clapper."

"I think he'd appreciate that."

With that, I made all the arrangements. Every Thursday I promptly got on the bus and rode to church. Now however, I helped Mr. Clapper by taking out the garbage, washing windows, painting and helping with the lawn and landscaping. In winter, I shoveled snow on both Thursdays and Sundays. The church paid me two dollars a week, year round.

"Mom, this worked out pretty good. It sure beats singing!" Mom smiled, knowing that everything had worked as it should and I was serving God, just in a different way.

⌂

I recall several times anxiously awaiting, in fear, the obnoxious civil defense horn. We students were always prepared for disaster, even the unthinkable – a nuclear bomb. Shelters were designated with funny looking deep mustard colored signs. There were several cat and mouse showdowns that Fall between President Kennedy and Russian Premier Khrushchev. Several times I expected to see missiles flying in the sky above our lunchtime recess. When the practice horn was sounded, we hastily and efficiently moved toward a safe area of the building. We were trained how to hide under our desks and to not forget a key element of that training – darkening the room by drawing the window blinds.

Despite the tension, as a country we had a time for joy as Astronaut John Glenn circled the earth three times aboard his Friendship 7 capsule. Preceding his orbit were the sub-orbital flights by Alan Shepard and Gus Grissom.

⌂

One Saturday in December, when the church youth choir went caroling at Country Manor Nursing Home, rounding a corner, Susanna said she noticed something very familiar. It was then, she said, that she remembered all the boxes and bags of Christmas ornaments had mysteriously disappeared from Mom's basement storage shelving.

Country Manor probably knew more about how and when it had received the eight foot aluminum tree with its single color ornaments and spinning color wheel and base than any member of the Olsen family – except Mom – and she wasn't talking.

As for our tradition of tree cutting, decorating, and fellowship the first weekend in December, it was reborn and well once again.

1963

A little over 17 years after returning from the Pacific, Coach Fox died at the young age of 41. The gloomy weather that early January day of his funeral only added to the depression and grief. Just as First Swedish Church had been for Miss Severson's funeral five months earlier, St. Peter's Church was packed to capacity. Tears of sorrow were everywhere. The small sanctuary was packed with many of the boys who had played baseball during Coach Fox's tenure. Coach Fox had given his time so freely. Several attendees, including me, were noticeably uneasy as the priest repeatedly forgot Coach Fox's name.

This was a special day for me too. Dad made special arrangements to leave work early so he would be able to take George and me to the funeral. Dad didn't talk much but we knew he was saying a lot; he had lost a fellow veteran on this battlefield of life.

⌂

"Buddy, come to town with George and me. I need to pick up several things at the lumberyard and we could use your help. I'm glad they have decided to open Saturday afternoons." Dad liked his new baby blue F100 pickup. Pulling the back forward, Dad slipped several items behind so we could ride comfortably three abreast. We first stopped to pick up gas for the tractor at Dad's cousin's service station. Having trouble keeping thieves out of his above ground tank, Dad decided he would start hauling gas cans rather than let it be stolen away. Always one for a good conversation, Dad took what seemed like hours to complete the transaction.

Returning to the driver's seat, George pointed toward the brown car in the distance. "Dad, there's Uncle Theodore's car parked in front of the Railroad Tavern."

"He's probably playing Pinochle or Cribbage. It must be a big game; I can see several cars around back."

Making two stops for Mom, we finally got to the lumberyard at 3:00 p.m.

"How's the missus Leif? We have your order ready to load." Walking from behind the counter, Mr. Arnold met us at the front door.

"Boys, go out with Mel and load it up. Put the gas cans on the sidewalk before you pull into the drive! We don't want anything to go wrong. I'm ready to go home and take a nap." Turning again to Mr. Arnold, he said, "Alvin, what's wrong? I can see it in your face."

"I'm glad you sent the three of them outside. Anna called and said Theodore got into some kind of ruckus at the bar. She told me to tell you to call home as soon as I saw you. You can use my phone in the back office."

We had just finished loading the pickup when Dad hurried out. "George, slowly pull the truck across the street; pull it forward into that front stall so no cars are between you and the stop sign."

Inquiringly I looked up and said, "What's going on Dad? I thought we were going home."

"It's probably a good time to teach you both one of life's lessons." Walking faster the closer we got to the Railroad Tavern, Dad swung open the bar door like a western marshal ready to clear the place.

"He's over there. He keeps dozing off. He got hit pretty hard."

"Who hit him?"

"He had too many drinks. When I stopped serving him, he began to argue with me. He took a wild swing, so I shoved him back into that chair, where he's been ever since. His color isn't very good. He isn't feeling very well either. You're his brother, right?" Dad didn't answer the question.

In a stupor, Uncle Theodore pleaded, "Come on Leif, jus' one more beer and then we can go." Sadly, Dad had probably heard this many times before.

Grabbing Uncle Theodore like a soldier carrying his comrade off the battlefield, Dad sarcastically responded to the bartender, "Thanks for your help. I'll take care of him."

Dad looked to George and said, "Do you still have the keys to the pickup? Tie down the load and head straight out of town toward the farm. Buddy, come with me." Opening the driver's door he directed, "Jump in the middle; I need someone to keep him in a comfortable position. Hold your nose, he will likely fall against you. If he lies down he will be a goner." Refocusing, wiping tears from his cheeks, he added, "George, I'll follow you until the dogleg cutoff. I'll take him directly to his farm. Tell Mom where we've gone. Pull the truck straight in the driveway and leave it in the turnout. We can unload it tomorrow after church. Drive slowly; be careful of the ice patches."

Growing up on the farm, George and I had plenty of off road driving experience. Driving a brand new, loaded down pickup down an icy road was something neither George nor I had ever experienced. Once in a while, perhaps in anticipation of a situation like this, Dad let us drive the car down the gravel roads. Of course, Mom knew nothing about that! I could hear George shifting like a pro. Heading due west, Dad and I quickly came up behind him.

Seeing the pickup coming in the driveway, Mom frantically ran out the screen door. Bringing the truck to a stop, George intercepted her just short of the corn crib. "Dad had to drive Uncle Theodore home. Buddy went along to help him sit up. Mom, Uncle Theodore didn't look like he was going to make it this time."

Sensing George's calmness, Mom asked, "Did you see any deputies?"

"Dad was behind me until the dogleg. I figured he could explain the situation if it arose."

Dad and I were exhausted as we came in the back door well after 6 o'clock. "Theodore won't need his car for a few days. I told Millie to call us if he took a turn for the worse. Without a driver's license and having no insurance, Millie will be pretty dependent on others' help. Buddy, before we go to bed, be sure and pull the pickup into the crib. I guess I'll put off my project until next week."

Mom asked, "Was Theodore all right when you left?"

Looking sad, Dad responded, "He looked terrible. He was spitting blood. The only thing we could do was prop him up in the dining room chair. Millie seemed to have him settled down when we left. Thanks for the help Buddy... you too George."

Then turning to George and me, Dad asked, "Well boys, what have you learned today?'

"I never want to touch that stuff! That cigarette smoke almost made me gag! The bar smelled even worse than Mom's old chicken coop!"

George then asked, "Dad, why does Uncle Theodore drink and you don't?"

"We each make decisions. I would be lying to you if I said I never touched Satan's Potion. After I entered the service, it became clear to me that having a clear mind – all of the time – was best for me. I also believe family is more important than the other option. Boys, that is something you may want to emulate."

Together we chimed, "Emulate? What does that mean?"

"It's my word of the day. The first to find its meaning gets to be served ice cream by the other two. Come on Anna, let's see who ends up serving whom."

Since I was closest to the bookshelf dictionary, Susanna and George dipped. It was funny though, when we looked at our meager servings, we suddenly realized why it had taken them so long to serve us. The five quart container was empty and sitting in the sink.

Bringing the dishes to the kitchen sink, Mom laughed, "Boy that tub didn't last very long. I just bought it off the ice cream truck this afternoon." With that we all sank into our Living Room seats as Dad turned on The Lawrence Welk Show.

◌

In 1959 it was Jose, 1960 Hector, 1961 Angelina, and 1962 Enrique. In 1963 a second girl joined her older siblings. All five were already on board by the time the big yellow bus stopped to pick up the Olsen trio.

Several Mexican families had been coming to the vege-table farm, just one section east of our farm, for many years. Migrating to Providence to cut asparagus in the spring, they would eventually travel further north during the summer harvests of tomatoes, potatoes, sweet corn, peas, beets, and onions from other vegetable farms scattered throughout the upper Midwest.

These same migrant families would always return just in time to start the school year in Providence. As the tempera-tures dropped, they would generally remain until their wood fires could no longer supply adequate heat to their living quarters.

Cute as a button, Maria had prepared herself for her first full day at Providence Junior High. At the time, it never occurred to me that one of their greatest hardships was the fact that every year these migrant students changed schools several times during an academic year.

At the end of each harvest season, some of the weary families chose to abandon migrant work and seek employment in one of the new nearby factories. Some were even hoping to invest their meager earnings into an area apartment or small house. The lure of steady employment far outweighed the toil and sweat promised by another year in the fields. Some, however, seasonally migrated year after year to the same railroad car homes located just on the edge of the productive fields.

Unlike her older siblings, Maria easily mixed with the other children on the bus. Her English had obviously become second nature, even before she left the Valley. She soon found out that speaking English brought her new friends.

However, these newfound friends in the schoolyard appeared standoffish when she invited them to come over to her home. Her home was unlike their wood framed, painted houses on tree-lined streets. For that matter, the railroad cars didn't even compare to the rundown farmhouses of the tenant farmers.

"Why won't any of the girls stay over with me?" I heard her ask Teri Mazzocco one afternoon. I sensed this question was awkward for the vegetable farmer's daughter. Although she acknowledged the question, Teri never appeared to cross the forbidden barrier of socializing with the migrant workers. I wondered, "Was this the way Dad, he too the son of immigrants, had been treated by his landlord? It seemed condescending, a trait I made up my mind to avoid."

⌂

Springtime brought new teams and new coaches. It was again time to move upward and onward. Since only 14 boys tried out, some may have won a position on the Pony League Giants solely by default. By league rules, teams could carry up to 16 players. The team was comprised of 12–14 year olds.

Volunteering as a baseball coach now became a serious undertaking, since there was only one team and it was a "traveler". Four area towns formed a League, including Big Stone, New Bergen, South Lake, and Providence. Practices were limited to Wednesday nights with games held every Saturday or Sunday afternoon.

Arriving early for the start of our first practice, Mom was startled as she and Dad dropped me off saying, "Aha! My hunch was correct. Leif, quick, look over there. She never mentioned her husband was going to be the new Pony League coach when Marvin first introduced me to her in the bank last fall. Sure enough, that is Sara with him."

The team quickly recognized him as the tall, thin visitor who had watched our practices late last summer. We learned Coach Ziegler had been hired by the school board to become both the junior high math teacher in the fall and the head varsity baseball coach next spring.

With most boys continuing to mature physically, my size and stature started to work against me. At first I believed I was being assigned the position of team bench warmer. At five feet tall and weighing 115 pounds, I was largely relegated to keeping score on the outfield plywood scoreboard during home games or in the scorebook at away games. I also carried the team's equipment and played catch with the other substitute players.

Nearing the end of the Pony League season, Coach Ziegler pulled me aside one afternoon after midweek practice. "Buddy, I've been studying your batting average for the season to see if I can find the reason why it hasn't improved as the season has progressed. You are now 2 for 20 and have gone hitless in your last 16 at bats. Usually when an 11 or 12 year old's eyes change and are corrected, their hand/eye coordination improves. Yours has not. I've got a couple of ideas."

After a few simple vision tests, Coach Ziegler concluded that my left eye was by far my dominant eye.

"Let's try something during our last game. I want you to bat only left-handed. I think that's how God's designed you. No matter what the outcome, I plan on using this game to fine tune you for next year's team. I may take it one step further, but I'll decide that if the opportunity arises."

⌂

Our last League game was at South Lake. With similar 1–8 records, the only consolation for the winner of this game was not being awarded last place. When the lineups were posted, it soon became evident that Coach Ziegler had indeed shuffled the lineup in order to test some additional new theories.

One of his theories was tested early. South Lake had only one strong pitcher, right hander Alex DeVleer. We had seen him earlier in the season during a game in which he had humiliated us by allowing only one run and two hits.

Buster patiently coaxed a walk off of Alex. Each pitch was well out of the strike zone. Buster had even helped Alex's efforts by embarrassingly swinging at two bad pitches. After a brief catcher/pitcher conference it was my turn to bat. South Lake seemed somewhat confused to see me in the lineup, much less batting from the left hand side.

My hands seized the bat's black electrical tape as Alex's first pitch blazed, belt high, straight down the middle of the plate. I swung late and it lined directly towards the third base coach's box. Third base coach Vaughn skipped out of the way.

Yelling from his bleacher seat near the backstop screen, I clearly heard Dad coax, "Concentrate Buddy and choke up a little. It will lighten your bat!"

Alex's second strike was well on its way – not incoming this time but outgoing! The line drive was hit so hard that Buster was on his way to third by the time it first scuffed the new mown outfield grass. Possessing what seemed to be eyes, it was on its way to the right center coffin corner. Skipping over the low rope, Buster rounded second and third, easily trotting home for our first run. Starting out from the nearest side of the box, I dug my steel spikes into the hard clay as I rounded first. I made it to second standing up.

"Boy did that feel good!" I later told Coach Ziegler. "I saw the ball just as if I could smash it like a pumpkin!" Even though Alex was considered a good fastball pitcher, this afternoon, more powerful bats overwhelmed everything he threw.

Coach Ziegler later confided to me: "I believed if Buster could successfully reach first base as the leadoff man, batting left-handed you may have a chance of advancing him to third with a hit that tailed behind him. If the first baseman held him close to the bag, and your natural pull to right field, the ball should land in the gap between fielders and result in an extra base hit for you."

Before our third turn at bat and already behind by four runs, South Lake Coach DeVleer decided he had seen enough of his son's pitching. Lefties were as uncommon as pitchers as they were as batters. New entry, Keith Baaken was a straight over-the-shoulder lefty. This was to be my first time seeing the ball delivered from the first base side of the mound and my new side of the plate. Keith relied heavily on the fact that his natural curve slid inside and down to the right handed batter. I theorized that if he pitched the same to a lefty batter, the ball could be lifted high and long. If a left-handed batter slightly crowded the plate, when extended, the shaft of the bat would be at its most powerful position. Coach Ziegler confirmed my thinking by adding, "Dig in and move slightly closer to the plate so you take the ball at the beginning of its curve."

He was right! This time the ball sailed well over the corncrib fencing between the center and right fielders. With straight center being the deepest part of the diamond, making these minor adjustments, I was able to unconsciously pull it away from the deepest points and land it ten feet beyond the 250' corn cribbing fence line. Coach Ziegler was 2 for 2 in the theory department.

Just before the bottom of the fifth I heard, "Buddy, put on the gear. With Bill sick again and Mark tiring, I want to try something different. Let's see what happens."

What? Did I hear him right? Am I finally getting my chance behind the plate?

After taking just two pitches the umpire called "Time". Quietly he said, "Turn around catcher. Did you forget something?"

"May I go back to my bag and grab it?"

Outside of the batter's earshot, he whispered, "League rules say that a catcher without a protection cup is to be removed from the game. Understanding your team's circumstances, I'll let you go this time and this time only. I wouldn't want to see you get injured. Remember, when you put it on, the point goes down."

I ran by the dugout and quickly grabbed my equipment bag. I headed for the nearest outdoor toilet – only to find it occupied. After some quick pleading, David Finch strolled out the door. "David, you left your magazine in here," I shouted, to no avail.

Since I wore a snap pouch supporter, the problem became a quick fix. I hustled back to the field. Most of the fans were unaware of my equipment problem.

"He had to go to the bathroom!" the umpire shouted to Coach DeVleer.

Offensively, it appeared Coach DeVleer was using the same experimental game plan as Coach Ziegler. I was unable to control two wild pitches, thus allowing unearned runs and additional hitting opportunities.

Larry Dreger was hastily losing both control and speed. With the game now tied, Coach Ziegler saw a chance to test another theory. He again called "time". Hoping to end the inning, Coach Ziegler took the opportunity to make an adjustment. He ordered George and Larry to make a switch, putting Larry in left field and George on the mound. The Olsen battery was alive again!

When the inning was over, Coach took me aside and said, "Remember how we talked about your dominant eye? Let's apply that same theory when you're catching." Then Coach proceeded to show me why I wasn't performing as well as I could and how I could improve. He finished with one more piece of advice: "With right-handed batters in the box, cheat way to the inside of the outside chalk line. Be careful; never cross over the chalk. For lefties, your sight line will be right over the plate and your throwing will not be restricted to any base."

It appeared Coach Ziegler had scripted the entire game. We handily defeated South Lake. I had gone 5 for 5 at the plate with two doubles, two triples, a home run, and an intentional walk. George shut out South Lake the remaining two innings, coming within a single of perfect pitching. There were no pass balls, no additional wild pitches. The sole runner was easily picked off first when a left-handed batter allowed me unimpeded vision and movement. The over exuberant base runner underestimated the speed and accuracy of my throw. From experience, George knew exactly where to place the pitch so as to maximize the chance for the pickoff play.

"Buddy, that worked well, didn't it? There is one more thing I need to tell you. I asked you to work the scoreboard for a reason. Even though, early on, you didn't play, you still watched the entire game from a seat slightly above the field. Also, by keeping the scorebook at the away games, as you readily saw, you were able to identify the strengths, weakness and strategies of the opposition. I have never let my catcher call a game before. I must say, you have become a well educated student of the game." With the summer over, we went our separate ways, now to become pupil and teacher.

Memories of Uncle Harry's imaginative calls danced in my head as I dozed to sleep: "Now up to bat for New York, all-star, and the League's only left handed catcher, Budddyyyy Olsen!"

◠

For me, Confirmation classes began that fall. The curriculum was set for the two-year instruction, starting with the Book of Genesis, progressing through the historical parts of the Bible, and completing the Old Testament by spring. At six, our class size was small. When one or two were absent, the sessions became hopelessly unproductive.

I knew for the next two years, every Saturday morning would be spent in a pseudo Sunday School classroom setting. With Pastor Buchanan fully retired and no longer living in the area, and Pastor Davidson's sudden resignation, the District's interim Pastor, Samuel Lawrence, was asked to lead the flock permanently.

My mind was not on confirmation these Saturday mornings. The long-winded, 2½ hour sessions were grueling. My thoughts were on other things that could be accomplished during that same time period. I had just begun to enjoy basketball. I thought this time could easily be used on a court.

⌂

Late one Friday afternoon in mid-September, math teacher Ziegler asked me to stay after class. I just knew it was about my conduct in class that afternoon.

"You all go to St. Bartholomew's, don't you?"

Stunned, I wondered how he ever came to know that. I also thought: You all? Where was he from? Me, go to St. Bartholomew's? Of course not – I would never want be thought of as a Sunday School brat. Besides, it would hurt my image. Then without thought, I responded, "Yeah, why don't you all meet us there Sunday morning?" Where did that '*you all*' come from?

He chuckled, "What time?"

"Well, church starts at 9:00 a.m. Meet me at the south door at 8:45." What had I done now? Would we even be there? I hoped Dad and Mom weren't planning on changing the routine.

The time was set. Again, I wondered: Why did he ask me? There were plenty of others, especially those who attended First Apostles. I was beside myself.

When we tardily arrived at 8:50, Coach and Mrs. Ziegler had already been introduced to Pastor Lawrence by the door greeters. It appeared my enthusiasm for the new visitors far exceeded that of the Pastor – something I thought was quite unusual. Bypassing the assigned ushers, I quickly walked the

Zieglers to the pew directly in front of ours. Our family was ushered in shortly thereafter.

From the beginning it became quite apparent Coach and Mrs. Ziegler were very unfamiliar with a liturgical service. Before being seated, I handed them six pages of announcements, readings, and promotional literature. In front of them were two large blue service books. Five hymn numbers were posted on the hymn boards located on both sides of the sanctuary. The bulletin order of service included names and page numbers for the different parts of the service. The order of service was divided into subparts. Latin words such as: Gloria Dei and Nunc Diminitis, along with Italian titles for the prelude and postlude. It likely appeared to them that the only two recognizable English words were *Sermon* and *Offering*.

Sensing their lost state, it suddenly occurred to me that the liturgy had become rote in just 12 years of childhood. I always knew what ritual was to happen next – when I was to stand, and when I was to sit. I also knew what responses I was to recite at the end of each printed prayer. After singing, chanting, and the readings from the printed pages of the service book, it was now time to sit. It was obvious the Zieglers were totally embarrassed as they slowly realized they were the only ones standing. Similarities to dog obedience school must have crossed their mind. The entire congregation patiently waited for them to correct their mistake.

For the Bible readings, however, we didn't need Bibles at the new, contemporary, St. Bart's; we had the scripture readings conveniently inserted into the bulletin. Those who were well prepared had pulled the insert from the packet; those who weren't, noisily fumbled through the assortment of papers. Wavering from the Scripture, Pastor Lawrence's sermon appeared to come more from the latest newspaper articles and philosophy books.

At the close of the sermon, Pastor Lawrence, just as his predecessors, paraphrased Philippians 4:7: "Now may the Peace of God, which passes all understanding, keep your hearts and minds in Christ Jesus." Even someone as young as I knew it was the end of the sermon, although I wasn't really sure what the verse meant.

Hastily closing the one hour service, the young acolytes raced out the side door as the pastor proceeded down the aisle to his appointed position by the sanctuary doors. I saw an overwhelming sense of relief come over the Zieglers' faces. All that remained was to be run up the chute for the anticlimactic cattle drive toward the exit.

My family warmly greeted the Zieglers after the service. In our world however, it was time to go to the restaurant for Sunday dinner in order to be fully ready for the afternoon NFL football game.

Coach Ziegler didn't say anything about church on Monday. Despite what appeared to be an embarrassing first visit, Coach Ziegler and his wife continued to attend St. Bart's. Late in the fall, the Zieglers joined. We never spoke about church at school or about school at church. These were two different worlds, the spoken and unspoken. For that matter, banking was never talked about either.

⌂

"The President has been shot." "The President is dead." Those words have forever been engrained in each of us old enough to remember that tragic Friday morning, November 22, 1963.

⌂

Saturday, November 23rd was very cold; however, something inside told me I needed to ride my bicycle the two miles to the vegetable farm. Starting with sunshine, the day became mostly cloudy as it progressed. The weather report forecasted an increasing chance of snow flurries. My heart was pounding as I rode down the dirt path leading to the railroad cars. I had seen them from a distance but never had I actually entered the camp.

Much to my surprise, the camp appeared to have been rapidly vacated. Six boxcars stood behind the bare leaf lilac screen. I had seen from a distance the large steel wheels had been removed, but I soon learned the large sliding door was welded shut. A small opening, two feet wide by five feet tall, had been cut into the smooth sidewall allowing me enough room to enter and look around. Pushing the heavy oil cloth tarp to the side, I discovered natural light diffused through two small end openings. Both were glazed with polyethylene film stapled to a wood frame.

Approximately 10 make shift beds had been built from tomato crates and wood pallets. Each was covered with various sizes of tarp. There were two box springs on the ground and six suspended tarp hammocks – large enough for a child. Two dim incandescent light bulbs hung from the ceiling – both were still burning. Direct wired from the transformer feed, apparently they glowed day and night. In the center, tomato crates were also used to support a piece of plywood making it into a makeshift table. Tomato crates were used to make chairs, with the very best ones being nailed together forming backs and legs.

Stepping back outside, I could see each home had a 55-gallon drum used for cooking, trash burning, and heating. A duct transferred the heat and likely some of the smoke into the rail car. One outhouse had been built between each car. The drifting fumes confirmed the same location had been used for many seasons.

Suddenly, I remembered the cheerful words Maria spoke on Wednesday afternoon as she stepped off the bus,

82

"Remember, the Lord will reward those whose toil is blessed."

With that the 11-year-old winked and added, "Adios mi amigo de Cristo. Go sow some more seeds!" With the end of the second grading period now complete, I knew Maria and her witness would receive the Lord's protection as they made their way back to the warmth of the Texas Rio Grande Valley.

⌂

With the Advent season approaching, Sunday School lessons were derived from the traditional Christmas stories found in Luke.

The Sunday before Christmas, we gathered in the church fellowship hall for a family reunion and dinner. Small presents were exchanged. It was readily apparent this year's attendance was small. Loved ones who had passed away earlier in the year were sadly missed. Burying his younger brother and childhood buddy made this Christmas especially hard for Dad.

1964

With the holidays long over and the snow slowly melting away, the time was rapidly approaching for my second year in Pony League. During the winter, Dad made several minor improvements to Connie. Adding lubrication fittings, everything rolled and moved much easier. In early spring, while farmers were in their fields, so too, Dad was in his – relocating the pitcher's mound and batter's boxes to different areas. This distance was now precisely 60 feet 6 inches. The regulation pitching rubber and home plate were re-installed. This year's alfalfa field was transformed into a ball field complete with duck cloth bags and a snow fenced outfield. With its close proximity to the creek, this poor producing, flood plain parcel was perfectly suited for its new use.

⌂

"Buddy, that is the most convoluted tournament bracketing I have ever seen in my life."

"But Coach Ziegler, with only six town teams in Itasca County that is the fairest I could come up with."

"All right. I'll take it to the other coaches when we meet in New Bergen next week."

Following the first year's success, two new Pony League teams formed and joined an expanded league of six teams. With a longer season of 15 games, at the end of the summer we remained second only to Big Stone. We were elated with our 12–3 record. The final standings determined the seeds for the all-team championship tournament.

Big Stone had an easy time against their Saturday morning opponent, New Bergen, but the Boulders had to go into extra innings against South Lake in the Saturday night game.

As second seed, we had to play the winner of the number three versus four seeds, West Fork. Although the towns were close in size, there was no closeness in the score.

With West Fork now safely behind us, our second game was against Riceland, a first round loser of the fifth versus sixth game. George was able to hold off Riceland through the first six innings. Reliever Peter Swann came on in the top of the seventh to secure our win.

It was on to the Championship Game against our arch-rival Big Stone, the number one seed, set for Sunday afternoon.

As Sunday afternoon's Consolation, Third Place, and Championship games were ready to start, it became evident there was a noticeable absence of players on all sides. Several boys, whose parents attended the more conservative area churches, would not let them participate in the Sunday afternoon finale.

With only an eleven-man roster, Coach Ziegler must have thought he would be forced to implement some of his observations discovered during last year's end of season game with South Lake.

It was during the sixth inning, and ahead by two runs, that Larry Dreger's arm finally gave out. Again, Coach called George in from left field. He substituted Buster Mazzocco in his place. I was in right. George's second throw was foul tipped and caught Mark Farmer in an unprotected area inside of his right shoulder. Mark fought back tears as he was helped from the field. Coach Ziegler's luck had just worsened that afternoon since our back-up catcher, Bill Schmidt, was one of the boys whose parents would not allow him to play on Sundays.

Because of the injury, another switch had to be made. With one out, men on first and second, Coach realized his dilemma was that he had no other catcher, except...

Coach Ziegler yelled across the diamond, "Buddy, put on the equipment!"

I thought: "If I am successful here, this will be for the prestigious All-County Pony League Championship. My name will be in marquee lights!"

Ben Armstrong was inexperienced but Coach thought he could hold down right field for two-thirds of an inning. I am sure Coach easily remembered the outcome of last year's game with South Lake. He knew I should be able to block wild pitches and pass balls. But how about under the pressure of this Championship game?

As I ran by, George yelled "Get Dad's catcher's mitt out of my equipment bag." Depressed that I had not played catcher for some time, I had purposely left Dad's mitt at home. George must have known better.

There it was, "Old Reliable", especially molded over time to fit my right hand. I stepped into the battery with confidence as I heard Dad say: "Remember it's just you, George, and Connie."

With one out and just one more inning to play, the Boulders' coach signaled for a double steal. He must have figured he might as well challenge the rookie, left-handed catcher. George's pitch was perfect, slightly inside to the left-handed batter. It was gone so fast that the streaking lead runner was tagged out easily by our third baseman who in turn threw to second with the same result. Once again I could hear Uncle Harry say, "Just like the big leagues, around the horn, score it 2 to 5 to 4. Nice job Olsen!"

Coach Ziegler remained guarded. Out of the inning, Coach knew the game wasn't over quite yet. With his favorite catcher in place, George reeled off nine strikes in the

86

bottom of the 7th to the Boulders' #7, #8, and #9 batters. The All-County Pony League Championship belonged to the Providence Pilgrims. Now, where can I find those lights?

⌂

My second year of Confirmation classes began just as summer ended. When Don Longley's parents officially transferred to another church just five members remained for the second year class. Pastor Lawrence complained that he was overworked and that he could not handle two confirmation classes at the same time. Rather than join the much larger first year class, the church council decided to rotate the teaching assignment between Mrs. Ziegler and Mrs. Thompson. The plan was for each to rotate instruction throughout the year. Upon receiving a passing score on the final written test, and demonstrating an ability to recite the names of the books of the Bible, in order from memory, I knew I would then be Confirmed.

Midway into the New Testament curriculum Mrs. Thompson asked to be relieved of her responsibility. Almost like I had been revived from a nap, I began to listen intently to Mrs. Ziegler's teachings from Paul's writings. She too spoke of his conversion as recorded in the book of Acts. Was this just a nice story? I had heard it before. However now, I began to wonder: "How could a light blind, and more suspiciously *speak* to, a man for three days?"

⌂

Dad quickly sensed something was wrong before he even saw anyone. Supper was not ready as he walked in the screened porch door at his usual time of 5:00 p.m.

"What happened?"

Tearfully falling into his arms, Mom made every effort not to club him with her arm cast, "I fell against a stainless steel preparation table in the hospital kitchen."

"Well at least you were in the right place at the right time!"

"Please don't make me laugh. My head is throbbing and I ache all over."

"Tell me how it happened."

"I went into the kitchen's walk-in freezer. I had bought several boxes of Eskimo Pies and had stashed them on an unused shelf in the corner. Walking out of the freezer, I felt a little light-headed as I latched the heavy door. I leaned against a nearby stainless steel table and munched away."

"Did you get an ice cream headache?"

"No, I don't think so... I just don't remember. I thought I felt fine as I walked away. I wound my way through the tables and equipment. I do remember that I was beginning to think I was in a maze. All of a sudden, the tile became blurry, I lost my peripheral vision, my fingers tingled and my knees buckled. Realizing I was falling fast and hard, I instinctively put out my arm to break the fall. I soon found out it couldn't support me either! "

"Then what?"

"That same table next to the freezer redirected my fall; otherwise I would have hit the floor with my entire body. Instead, I landed on my rump! While falling, I hit my arm on the table, causing it to break. Hearing my slurred cries for help, a couple of nurses' aids who were nearby, rushed into the kitchen to see what had happened. Picking me up by my armpits they walked me to an empty wheelchair and whisked me down to the emergency room."

"You better go get some rest. You look exhausted."

Almost like she knew she would be asleep for quite awhile, Mom responded, "I hope that patient didn't think his wheelchair had been stolen! I need to be at work early on Monday; we are training some new Candy Stripers. "

Mom went into their bedroom where she slept on and off for three days – mostly on. She was unable to attend church on Sunday, but she was ready to go to work on Monday morning. Although somewhat impaired by the cast on her right arm, she taught herself how to write with her left hand. She later told us that most of the doctors thought her writing was good!

"Buddy, I easily see how difficult it is to try and adapt to something that doesn't come naturally!"

Daily, for the next six weeks, Susanna drove Mom to and from work. Needless to say, the Holiday season was subdued.

1965

"You got home fast. Dinner is not quite ready. Go in and talk to your guests." Surprised by the number of cars in the drive, I returned home to a very large get together with family and friends, complete with Mom's great home cooking and congratulatory gifts for the Confirmand.

"It doesn't take long to photograph a group of five. Can I take off my tie?"

"You can wear it through dinner. You can take your suit coat off if you want to."

Palm Sunday was St. Bart's traditional day of Confirmation. Dressed in our pure white robes, starched crisply to show no wrinkles, we stood before the small congregation to confirm what we had been taught. Confirmation began the time when the church allowed us to go to the altar to receive the sacrament of Holy Communion. It also entitled me to become a member of St. Bart's.

The few times, since I was not good about getting it into the hamper, my baseball uniform was laundered, it seemed to shrink! It may have been the malfunctioning single selection dryer that Dad and Mom had purchased in 1959, but more than likely it was the fact that my body was growing. To this day I remember Mom's first commandment of laundering: If it is to be laundered, it must be in the hamper, period! If it's not, then it is worn dirty or you are responsible for washing it yourself.

At the beginning of the year, it seemed shirts were grossly oversized. The flannel cotton was durable but not the least bit light in weight. Medium appeared to be small and large was only for those who had the physique of Goliath. There was no such thing as a real medium. Eventually, by the end of the season, the shirts began to fit the trim golden tanned torsos. Confidently, I concluded it was the result of enlarging arms and chests, not of laundering.

Throughout the summer, both my Pony League and George's Babe Ruth teams remained mediocre. I recall one of George's games in New Bergen. In the bottom of the seventh inning, with bases loaded and two outs in a tie ballgame, mentally George pitched aggressively; he was prepared to go into extra innings. He only needed one more out. A New Bergen pitcher named Peltier hit a hard grounder back to George. Seeing the force play at the plate as his best option, the play turned into disaster when catcher Bill Schmidt failed to step on home plate.

⌂

Our interest in 4-H animals, hunting, trapping, and fishing began to fade as interscholastic sports and girls became more important. Money we accumulated from marketing the livestock was supplemented by part time jobs sacking groceries or working as hired men for local farmers, including Ed Davis. I received my first raise and now earned five dollars every two weeks at the church. Extramural church activities became optional; worship attendance was compulsory.

⌂

We were tied going into the bottom of the seventh. South Lake's pitcher Alex DeVleer remained un-hittable. Yes, Alex had held us to no hits but Larry Dreger had held South Lake scoreless, too.

With two outs and the potential for extra innings, it was my turn to bat. Alex rang up two strikes against me. I expected the third fastball to be directly over the plate. On its way, I hopelessly swung way ahead of his newly acquired changeup.

Now I had been having trouble with gas for some time. Doctor Fitzgerald believed it was a food allergy, but he wasn't quite sure. Sure enough, just as I swung, I passed gas. South Lake's catcher, uncontrollably, began to laugh so hard he lost track of the ball as it skirted through his feet toward the backstop weeds. Seeing the opportunity, I sprinted to first and headed toward second. As the catcher struggled to hold back tears, he made a weak throw back to Alex; I scooted to third. With two outs, the whole game was suddenly in jeopardy. During the play, Alex totally lost his concentration. He then threw a marshmallow to Larry Dreger. The hard liner didn't touch the field until it reached the base of the center field fence. Officially, mine was scored as a pass ball – against South Lake's catcher – score it an unearned run. Final score: 1–0. I'm not sure how Uncle Harry would have announced that play.

This has become a lifelong memory of my final game as a Pony Leaguer. As I embarrassingly walked to the family car, I noticed even Coach Ziegler and Umpire Hendricks both had gotten a chuckle out of the whole incident.

"You really gassed them tonight Buddy!" Marty Polanski yelled as he got into a shiny, red, four door sedan.

⌂

"Where did you get those baby blue eyes with just a teasing of freckles?" Then with her own deep brown eyes twinkling, she approached me and said, "You are a handsome one you know." So went my first introduction to Tina Polanski. Tina had driven her parents out from the City to visit their cousins, our next door neighbors. Marty had told me during lunch hour on Friday that he wanted me to see his cool cousin. He said she would be at their house all weekend and that for sure she would want to see me. Late Saturday afternoon, having finished my few outside chores, I was startled when I looked up and saw Marty and his seventeen year old cousin had joined me in the barn. The tight-fitting, button front white blouse that was partially unbuttoned told me she wasn't properly dressed to go to Saturday evening mass.

After closing the barn door, Tina suggested, "Let's go down to the creek and wade in the water." I didn't find that to be unusual; Marty and I frequently fished in the creek or just walked along the banks looking for wildlife or other signs of nature. After a short time, Marty's younger brother Alan came along to join us.

"Anyone up for Hide and Go Seek?" We boys concurred; it sounded like a great idea.

"Scissors beats paper. It looks like you're 'it', Buddy." The three of them hastily scattered amongst the hickory trees.

With the sun moving swiftly towards the western horizon, and, after an hour of looking in every canyon, tree and crevice, I surrendered to the fact that Marty, Alan, and Tina had probably gone back home since they were nowhere to be found.

Out of nowhere, the silence was broken, "Geronimo!" With that I was butted by what felt like charging cow.

Flying through the air and into the creek, I was working my way back to the surface when I heard a cannonball splash. Wiping my eyes as I broke the water's surface, I barely got my words out, "Marty, what in the heck are you doing?" when I discovered the encounter was much more than I expected! I soon discovered it was Tina Polanski who had flung me into that tranquil pool of water. Having hid beneath a small embankment, I was completely startled when she rammed me from behind. Her momentum hurled me into the deep temperate waters of Providence Creek. Playfully, dunking me a second time, I was startled to discover she had been skinny dipping. Mesmerized by the image below the surface, I had never seen a young woman's body. Something told me, Tina wanted to be sure that she was my first. Still thrashing in the deep water, I realized my shirt was being methodically torn off; it began floating down stream.

Instinctively I swam for my shirt, grabbed it and headed for the far bank. I knew what I had been taught, so without turning my head, I quickly ran up a low embankment. "What's the matter country boy? See some nature you didn't expect?" She taunted me with flirtatious laughter. "I'll see you again some day! Nice farmer's tan, handsome!"

I knew I had climbed up the wrong bank, but I also knew the winding creek very well, having walked every inch of it while running our trap line. Fording at a rapids, I carefully snuck back through the woods, entering the barnyard like nothing had happened. But it had.

Later, trying to sneak into the house through the back door, Dad looked up from his paper and asked, "Buddy, those chores sure took you a long time. I'm glad we didn't have any family plans tonight. How did you get all wet? Are you ready for supper? We've been holding it until you came in."

"I went to the deep water pool and dove in to cool off – kind of a spur-of-the-moment thing. I'll be right back down. I'll hang my wet clothes in the basement. OK, Mom?"

"What did you say? You dove in with your clothes on?"

Looking up again Dad slyly said, "What's new with Marty?" Marty didn't come over as he usually did on Sunday. Neither did he mention anything about Saturday when we rode the bus to school on Monday. He did say however that his bottom was still sore from a spanking received because he left Tina all alone in the woods. Apparently, her parents thought she could have gotten lost.

◌

Coach Ziegler surprised me when he approached me after church. "This winter I want you to try out for wrestling instead of basketball. I think you will do better in an individual sport. We will have new coaches since the School Board approved the entire program at Tuesday night's board meeting. It should help you both in discipline and confidence."

◌

"So you entered. I'm glad. I know you'll do well."

The Providence Service Club organized its first annual Draft Horse and Tractor Rodeo the last weekend in September. Several local businesses set up canvas tents and donated prizes to the community event. Small food stands were erected along with a large outdoor barbeque pit. Even the St. Bart's Ladies Aid, although now with greatly reduced numbers, planned a bake sale. A traditional cake walk was scheduled for the end of the day. Predictably, the Ladies brought their multi-colored ice cream social lights to add to the festive atmosphere.

As the name indicates, the competition was organized into draft horse and tractor competition. Not a pulling contest, the events were solely intended to display the skills of the driver or operator. Since draft horses were becoming a hobby rather than a necessity, the organizers provided five draft horse teams.

Paraphrasing the *Providence Purveyor* article as he read, Dad said, "The organizers have posted a $500 bond to offset the high value of the borrowed horses. A lone pair of

Percheron has been added to two pair each of Clydesdales and Belgians. The age and weight of each hitch has been matched as closely as possible. All horses are experienced working teams. The draft horse events include team handling, plowing, mowing, and separate freight and hay wagon slalom."

"Boy, those must be some good horses!"

"The tractor competition is limited to a 45 horsepower maximum. One tractor will be collectively used for the bucket loading event; otherwise, each farmer is to bring his own unit. Each contestant can enter with either a wide or narrow front machine. The tractor events include: separate grain and hay wagon maneuvering, disking, cultivating, and bucket loading."

Mom asked, "So what have you entered?"

Ignoring her question, Dad read: "In addition to the gift prizes, cash prizes will be given to the first and second place winners. Twenty-five dollars is to be given for first; ten for second. Each first place winner will get their entry fees back. An additional fifty dollars is to be awarded by Providence State Bank to a farmer if he wins both competitions. With the lucrative prize package, the number of entries is limited to ten in the draft horse and fifteen in the tractor competition. Only farmers who are experienced draft horse handlers can enter that competition. Each contestant must enter three events. A contestant can also enter a wild card event, using his best three scores to determine his overall placement."

Dad then directly responded to her question, "Both. I've entered the draft horse team handling, plowing, and freight wagon maneuvering. I'll pick up hay wagon maneuvering as a wild card event. In the tractor competition I've entered grain wagon maneuvering, cultivating, and plowing."

Mom confirmed, "That should be a full day, to say the least! You are definitely experienced; I hope you haven't lost your touch."

Using a fallowed field, the organizers planted corn in early July, expecting it to be knee high by the competition. Alfalfa had been sown for the mowing portions. Both the disking and plowing were to be completed on bare ground with the plowing event contouring the earth for the subsequent disking match. The wagon courses were laid out using color-coded studded T steel fence posts and barbed wire. The barbed wire served as both a telltale signal of a foul and a deterrent for both animal and implement.

"I am not as concerned about the tractor events; you've been getting plenty of training on the ball field. But, do you think you can still handle the horses?" Mom asked.

Dad confidently responded, "My father taught me well."

△

Finally, the big day arrived. A light overnight shower made everything crisp and clean. "It looks almost as good as the day you brought it home from Kuehl's," Mom said, somewhat startled as Dad proudly brought the tractor out the machine shed doors. Anxiously awaiting the competition, over the past month, Dad had meticulously greased, cleaned, and serviced his prized Minneapolis-Moline RTU.

"I'd better get going. It will take me a good hour to get to the grounds. Anna, please remember to bring along those three extra gas cans. I'll need one of the boys to fill two, but leave the third one empty. See all of you there." With that he flipped the light toggle, pushed the throttle bar forward, and disappeared into the early morning darkness.

Upon arriving, I quickly recognized all of the competing farmers. Unbeknownst to Mom or Darlene Davis, it seemed Ed Davis and Dad had entered into a friendly side bet. Both exhibited an almost childlike competitiveness. "I can't wait to get a piece of Darlene's pie."

"We'll see, Anna's chicken dinner sounds pretty good to me!"

Wisely, the draft horse events were scheduled for the cool of the morning, starting promptly at 8:00 a.m. Each of the contestants worked in rotating sequence. Each competitor had paid the $5 entry fee or $9 for both competitions, plus $2 for each event entered.

"That was very impressive; I guess your Dad did teach you well."

Dad had flawlessly completed the draft horse events, proving he could backup his boasting. He was the leader at the end of the morning. Arranging the others in their place, I proudly hung his name from the teacup hooks anchored into the large whitewashed tally board. Winning the first round guaranteed Dad got his entry money back for that round and at least $25 in prize money. He was now ready to move "Miss Molly" into place for the afternoon's competition.

After grabbing a quick sandwich, Dad nervously screamed, "Oh no! Molly won't start!" Quickly spotting a buildup of sludge in the bottom of the glass fuel filter jar, Dad immediately opened his tool box, conveniently welded to the right fender. Amongst the tools, Dad had a scattering of sockets and wrenches. First rehearsing each step in his mind, he quickly changed the four spark plugs. After rinsing the jar in clean gasoline, he proceeded to open the butterfly valve and drain the tractor's gasoline tank into the empty gas can. He then refilled the tank from one of the two full cans. Climbing back into the seat, he pushed the starter pedal; Molly's engine purred with a mere two minutes to spare. Because of his first round victory, Dad was scheduled to be the last contestant to enter the tractor maze.

Dad performed well through his first two events. Trailing Ed by half a point on a scale of one to five, Dad needed a perfect score of 5 on the grain wagon maneuvering course to be awarded his second victory. The last event for each contestant, grain wagon maneuvering appeared to be the toughest for all.

Stepping off the tractor, Dad briefly studied the layout. Climbing back into the seat, he jokingly shouted over the sound of tractor engines to Uncle Marvin, "You set that up with lots of room for error, didn't you?"

In addition to backing the wagon into the makeshift opening, the driver's total score would be determined by the final placement of the wagon's discharge door. A galvanized feed tub had been placed in a fixed location precisely midway between the rear studded T posts. Before entering the course, twenty-five corn ears had been counted and carefully placed in each farmer's high walled wagon. When Dad acknowledged he was in his final position, a bystander raised the discharge door to the measured, uniform height of 12" above the wagon's floor. Dad methodically raised the wagon box using his fender mounted hydraulic controls. The ears began to fall toward the empty bin. One by one, the sound was distinctive. To determine the score, the judge counted the ears that landed directly into the tub below.

Uncle Marvin yelled with excitement, "He's the first to do it! He's got twenty-five in the tub!"

"Whoopee!" Mom shouted from the sidelines.

However, the final task required the operator to drive out of the makeshift opening, and continue to a sharp left hand turn toward the finish line.

Dad beamed with confidence as he drove the RTU out of the opening. To score a five on the driving portion he could have no demerits in the remaining 80 feet. The sharp dogleg worked to his advantage. Unlike his competitors who drove John Deere, Oliver, Allis-Chalmers, Farmall, or Massey Ferguson, Dad's RTU was designed so the driver sat low and off-center, slightly to the left of center. The steering rod was mounted on the left side of the engine housing. In the field, this allowed a good view of a furrow but it was also beneficial when making sharp left handed turns. From his advantageous perspective, Dad maneuvered both tractor and wagon around the hairpin curve, without a scratch.

⌂

The $100 windfall had not been budgeted; for that matter, neither had a new furnace! Pulling a tablet out of his bib overall pocket, Mr. Clapper said, "Let's see, this will be due in 10 days. As I told you Leif, the gravity furnace burner was corroded beyond repair. This should give you and the Missus plenty of years of service."

Then, just as the chill of fall set in, Dad calculated he could replace the oil burner with a cleaner burning propane unit. This meant the dingy oil tank could be removed from the basement and replaced with an external tank. The total cost, exactly $90 – Dad and Mom had already tithed the first fruits on the first Sunday after the Draft Horse and Tractor Rodeo.

⌂

"Those trophies would make Barney proud of me! Maybe someday he will come and see them." Dad reconfirmed they were to be placed in the prime positions on the living room knickknack mantle. The two trophies, however, took second position to his most prized reward. For winning the draft horse and tractor rodeo, Dad received a large, solid brass western style belt buckle. Presented to him by Bank Vice-President Ziegler, the front side had been cast to read: *Providence Draft Horse and Tractor Rodeo*; the backside was etched: *All Around Champion – Leif Olsen 1965*.

Sadly, the First Annual Providence Draft Horse and Tractor Rodeo was also the one and only. Shortly thereafter, William Schmidt's Rolling Hickory Farm was subdivided, eventually to become a weekend campers' retreat for those looking for a respite from the rising crime and violence of the City.

Later that fall, Connie was dismantled as she gave way to the disciplined instruction of Coach Ziegler. Many boys purchased new fielder's gloves in anticipation that the next two years would be a time when the high school and Babe Ruth teams contained the most successful player mix.

⌂

"I don't know where they could be! Anna called me late this afternoon from the gas station at the intersection of Highway 72 and 51, just south of Rockford. That was six hours ago. That's a two hour trip from here! I'm worried they may have been overtaken by the snowstorm," Dad nervously spoke with Uncle Marvin on the phone.

"Do you want me to head out and see if I can find them?"

"No, it's better to heed the State Police warning to stay off the highways. Maybe I..." Suddenly, the phone went dead.

An early winter blizzard was forecasted for the Providence area. George and Mom left on Friday morning, traveling to Beaver Dam, Wisconsin to visit Mom's favorite Aunt Maxine. It was now eleven o'clock Sunday night; they still weren't home. Snow flurries were beginning to fall and the telltale southeasterly wind began to howl. According to the radio, roads were becoming icy.

"Susanna and Buddy, come here. Let's pray. Heavenly Father, you know the whereabouts of your servant Anna and our son George. We don't. Please Father, give them safe shelter if they are in trouble. Provide help for them if they are stranded. We come to you, Lord Jesus. As your disciples, we too need your protection from this storm."

Sleepy eyes soon overcame our vigil. Each of us tried to stay alert, but with no success. At about 3 a.m. we were awakened by loud banging on the screen porch door. The lone deputy illuminated his face by using his hand held flashlight. In the dim barnyard light, we could see his snow covered Itasca County Sheriff's car idling in the driveway.

"Leif, Anna and George are safe. However, they are both in the Rochelle hospital. We received a radio call, about an hour ago, from the Ogle County Sheriff's Department that your car was in a field about three miles south of Highway 30. Anna was in the driver's seat. May I come in and talk?"

Deputy Wiley continued, "George told us he had driven from Beaver Dam to the Highway 72 intersection. That was about 5:00 p.m. yesterday afternoon. George said that while the attendant filled the car with gas, Anna went inside to use the restroom. Apparently, just north of Paw Paw, according to George, Anna blacked out. As quick as he could, George said he grabbed the steering wheel but he could not control the gas pedal or brake. With the icy conditions the car catapulted the roadside ditch, landing full speed into a harvested soybean field. The wheels immediately became mired in the heavy clay soil; the car's momentum halted. Fortunately, a sanding truck driver, from his elevated cab, could see the fresh tire ruts. He stopped along the shoulder and immediately called dispatch. No passing car would have been able to see them. Both are alert but both have several bruises and sore stomachs. Those new seat belts seemed to have worked. The Ogle County deputy said the windshield shattered but it miraculously stayed in the frame. I'll be back in the morning to escort you to Rochelle. Your car may be a total loss, but your wife and son seem to be all right."

1966

Winter wrestling was indeed a learning curve. All too often I found myself looking at the roof framing. At 112 pounds, I slowly learned to use my leg strength instead of trying to steer wrestle my opponent. I finished the junior varsity season that spring with a record of 8–4, having to sit out half of the meets because I had been beaten in the pre-meet "wrestle-offs" by my teammate, Buster Mazzocco.

⌂

To me, Kitty Thompson's mother had two different personalities. I was in Myrt's Grocery one Saturday afternoon when I heard all sorts of commotion from the nearby canned foods aisle. Arnold Thompson was small in stature with thick black, curly hair brushed forward barely enough to cover his rapidly receding hairline. Quick to bark when Victoria wasn't around, his demeanor was now quite different. Screaming one order after another, the gruff, somewhat vulgar voiced Victoria had both Kitty and Arnold scurrying to meet her every wish.

One Sunday morning I got a taste of their true home life. Kitty hastily slid into the pew just as the Prelude finished. Unlike her mother, Kitty was shy and preferred to sit further back in the church, not the first row center as her mother insisted. With a cold glaring look, Victoria's scolding could be heard during a brief pause in the music, "We'll talk about this when we get the hell out of here! Oops."

The entire congregation gasped. You could have heard a pin drop!

Pastor Lawrence quickly stood. Aunt Ella, realizing the predicament, began playing the first hymn. Kitty immediately bolted out of the pew, turning the corner and then blasting out the double, front entry doors. Only the music muffled the doors. Her mother's tears of embarrassment were the more telltale, for the chasm between mother and daughter was quite visible.

I believe that was the last Sunday the Thompsons attended St. Bart's. As far as I know, they never joined another church.

"I was inserting a contact lens that morning," Kitty later confided. "I lost the lens when it flipped out of my eye, bounced off the bathroom vanity, and lodged into the throw rug beneath."

Fortunately for Kitty their house was within walking distance to the church.

That Sunday afternoon, while she was napping on the couch, I went up and kissed Mom on the cheek. Opening one eye, she asked: "What did you do now?" That was her way of acknowledging she was being buttered up.

"Oh, nothing. I just wanted to thank the Lord for you, Mom."

"That's sweet Buddy. Now tell me what this is really all about."

"I'll tell you *someday*."

Slowly sitting up, she said, "I want to give you something." After stepping out of the room, she returned with a small New Testament in her hand. "I found this amongst Mother's belongings. I want you to have it."

"What is it?"

"I gave this New Testament to Harry when he was confirmed back in 1922. You will find the brief note I wrote inside; I was only ten, myself. I put a bookmark by a verse I chose specifically for him: I Corinthians 10:13. Read it sometime."

⌂

Baseball remained my favorite sport. At this level the high school and Babe Ruth rosters were reduced to fourteen players. This year's team contained a good mix of seasoned veterans. Although Coach Ziegler remained optimistic, Mark Farmer was not fully recovered from his shoulder injury. Bill Schmidt was sluggish behind the plate; he had gained a significant amount of weight over the winter months. To Bill, partying and socializing were much higher priorities than baseball.

As the new season progressed, Coach Ziegler repeatedly asked me to warm up pitchers both before the games and during our at bats. I was a steady player even though I was rotated between right field and the occasional catching assignment. Bill Schmidt's durability carried us through the season but not on to the Babe Ruth League Championship.

"When you catch, I'm disappointed in the number of pass balls you let by. You seem to be having trouble with them. Now that you can see better with your new contact lenses, let me give you a couple of tips.

"Instead of trying to swat the ball into the dirt, as I have seen you do, turn your mitt over. Turning it over will naturally force you to rise up. The ball is then blocked by your entire body. Also, keep your chin tucked in; there's a slight opening between your chest protector and mask, in the area of your Adam's apple. You want that protected."

⌂

Early Fall brought my fifteenth birthday and, as a sophomore in high school, I was no longer at the bottom of the barrel – at least in grade. Steadily I was increasing in stature and strength. I was able to secure a summer job as a laborer with a local building contractor. The long hours and physical requirements helped tone my physical strength. It was about this same time when Coach Ziegler set up a weight training room just outside the locker room area. Coach said he had received several used weightlifting apparatuses from an acquaintance at a junior college program. Coordinating with the varsity wrestling coach, the two supervised its schedule and use.

◯

"Boy, you really pounced on him!"

"That distraction didn't hurt either. Thanks."

With that said, we were alarmed by the loud *rap, rap, rap* just before the bedroom door slammed open. With her arms crossed and her oversized wooden spoon in hand, Mom stood steadfastly in the door opening. Throughout our childhood, Mom's choice of punishment was this same large wooden spoon. Properly placed, she could easily bring her point home when she had to. Secretly, we hoped someday it would splinter and break – naively believing it wasn't replaceable.

"Who pounced on whom? Buddy did you get into a fight at school?"

"Not really." I proceeded to tell her about my encounter.

Freshman, Ike Thompson's, badgering continued throughout that afternoon's wrestling practice. Ike was large for his age, but not necessarily blessed with wisdom.

"I had a difficult time beating Buster Mazzocco in the wrestle-off. By the time Coach Frantz whistled the end of practice, I had had enough of Ike's constant yapping. The practice mats were rolled, however the newer mat remained in place for tomorrow night's meet.

"Never one to know when to quit, Ike shouted from the far side of the mat, 'I think I just saw your Dad walk in the locker room door. You know the guy who just can't stop bellyaching about how America is drifting into Satan's hands!' That was all I could take! As fast as I could, I sprinted across the mat, startling Ike. Getting nose to nose, I felt blood rushing to my face as I screamed, 'You lousy fat slob! Everything you have has been given to you on a silver platter. Without veterans like my dad, you wouldn't have your freedom of speech! You are a disgrace to the man whose name you have been given!'

"At that precise moment, from the elevated jogging track on the other side of the gym, George clapped his hands loudly. The distraction was just enough for me to drop down and drive my shoulders into Ike's knees. Falling first to his butt, then to his back, he was in perfect position for a Reverse Nelson. Getting my body perpendicular to his, I tightened the noose with all my strength.

"Superficially, Ike surrendered, 'OK, OK, I'll say I'm sorry.'

"So I said, 'Well, let's hear it!'

"With that he tried to wiggle his way out of the predicament. I regained my strength, putting him back, this time in a cradle. His nose was soon touching one of his knees, and his other leg was stretched out on the floor. Sinking my chin into his chest bone, he tearfully mumbled, 'I said, I'm sorry!' I asked him for what and he said 'I'm sorry for what I said about your dad.' I made him repeat it and he begged, 'I'm sorry! Please let me go. This really hurts.' I don't think he'll demean Dad again!"

"You kind of overreacted didn't you Buddy?"

Remorsefully I responded to her question, "I suppose so. But, I would do it again if I heard him repeat those words."

Then, hesitating for effect, she stated her true heart, "It was probably a good thing I wasn't there; your Dad is a great and honorable man."

"Would you have kept us apart?"

"No, I would probably have used this on him," she said, waving her wooden spoon in the air. "Obviously, Arnold and Victoria have never spanked him."

With a drill sergeant-like demeanor, she concluded, "Now go to sleep boys. You know I'm here to protect you. Did you say your prayers? ...That's what I thought. Get down on your knees and let me hear them." With those words, we were subtly reminded that as long as we lived in this home, she and Dad were in charge.

Before drifting off to sleep, I grabbed my Bible and looked up I Corinthians 10:13. "No temptation has overtaken you that is not common to man. God is faithful, and he will not let you be tempted beyond your strength, but with temptation will also provide the way of escape, that you may be able to endure it." Temptation, strength, escape, and endurance; was she prophetically forecasting my destiny or had God used her as His messenger, giving her timely angelic words of wisdom to pass on at this, the start of my adolescence?

Ike never gave me any more trouble. Not necessarily the result of our encounter, he matured significantly simply by changing his outlook on life. Ike became Providence's first and only All State wrestler when in 1970, he went 26–0 to become the 165 pound weight class champion.

⌂

With Kitty also gone, only one Confirmand remained a regular attendee of St. Bart's. Slowly, I had seen my school classmates drifting away from their own home churches too. A growing number of my school classmates, however, were becoming more involved in other Christian youth activities and movements. Some were even downright pushy, asking me such things as: "Buddy, are you born again?" or "Are you a Christian?" with the follow-up, "How do you know?"

Mae Lynne Davis, in particular, was the pestering sort. With the help of her brothers and the oft hired Olsen boys, her father successfully cultivated our 120 acres plus his own 320 acres. Her brothers had never been in sports but all of us had raised livestock for 4H projects. Our families were trusted neighbors. The Davises didn't go to St. Bart's; First Apostles was their family church. Over the years I had noticed Mae Lynne skillfully managed every task with determination and conviction – traits not unlike my mother.

Always neatly dressed, her skin remained bronzed from outdoor chores well into the winter months. A tall, slender girl, at 5'7", she was always seated front and center for class pictures.

We always spoke in a neighborly manner, however, she seemed to be uneasy and in a hurry when I attempted to strike up a longer conversation.

1967

After the New Year, Coach Ziegler approached his entire Babe Ruth prospects hoping to encourage them to remain involved in a winter sport or work independently through his weight training programs. In mid-February he started indoor drills for the spring high school and summer Babe Ruth teams; both were essentially the same team. Although disappointed the previous year, Coach Ziegler believed this year's well was deeper. He strongly believed this team could secure the championships that had eluded him previously. The next hierarchal step, success in Legion ball, would likely foster new aspirations for those players. Dreaming to himself, he must have thought these high school and Babe Ruth seasons could be the tune up needed to take these boys to new heights.

△

The gymnasium was old and without a great deal of room beyond the basketball court's borders. Although I was getting bigger, reflecting some of my father's size, I was still smaller than most upperclassmen. A fitter, trimmer Bill Schmidt, having done well his senior year in football, was confident he would return to his first team catcher throne. Approximately 50 pounds heavier and two inches taller, Bill was aware of the accolades I received in 1964 following the All-County Pony League Championship. Essentially, this spring's high school team would be the same; however, there were no Sunday games in High School League baseball.

The springtime weather was slow to improve. Early spring training remained in the gym. Physical conditioning and simulated batting, with fully equipped batteries in place, were part of the routine training. Coach wanted each player to be comfortable in the batter's box, developing an eye for pitches without the necessity of swinging. Defensively, precise catching and throwing were stressed. Coach Ziegler even wore a complete umpire's uniform.

Using his imagination further, Coach Ziegler developed a fantasy game for the team. Each player was scheduled fantasy "at bats". Teams were assigned and equipment manager, Pat Davis kept a score sheet and posted the score on the electronic basketball scoreboard. Coach prepared a deck of cards for the three inning games. Each deck contained action cards: an ace being a single, a king a strikeout, 4s or 8s indicating a walk, etc. Although they did not swing the bat, pitchers threw to the catcher and the batter ran the bases. Drawing the joker was as an automatic out; a double play if there were base runners and less than two outs.

In every aspect, Coach Ziegler was determined to develop a strong and fast team. Coach Ziegler expected his team to be disciplined.

I could sense Bill Schmidt's competitiveness. He had few friends and was determined not to let anyone challenge his self-appointed position as the team leader. After eighteen months of rehabilitation, Mark Farmer had rejoined the team for the spring practices. Mark played catcher for many years prior to his devastating injury. Mark's rotator cuff and shoulder muscles were healing ever so slowly.

Possessively, Bill saw underclassmen as the primary threat. Although overlooked as the team captain, he intended to steal leadership by using his physical prowess, a trait that had made him a good linebacker. However, Bill was nearing disqualification for poor grades and social misconduct.

Believing Mark was his primary challenger, Bill showed no pity for Mark's slow healing, constantly shoving and pushing him almost to the point of assault. None of his peers had the backbone to take him down. He wallowed in his belief of invincibility.

Bill did not limit his pranks in the locker room to knotting shoe strings or applying Heat Balm to supporters and underwear. Trips to and from the showers meant a run through his gauntlet of snapping towels. Drying towels, for some reason, repeatedly disappeared or somehow become water soaked when an unobservant underclassman turned his back.

Although I received the same treatment as the other underclassmen, Bill decided it was time to take it one step further with me – after all I was the unknown in the equation.

The varsity team shared the gymnasium with the junior varsity during wind sprints. Because the teams were combined, on the whistle, one half of the boys on each end of the gymnasium sprinted towards the opposite end. Bill slowly drifted latterly toward the end opposite me. His first opportunity for a head-on charge was frustrated by my ability to anticipate the movements of the oncoming bull.

Using an innocent hazer, his fourth try, however, was successful. Without a clear avoidance path, I was sent sailing backward, by the former linebacker, to the unyielding hardwood floor. "Get out of my way jack! Can't you see where I am going?" The floor was somewhat forgiving to my body, but not to my head. With a bump the size of a plum, suddenly I realized how Buster Mazzocco must have felt so many years before.

This time, there was no coach, team, or fatherly sympathy. I sat in the bleachers the remainder of practice. After all had left the gymnasium, Coach Ziegler came along side of me. He reminded me there would be bullies, such as Bill

Schmidt, throughout life's journey. He ended the conversation saying: "Buddy, how bad do you want it?"

When the ball fields dried, it became evident Mark Farmer's recovery would be slower than anticipated. Bill was awarded the starting catcher position; I received the starting right fielder's position. Bill continually attempted to splinter the cohesiveness of the team. Bill successfully convinced several bench warming seniors that the underclassmen were unnecessary position fillers, stealing their own attempts for stardom.

"David! I'll meet you in the parking lot at seven. I'll have a full tank of gas so we can go wherever we want." Overhearing the conversation, I was surprised when Bill shouted, "Hey Olsen! Do you want to join us? After all it is Thursday night!"

"Sorry, I've got to study tonight; I have a big test tomorrow." I didn't tell him it was for Health.

⌂

As I said before, David Fox's leadership as team captain was being eroded by the pranks of several others. David never participated beyond the small stuff. With our first game and the end of the fourth grading period rapidly approaching, Coach Ziegler remained hopeful the team's vigor could be harnessed into a successful team. Big Stone was to be the first opponent.

Coming off a championship year seemed to add to their personal expectations. With Big Stone ahead most of the game, Coach Ziegler surprised all of us by bringing in George during the bottom half of the sixth inning to face the Boulders' #2, #3, and #4 hitters. If George was able to keep us close, Coach Ziegler had the heart of our lineup for the top of the inning. We would be leading off with Buster

Mazzocco followed by Kenny Stahl, Larry Dreger, and, hopefully, Bill Schmidt and David Fox.

"Coach Ziegler, I think I have a case of the stomach flu. It's been going around you know." Despite his self-diagnosis, Bill was able to catch the first five innings without further complaint. Suddenly, as the air became more humid, between pitches, we all heard a loud: "Oh no...!" Bill ran awkwardly from the playing field, then sprinting to the nearby corn field. His disgusting sounds seemed to be amplified back toward the ball field – including a bad case of the dry heaves. Bill also had the misfortune of prolonged diarrhea – not surprisingly, no one offered to come to his aid.

"Since no one called 'time out' and your player left the diamond, your catcher is disqualified. You need to substitute a new one," the High School League umpire said to Coach Ziegler. Coach Ziegler looked relieved, probably thinking he had received an answer to his prayers.

Mark Farmer was brought off the bench. George allowed two hits to the #3 and #4 batters and with men on first and third, their #5 batter was due at the plate. Sensing an opportunity to execute a delayed double steal, the Boulders' coach signaled the green light. Although Mark had seen this situation many times, he threw wildly towards the first base side of second. Seeing the weakness in his throw, the runner on 3rd sprinted home unchallenged.

From my right field vantage point I could clearly see Coach Ziegler's frustration. Now up by two runs, the Boulders' strong pitching and good defense prevailed through the remainder of the game.

A discombobulated team went back to the awaiting bus and the quiet trip home. Usually a man of few words, Coach Ziegler's displeasure was both sensed and heard. With the weekend upon us, each of us had a chance to revisit our priorities. Team expectations had been high and the hopes of an unbeaten season were now a thing of the past.

△

As a family, we continued to attend worship at St. Bart's Church. With more new families, a late morning, second service was added. The early service was moved to 8:00 a.m. and limited to precisely one hour. Sunday School was held between services. Early service was the norm for our family. With my newly obtained driver's permit, George and I began to make a quick show and leave. I was convinced High School Sunday School was not for me. After all, the Sunday paper contained sports scores, comics, and other interesting sections. I believed that was much better reading than Sunday School lessons. Christian holidays came and went. It appeared they had become a reunion for those who did not attend the rest of the year.

△

Monday morning rumors were rampant at Providence High. We knew for certain several students had been detained by the police following a spring party. It was said that all had been turned over to their parents' custody. It was rumored several athletes were involved. School administrators now had to deal with the end of term grades and possible disciplinary action.

That afternoon, Coach Ziegler hastily called a combined junior and varsity team meeting just prior to practice. We were told to dress for practice but to remain in the locker room. With over thirty of us crowded into the small locker room, missing persons were not immediately discovered. Coach Ziegler re-stated the school's position regarding poor grades and social misconduct. He didn't name names but it soon became apparent – Bill Schmidt and underclassman David Finch were not in the room. Both lockers had been cleared and both steel locker doors had been purposely left wide open. The message was clear.

Although shortened, Monday's practice had a new sense of purpose. Coach Ziegler repeatedly encouraged the leadership of Captain Fox and alternate captain Kenny Stahl. In two short days the second game of the season would be upon us. With our upcoming second road game in New Bergen, no one wanted to return on a losing bus ever again!

Sensing urgency, Coach Ziegler had revisited all of his options. Falling back to his success in the All-County Pony League Tournament, he moved Buster Mazzocco to third base, David Fox to shortstop, and Buddy Olsen to catcher. Did you hear that? Yes, me! George and Larry Dreger would pitch, alternating between left field; Mark Farmer would be the back-up catcher. Peter Swann would be in center and Alan Jones in right field. Don Longly would be at first and Kenny Stahl would remain at second. With the addition of a junior varsity player, there were now five back up players to round out the team. Both Peter Swann and Don Longly could pitch if needed.

With a new sense of enthusiasm, the bus left for New Bergen, just 18 miles north. Arriving at the field, out the bus's window, I noticed the Davises' beige Ford Galaxy 500 parked strategically beneath a large oak tree. In the passenger seat I could see Mrs. Davis. I saw Mae Lynne was behind the wheel. I knew this meant she had passed her permit test.

◠

Putting her head between the backstop pole and the dugout, Mae Lynne called to me, "Well done, Buddy. What an exciting game! Honestly, it is my favorite play in baseball! Discipline, accuracy, and timing must be precise."

At first not knowing who was commenting, I lethargically responded, "Yes, it was an exciting game."

"With a man already on second, and one out, you could not afford to open the flood gates!" Her enthusiasm was catching.

I sat up and replayed the play in my mind as I described every detail to her. "It was a beautiful hit, solid and strong. Sailing deeply into left field, George snared the ball backhanded, chest high; spinning with all of his strength he let the ball fly! He had been taught to anticipate all options even before the pitch is thrown; if the ball comes to you, make your throw to the base ahead of the runner. George knew his throw was to home plate. He knew the strength of the hit would clearly advance the runner beyond third base. His smooth, natural response was perfect. The Viking base runner charged full steam for the plate. George's throw had to have the precise height needed for the cutoff man. But wisely, Peter elected not to interfere with the low throw and imminent play. Stepping aside just in time, George's throw bounced precisely where Peter had stood. The carom, a mere 2 feet off the ground, landed perfectly into the web of my mitt."

Like a bulwark, I had positioned myself between third and home, standing in the batter's box. The impact put me back onto the plate, smothering it completely with my back. "After hearing the umpire's call: 'Runner's out!', the next thing I remember was you yelling 'Get up Buddy, get up!!' Your yelling woke me from my daze. Sensing no one was concerned with his running, the aggressive hitter was on his way to third. I spotted him in my peripheral vision. Buster was in perfect position and ready for the put out. If you hadn't been there yelling at the top of your lungs, that third out play likely wouldn't have happened."

"Yes, but your play was perfect! With only two umpires, Umpire Hendricks had to sprint as fast as the runner."

I grinned as I remembered the call, "Runner's out!"

The rivalry was as strong as ever. The positive outcome was not clear until the bottom of the 7th inning. Final score: New Bergen 3, Providence 5.

Hearing Mae Lynne's intensity ignited my enthusiasm. This new sense made the return trip back to Providence sail by.

$\bigcirc$

By the end of the season, Coach Ziegler had instilled a great deal of confidence in his players. West Fork was to come to town for the final game of the year.

Well ahead in the district standings, George breezed through the first five innings of the game. Up by two runs, the late season heat finally sapped George's strength. Peter Swann was brought in to pitch the remaining two innings. Having worn all my gear for the better part of ninety minutes, the heat had sapped my energy, too. I believed our two run lead was precarious. Peter held West Fork to a run in the top of the sixth, however his wild pitches had loaded the bases. Fortunately, I blocked his fourth ball from going toward the back stop. An overanxious batter helped by swatting at the low and away ball. I quickly tagged him for the third out before he realized he could have sprinted to first.

Losing to cellar dwelling West Fork was just not in my playbook. Starting out the top of the seventh just as he finished the top of the sixth, Peter's third wild pitch to the second batter was enough for me!

"Time out ump!" Jumping to my feet, the plate umpire waved time out as I broke from behind the plate. I threw off my shin guards, chest protector, and mask before I reached the top of the batter's box. Realizing I had no other option, I decided to keep my cup in its place. Still holding the ball in my mitt, arriving at the mound, I screamed, "Peter, go put on those pads! I'm not killing myself trying to stop your wild pitches! If you can't accurately throw my pitches back, then at least I can walk in there and pick them out of your glove!"

"But...what do I use for a glove?"

"You won't need to worry! This mitt is for right-handers anyway; just hold it against your chest; I'll put it right in there! On second thought, hold it about six inches in front of the chest protector! You heard me, now give me your glove and get in there!" Thankfully Peter was a lefty. Dumfounded, he was visibly shaken, as he walked toward the mound. Lastly, I yelled, "You won't need a cup either, just stick that mitt in front of your chest; I'll do the rest."

Later I was told we were the only two who did not see Coach Ziegler rolling in laughter from the back corner of the dugout. Nine strikes in a row later, the game was over. The umpire must have planned an early supper as he was apparently complacent about the two position switch and the league's rule on a catcher's cup.

Putting his long arms around me, Coach Ziegler hugged me as we walked to the locker room. "You do get a little stubborn every once in a while, don't you?" He was still laughing when I heard him phone Mrs. Ziegler from his locker room office. "I'll be home early; Buddy became his own self-appointed relief pitcher tonight!"

⌂

Late summer brought the 9–1 season to an end. Coach Ziegler recognized that many of his veteran players would be moving on to new lives beyond their high school days. He knew a few of the best players might receive a chance to play at the college level. However, no one appeared to be Division 1 caliber. Hoping to be drafted, minor league city teams were also likely beyond the abilities of many of these players.

However, in 1967, another team was drafting. America was deep into the Vietnam Conflict. And, like all other American towns, young men from Providence registered and were being called by the local Selective Service Board for review. Electing not to play Legion Ball, Bill Schmidt enlisted in June and had gone to boot camp by the Fourth of July.

Deferments were limited to health or family circumstances, including farm obligations, or to those pursuing a higher education. Boys slightly older than me soon became my heroes. Sadly, unlike those before them, these courageous boys were never publicly recognized for their valor.

The outside world offered sex, alcohol, drugs, and musical lyrics full of innuendos. It was less than two years before this bird too would fly out of the nest. Would it soar? What words had found fertile soil and what had fallen among the rocks? Only God knew.

In August, Mae Lynne began working at Hendricks' Drug Store as a cashier and stocker. Mr. and Mrs. Hendricks had no children. It was well known that cooperative students who worked for them would likely be the recipient of a well-funded college scholarship. It was rumored that the Hendricks freely determined the size. In September, Mae Lynne's class schedule was coordinated so she worked on the job the final three periods of each school day. Her work day however didn't end until the store closed at 6:00 p.m.

⌂

"Go ahead. I know she's home; I just talked to Darlene about an hour ago. We'll go into the Living Room, that way you can have privacy. Leif, leave him alone! Get in here!"

"Remember Buddy," my Dad told me, "I had to ask Grandpa Carson the first time I wanted to take out the lovely Anna. I don't think he expected it. Until the day he died I

120

believe he was still shocked it was me who asked him for her hand, too. Buddy, your mother will never admit it, but she asked me out from then on! At 27, I think she was afraid of becoming a spinster!"

"If I wouldn't have, today you would be the oldest bachelor in the world! Don't kid yourself, I had my eyes focused on the ultimate prize! Go ahead Buddy, we'll leave you alone. You might want to pray first or do you think you've got what you're going to say under control?"

They were still laughing at their jousting when I heard the first ring in my ear. "Quiet down!" My hands were shaking and my voice quivered, "Hello, Mrs. Davis, this is Buddy Olsen. Is Mae Lynne there?"

Even though the phone mouthpiece was muffled, I could hear her yell, "Mae Lynne, it's Buddy." I heard snickering in my earpiece.

"Is that you Marty? Get off the line!" I never heard a click.

"Hi, Buddy, what's new?" For some reason, I suspect that that first phone call was heard throughout the area. Hard telling how many eavesdroppers were on the party line that night.

So it was, just after my sixteenth birthday, I asked Mae Lynne Davis to a movie; it was the first date for both of us. Not surprisingly, her acceptance had come with limitations. With my permanent driver's license in hand and the new Coronet clean and gassed, I drove the short distance between driveways to their stately farm house.

⌂

The Davises' lane was long and winding. The approximately three-quarters of a mile length was terminated on both ends by in-ground cattle guards. The beautiful trees looked like tin soldiers marking the edge of the roadway. Just beyond I saw the purebred Aberdeen Angus cows with calves grazing freely amongst the white oak, shaggy bark hickory, and black walnut trees. The driveway meandered across the second cattle guard near the red stained, wood frame barn, the cow yard just off its south side. The mow door conveniently faced east allowing easy loading of the hay bale cubes. A newly constructed wooden corn crib stood majestically along its north side. Just slightly behind the barn, a concrete silo with a bright galvanized dome, stood sentry over all of the buildings.

Mr. Davis had built a machine shed to house his implements. Dad told me frequently, "Emulate Ed Davis; a wise farmer puts all of his machinery away before nightfall. Mr. Davis' parked, Oliver tractor told me that this day's farm work wasn't complete. Behind the tractor were two flat bed wagons loaded with bales of freshly conditioned hay. Since no rain was forecast, they could remain fully loaded while sitting under the shelter of the crib's driveway. This allowed the hay to further cool as a precaution against a tragic barn fire, ignited by hay that had spontaneously combusted.

All of the alarms sounded my approach. The chorus of bleating calves joined the bellowing cows. Barking in harmony, the Davises' rust colored Chesapeake, Bouncer, ran alongside the approaching car, easily peering into the partially rolled down window. I hoped he wouldn't slobber.

The two-story Victorian home was reminiscent of an English countryside manor. Its siding was painted brilliant white; the house was trimmed in black. The expansive grass lawn flowed beneath the trees. The gentle breeze seemed never ending.

Then reality hit! Mr. Davis met me just inside the front door. He reminded me that we could go to the movie, grab a treat... and that we were expected to be home by 10:30 p.m.! Mae Lynne quickly told me *The Greatest Story Ever Told* was being shown as a special Saturday night feature film at the Little Fork Theater. She told me *Valley of the Dolls* would be off limits.

To this day, I believe our parents had talked before that first date night. Taking their child's well-being seriously, each likely agreed to the ground rules of dating.

◌

The fall football schedule was highlighted by the Homecoming Bonfire, Parade, and Dance. Rumors abounded – who would take whom? As our physical bodies continued to mature and eyes began to glaze, was it also a time for a steady commitment?

After breaking the ice with our first date, Mae Lynne and I had gone to movies, ate popcorn, and enjoyed each other's company. She had supported me earlier in the year by attending baseball games but had somewhat drifted away when her schedule became more demanding. Her church appeared to have an active high school program for the youth. Some at First Apostles would not allow their children to attend dances, go to movies, or date. It was quite apparent Mae Lynne's parents heavily restricted her socializing outside of church activities. When we went out on a date, we were under the same guidelines and rules as that first date.

Friday morning, after Math and before lunch, I realized it was time for my decision. The boy's locker room talk was that I would be asking Jill Benedict to the Homecoming Dance, despite the fact that I was seeing Mae Lynne. Jill's family had just moved from Missouri to Providence where her father found work as an engineer in a local factory. Her step mother was an elementary teacher in Big Stone. It seemed wherever I went, her smiling face appeared. A few of Jill's newfound friends likely conspired to fuel the locker room flame. I knew Jill would not have the same restrictions as Mae Lynne. The peer pressure was not unlike that I faced on the ball field.

Coach Ziegler knew I was scheduled to go from Math class to lunch.

"Buddy, bring your lunch into my office." Believing it must have been of the utmost importance I stopped by my locker and picked up the brown paper bag. Casually sprawled behind his desk, with his feet propped up, it appeared he wasn't totally prepared for the conversation.

"What are your plans for next spring? With the loss of several veteran players I thought it would be prudent to talk to each of you, the ones I am expecting to play in the spring. Since you aren't participating in a fall sport, how do you expect to stay in condition until wrestling practice begins again?"

I knew my answer had to be tempered. He would not expect a 16 year old with a shiny car at his disposal and a new driver's license to lead a life of disciplined training and celibacy, did he? I knew he would not buy the fact that I believed girls were part of my training.

After those first few minutes, I thought I knew his reason for the meeting. Grabbing a long piece of paper, he began: "Look over this schedule. I want you to sign up for specific times when you can complete this regimented schedule of weightlifting and running." Although he was not allowed to supervise the baseball team until February 1st, his determination and resolve were apparent.

Just prior to the end of the meeting, varsity wrestling Coach Frantz appeared at the office door. Silly me, I was beginning to think this meeting was an impulse. After Coach Frantz praised my first two seasons on the wrestling team, I began to get the feeling the meeting was orchestrated. Now weighing 135 pounds, he encouraged me to continue to be a part of the team as a junior. "As you know, Kenny Stahl, our

127 pound wrestler, graduated last spring. With a small weight loss you should be able to capture that spot. Remember, in wrestling it doesn't matter if you are left-handed."

I then signed a covenant, confirming my commitment to follow the training program. A new trend had started – the commitment included both academic and social conduct.

Only after Coach Frantz left, did Coach Ziegler verify the real reason for the visit. "Who are you going to take to the Homecoming Dance?"

And I had foolishly thought the only pressure would come from my peers! What is this, a conspiracy or the Gossip Room?

Excusing himself just as the bell rang, he concluded, "See you in church on Sunday." Coach Ziegler had never before acknowledged our common church affiliation. He knew that despite all the outside activities, he could still count on me as a regular on Sunday mornings. He also knew he could count on me to usher or count the offering if he was short of help. "The way I see it, you can go with your head or your heart."

"Now what is that supposed to mean?"

I could hear him chuckle loudly as he walked down the hall.

Sitting behind Jill Benedict in class, I was convinced my plan would be the best. Her over-the-shoulder length brunette hair was more interesting than the problems being chalked on the board. Mae Lynne was seated front and center, well away from these back of the room distractions. Following Study Hall, Health, and English, I figured I would have at least two opportunities to make my move. Jill was in all three of my classes; Mae Lynne was in none. Besides, I was shorter than Mae Lynne! My decision was made. I asked Jill.

Our junior class had scheduled to meet that Friday night in order to begin building its parade float. The location was secretly distributed to all class members at a late afternoon assembly. A previously undisclosed, secluded barn had been chosen. This unofficial start of Homecoming Week was traditionally also the time when the gossip mill would presumably quit because Homecoming Dance commitments were to be made no later than today. Coach Ziegler's plan would go into effect the Monday after Homecoming Week. I was set to enjoy both the upcoming week of preparation and the activities that followed.

Old barns were dwindling in number. As I said, the secluded place remained a secret until the end of classes on Friday afternoon. What wasn't expected – it was at Jill Benedict's hobby farm, right on the main highway! Also unexpected, Mae Lynne volunteered to have her Dad's tractor and hay wagon driven to Jill's farm.

Coldly looking at me throughout the late afternoon assembly, Class President Mae Lynne politely but firmly, in front of the entire junior class assembly, asked: "Mr. Olsen, you don't mind picking up Dad's tractor and wagon and driving it in to town, do you?" Suddenly, my attendance went from elective to obligatory. Later, as we walked to the school bus, she completed her plan saying, "I'll drive you home after we get done tonight." My anxiety level tripled. Arriving home, I did my evening chores, changed clothes and walked through the pasture, taking the short cut to the Davises' farm to pick up the tractor and wagon. Surprisingly, Mr. Davis had not pulled them into the machine shed. The tractor's steel seat was both wet and cold; the cushion had been removed. The drive into town was frigid, windy, and drizzly. I pulled my collar up as far as it would stretch. I thought I was going to shiver right out of my overalls. I wondered if I would ever warm up.

While others worked feverishly, several students, in-cluding Jill, frequently disappeared to the remote corners of the old barn. Giggles and laughter echoed throughout the barn. A new odor permeated the air. I, along with most others, knew it wasn't manure.

English teacher and junior class advisor, Miss Grainger, later made a cursory appearance just to see if all was proceeding as planned; it was. I found her behavior a bit unusual in that, even though it was near dusk outside, she still wore her sunglasses, including while she was in the barn. Despite school rules that forbid smoking at school-sponsored activities, I could see a strange looking cigarette partially hidden by her palm.

Needless to say, the ride home with Mae Lynne was awkward. In my mind, we couldn't get there fast enough. "How's your family? It's been a beautiful Indian Summer, hasn't it?" Somehow Mae Lynne was able to overlook the evening's blustery cold rain.

"Goodbye Buddy, I hope next week goes well. It will be a busy week for both of us." Seeing the remnants of a red sunset, she parted saying, "Maybe the weather will improve when you've gotten over your whim!"

⌂

The sun was shining brightly into my eyes; the highway traffic was heavy as I tried to turn left into Jill's family's hobby farm, located just outside the western city limits. Dressed in my new tweed sport coat and smartly polished dark olive wing tips, I sensed the evening might be rough when I walked up the heavily cracked sidewalk to the dilapidated back porch door – barely hanging by one hinge. With the front door blocked by boxes and old appliances, the back door appeared to be the only entrance. The rear porch smelled of mildew. Broken windows were covered with brittle plastic sheathing. I wasn't sure if anyone was home, including Jill.

"Come on in. Do you want something to drink? There's cold beer in the refrigerator."

"No, I don't drink."

Coming out a side, catch-all room, Jill said, "Well, what do you think?"

I was startled! "Jill?"

Her shoulder length brunette hair was probably lying on the floor somewhere in the house, certainly not at a beauty salon! The color for her short, bright red hair had obviously come out of a bottle. Her skirt was tight and very short. Her brown suede boots rose to just below her knee caps, the hem of her skirt 10 inches above.

"We need to stop at Jackie's before we go to the dance." Jackie and Jill were inseparable friends. Jackie had dated Larry Dreger for over a year, wearing both his school ring and letter jacket as a sign of their going steady. I never socialized with either of them. I knew Jill was inseparable from Jackie but I assumed this evening would be different. Foolishly, I thought I could change her.

I awkwardly pinned my brown tipped yellow mum onto her lime green and gray, loose-fitting blouse. "I thought you told me you were going to wear a dark rust colored dress?"

"Sorry; after talking to Jackie, we changed our minds. Besides, this outfit goes better with my new hair!"

"If you say so."

We proceeded to the car and our next scheduled stop, Jackie's house.

"I'll be just a minute." I soon realized Larry's Barracuda was parked on the street, just around the corner. After about ten minutes, Larry, Jackie, and Jill burst out the front door and made a direct beeline to my car. Both girls carried oversized, matching purses.

"It's OK if they come with us, isn't it?" Before I could respond, the three of them were in the car, ready to go. An awful, stale odor entered the car. I put it off as coming from their clothes or Jackie's old house. "Before we go to the dance, let's head towards Little Fork." Still about a half hour before the dance was to begin, I thought the trip would be harmless.

Just outside of Providence, I cringed when I heard the unmistakable sound of one of the new aluminum pull tabs. The smell of beer quickly engulfed the car. A second "swoosh" followed shortly thereafter. Then from her front seat position, excitedly, Jill announced, "Let the party begin!" as she reached in her oversized purse and pulled out a half-pint bottle of Southern Comfort whiskey. At the same time a pack of Parliaments fell onto the front seat. "Buddy we'd offer you something, but you have to drive! Remember, you said you don't drink. You are the perfect date!"

And drive I did — for what seemed to be hours. About the time I thought we should head for the dance, they were "not quite finished". When it was emptied, each container was littered out the window, the last being an empty vodka bottle, thrown so it exploded in the roadway just ahead of an approaching car. As it passed, I recognized the beige Ford Galaxy 500.

⌂

A metamorphosis had occurred in the cafeteria. The lunchroom tables had disappeared and beautiful fall decorations skirted the columns and covered the walls.

My anxiety mounted as Jill and I entered the school. Jackie and Jill quickly went to the girls' restroom. Larry thought he should "go" too. I thought it was probably good for him, too. This gave me a chance to get lost amongst the crowd, hopefully finding comfort among my closest friends. Mark Farmer and Karen Rae Armstrong were seated alone at a table of four; around the side of the stage, in a quiet, secluded area. We talked about the events of the early evening. When the three rowdies reappeared, I quickly pulled up from the table. I heard Mark and Karen Rae say "We'll pray for you." I slithered across the dance floor hoping no one had figured out that Jill was my date. How foolish a thought! Everyone knew WHO had taken whom!

The rest of the evening went easier. Fortunately, Jill and her cronies became so engrossed in each other that we missed the 11:00 p.m. last dance.

Just after we pulled out of the school parking lot, Larry inquired, "Do you think they'll get married?"

Sarcastically, Jackie responded, "She's such a goody two shoes; it serves her right!"

Naively I asked, "Who are you talking about?"

Jill quickly responded, "Didn't you hear? Kitty Thompson is PG. Buster Mazzocco is the father." Jill noted Kitty had not been in school the last two weeks. Not yet sixteen, Kitty was thrust into the challenges of a mother's life.

Jill said, "You can take me back to Jackie's. I'm staying with her tonight. Her parents went to Wisconsin for the weekend – they left us a refrigerator full of beer!"

⌂

Coach Ziegler was very surprised when we ran into each other at the church door for the 8:00 a.m. service. "Well how did your date go? Did you follow your head or your heart? I saw Mae Lynne driving the tractor and pulling the empty hay wagon out of town at about seven o'clock last night. I could see she wasn't dressed for the dance. Starting tomorrow, maybe the spring training we talked about will go better."

What else did he know?

Sunday afternoon was awfully quiet at home. "I think I'll go vacuum the car." Getting no reaction, I proceeded to the garage carrying Mom's trusty Electrolux. Air freshener in hand, I brought cleaner to brighten the beige vinyl. The usual gravel on the passenger's side was not all I discovered. Two of the aluminum pull tabs and three Parliament cigarettes were nestled behind the seat. I looked for vinyl cuts but fortunately found none. I quickly grabbed the pull tabs, wrapped them in a paper sack and buried them in the bottom of the half full garbage can. The rest of the afternoon was unbearably uncomfortable. I headed for bed, said my prayers, and was asleep as soon as the sky blackened.

Anxiously, I plodded through Monday morning. I was nervous about both the expectation of encounters I anticipated and those I believed were probably looming. After leaving his office, I saw Coach Ziegler snickering as he rounded the corner, likely anticipating what was about to occur.

How could three people, in a large building, be at the same place at the same time? An obviously hung-over Jill sluggishly plodded down the hall. Unfortunately, Jill, Mae Lynne, and I all approached the corridor intersection at the same time. Who was going to talk to whom?

The encounter never developed once Jill spotted Jackie coming down the adjacent stairway. "There you are! I've been looking for you all morning. Here's your blouse, I think I got the stain out. Sorry, I can't do much for the burn hole".

With Jill out of the way, Mae Lynne called to me, "Did you have a good time Saturday night? Just before the coronation, several of us saw you scurrying around the halls. You looked like you had your hands full! I should have offered you either a bridle or, better yet, the cattle prod I still held in my hands." Suddenly I remembered I was supposed to take it off the float and get it back to her dad. "Maybe sometime we can talk about it."

Whoa, I'm in charge here! Who does she think she is, leaving me speechless? Uncontrollably I blurted, "How about after school next Friday? I'll meet you at the Dairy Del."

"I can't be there until after work, but 6:15 will work fine. I wouldn't miss it for anything."

⌂

"Ok, Mr. Olsen, if you're so smart, who said: For God so loved the world that He gave his only begotten Son, that whosoever believeth in Him shall not perish but have everlasting life?"

"That's not fair. You know, Mae Lynne, you're starting to get on my nerves. Since you don't kiss, I don't suppose you dance or play cards either. Where in the Bible does it forbid them? How about having to eat fish on Fridays? Am I going to hell because I kiss and dance and play cards?"

"Who did you kiss, your Aunt Ella? Oops! Sorry, I didn't mean that. I've seen you dance, if that's what you call it! I'm not sure about your kissing, but if *you* go to hell, it won't be on account of whether you kissed, danced, played cards, or didn't eat fish!" Still focused despite my poor attempt at diversion, she continued, "So you believe in hell do you, but you aren't willing to have a personal relationship with the only One who can keep you out of hell?"

Making another attempt to trip her up, I said: "Oh yeah, then what does inerrant mean? Dad says that is why Pastor Davidson was forced to leave St. Bart's. He preached that the Bible is inerrant and the District said he was the one that was wrong."

"It means that the Bible is true, without error. If it says something, it is true. Let me give you an example. For three days, Jonah lived in the belly of a great sea monster, right? Do you really believe that?"

"I am not sure."

"Are you also not sure you're a Christian? When you read your Bible, how do you determine what is true and what is not? Have you ever seen the wind? You've seen <u>effects</u> of the wind but you have never <u>seen</u> it! If someone tells you 'the wind blew it over', you still believe them, especially if you saw the tree fall during the storm, right? Isn't Christianity really whether you believe the Bible in its entirety or not? To answer my original question, Jesus himself said to Nicodemus: 'For God so loved the world that He gave his only begotten Son, that whosoever believes in Him shall not perish but have everlasting life'. If you are indeed a Christian, what authority do you have to question Jesus?"

"Jesus didn't say that. It is 'according to St. John', at least that's what they say at St. Bart's."

Pulling a small Bible out of her purse, she said, "Here, read it!"

Putting my foot in deeper, I said: "I don't believe it! Jackie was right; you really <u>do</u> carry a Bible with you all of the time." Pausing, I continued, "Wait a minute. Are you saying that if I don't believe what Jesus said, as reported by John who was an eyewitness, then I am not really a follower of Jesus Christ?"

"Yes."

"Uh...maybe you have a point."

"I am not asking you to be religious or to follow man-made rules. I am asking you to have a personal relationship with the Savior. Buddy, you're lukewarm! While you are at it, take some time to read about that! Once upon a time, I didn't know I had a void either. My peace extends beyond this world, to the eternal world. This life is only temporary."

In my mind, I suddenly remembered: the Peace of God that passes all understanding. "So <u>that's</u> what it means!"

"What what means? Buddy, are you listening to your head or your heart? My belief is in my heart."

"The Peace of God that passes all understanding; that is what they say at the end of the service. Now I think I know what it means. Let's go back, you're moving way too fast... Am I listening to my head or my heart? What is that supposed to mean and where have I heard that before? "

"You tell me."

"I need to gather my thoughts; we'll talk about that later."

"Oh yeah, one thing I forgot to mention. Last Sunday morning, Dad went out to the garage and found the left rear tire was flat on the Galaxy 500. Since I had taken it to Little Fork before heading into the dance, he said I was lucky the large piece of glass he found had not punctured a front tire. He reminded me how to steer the car if I ever had a front tire blowout and started to skid. It was a good reminder. Do you want me to teach you what he taught me?"

"No, I'm a good driver." Realizing I had been caught, I humbly said, "I already know what to do."

1968

1968 brought the Winter Olympics to the mountains of France. A former Providence exchange student won a position on the French bobsled team. Apparently a local heroine, frequently interviewed by the media, the Grenoble native spoke openly of both his Christianity and his high regard for America and its World War II veterans. Not coincidentally it seemed, commentators quickly went to a commercial break just as he transitioned between sports and real life.

In 1968, America was heavily engaged in the Vietnam War. The Communists were waging a fierce counterattack. Television's covert power became apparent, as the war's opponents learned an effective way to bring the country to its knees. It was called "The Living Room War". Every night, news reporters brought gruesome details to the nation's living rooms. The detail contained in these broadcasts handcuffed our country's effort and the troops we asked to do the work.

⌂

With Susanna off at college and George having his own used car, Dad and Mom extended my responsibilities to include maintenance of the two family automobiles. In exchange for keeping both vehicles clean and serviced, I was permitted to use the older car as if it was my own. Dad and Mom paid the insurance, while I paid for my own gas, with strict orders to always keep the tank full. Dad and Mom paid for all maintenance as long as the manufacturer's maintenance schedule was strictly followed. I was required to keep a record of all work completed.

The self serve car wash in New Bergen was well known by consumers as the best around. The owners equipped the bays with powerful trigger sprayers, using the best detergents to wash away even the toughest road salt. Water was heated to enhance the cleansing action. In addition to the spray guns, separate soft horsetail brushes were available for gentle scrubbing. Chamois towels were provided in the covered drying area, which was set aside for waxing, vacuuming, floor mat cleaning, and detailing.

Dad frequently praised the appearance of both of his vehicles. He was confident he had made the right decision. Both the 1965 four door Dodge Monaco and the 1967 two door Dodge Coronet 440 were backed into the spotless garage, always ready to go on a moment's notice. Dad justified backing them in, claiming it was easier for me to check the oil in our slightly undersized garage.

Preston Brothers knew that both cars had been sold into good hands. Each time I entered the bay, service manager Lester Wiley beamed widely as his puffy, red cheeks communicated his joy. A fellow Legion member with Dad, both service manager Wiley and Dad knew well maintained equipment would provide years of dependable service. Dad had learned this lesson from his father while taking care of the family's farm equipment and draft horses – lessons he now passed on to me.

The Coronet 440 was especially striking when I completed working on it one unseasonably warm Saturday afternoon during the late January thaw. Removing the heavy amounts of road salt and sand with the power wash nozzles, I drove it to the forward bay area for the remaining work.

I knew her name. Older than me, I remembered she had been a varsity cheerleader for the New Bergen basketball team. For approximately six months I had caught a glimpse of her at the New Bergen Grain Elevator when I picked up ground feed for our few remaining livestock. I knew she also worked as a candy striper at Providence Hospital, just as she had done throughout high school.

"You're Buddy Olsen, aren't you?"

"Yes."

"I'm Cory Sullivan. I've watched you during your baseball games. You're a pretty good catcher. After high school, do you want to continue to play?"

As we both dried and waxed our cars, it occurred to me that she appeared to have the same desire to keep her 2+2 1967 deep blue Mustang as clean and shiny as I did to keep Dad's mint green Coronet 440 fastback. During our conversation, I learned she had spent all of her savings to buy the car, a graduation present to herself.

Quite unexpectedly, she said, "Do you have any plans for tonight?"

"What did you have in mind?"

"Would you like to go to a movie and then grab an ice cream cone?"

"Sure!"

"Do you know where I live?"

I full well knew, however I slyly said, "I think so. I'll pick you up in an hour." She proceeded to give me detailed directions.

"OK. Sounds like fun. I'll enjoy a night out."

Running down the second story stairs, I told Dad and Mom, "I'll be home by curfew. I'm going to a movie. OK if I keep the Coronet?"

Dad mumbled, "I suppose."

Much more attentive, Mom inquired, "With whom? I just saw Mae Lynne at Hendrick's. She didn't say you had a date tonight."

"Just a girl from New Bergen."

Having quickly dashed in and out of my bedroom, I spent only enough time to splash on some English Leather and change into my best jeans, shirt, and boots. I eclipsed the ten mile round trip in record time.

Unbeknownst to Cory, I was suffering from the same all work and no play symptoms she had. I had carried gypsum board every afternoon, all week. Even though the money was good, it was very hard work even for my youthful body.

Cory was standing at the end of their short driveway when I came down the blacktopped township road. She too had changed clothes. She smelled like a sweet flower. Hurriedly, she let herself in the fastback's oversized passenger door. The bucket seats did not prevent her from moving closer. Her radiant smile and perfect teeth complemented her strawberry blonde hair, light freckles, and green eyes.

We talked lightly during the 50 mile drive to the theater located in a southwestern Chicago suburb. We chose to see *The Graduate* at the Paramount Theater. Arriving in the side parking lot at 7:25 p.m., the marquis indicated the show was to start within five minutes. Parking quickly, we jogged hand in hand to the ticket booth. Realizing what we had unconsciously done, we both looked at each other and experienced a flush of warmth.

After I paid the ticket clerk, it seemed natural that we again hold hands. We proceeded to the refreshment counter and walked arm-in-arm to the single, wide screen theater. The lights had been dimmed; the previews were just beginning. With our single tub of popcorn in hand, I asked as I motioned with my head, "The back of the theater OK?"

"That would be just right."

With only a few attending the show, we had the back corner all to ourselves. As the movie progressed, our bodies became more entwined. Although the ambient temperature was probably cool, the temperature inside seemed to be getting warmer!

As the credits rolled down the screen, we leisurely strolled back to the parking lot, hugging and holding on like we would never let go. We agreed to forego the ice cream and reserve the rest of the evening as a time to watch the submarine races.

However, the trip back to New Bergen was not to be without interruption. Shortly after I left the theater parking lot, a city black and white signaled me over. Very well groomed, the officer looked familiar – and very large through my window. He had a revolver and night stick on his belt.

"While turning onto Broadway, you failed to signal your change of lanes. Let me take a look at your driver's license. Turn on that left blinker again... Look at the dashboard indicator, see how its glows solid? You have a burned out bulb. You better stop by the garage and get that fixed tomorrow morning. You're a long way from Providence," as if to be reading my address from my driver's license. "Cory, I mean Miss, let me see some identification." Returning from his car, he gave us an additional word of advice: "It would be best if you and the young lady drove straight back home. I wouldn't want to see you around here later tonight. We will be enforcing an early curfew. There have been a lot of disturbances in Chicago again and we hope it doesn't spread this way. Please, do as I say. By the way, another officer may have given you a ticket – not a pass." With that, Sergeant Wiley motioned us to drive away.

Sensing her worry, I spoke first: "Whew. I just figured out who he was. I wondered how he knew your name without looking at your driver's license first! He's the Preston Brothers' Service Manager's son. He had been a deputy for Itasca County. He must have just gotten out of the MPs and is now an officer here. I think he knew who he was stopping before he asked for my driver's license. He probably saw the dealer decal on the trunk."

Although more cautious, we did not heed Sergeant Wiley's advice. "It doesn't look like we will see any submarines tonight…much less water deep enough for them to run in."

Cory politely laughed – fully participating in the joke. She also accepted my kisses. The rural setting offered endless places to "park". We soon established this newfound infatuation was mutual. This was the beginning of several weekend dates with Cory Sullivan. It soon became evident that Friday and Saturday nights would need to be supplemented with a few Sunday or Thursday nights–if there wasn't a wrestling meet. Movies, popcorn, and ice cream soon became secondary to our time alone on some deserted back road or cornfield turnaround. Even though the outside weather was cold, we were warm inside.

Dad and I were in the garage one Wednesday evening early in March. Wednesdays remained traditional church nights for some families, but not for Cory's or ours. Cory had called earlier in the afternoon saying she had come down with something. "It came on just after our Sunday night date. We won't be able to go out tonight. I have a fever and sore throat. I hope it's not mononucleosis."

"Mom and I don't think you should see Cory anymore."

"What! Why not? It doesn't matter to you who I date, does it?"

Ignoring my question, he continued, "You know her dad has joined our carpool and she volunteers at the hospital, but now she is in your mother's department. If nothing else, this might help you learn: young girls have a tendency to chatter."

As it turned out, it was for the better. Although we had a physical attraction, Dad and Mom could see continuing this relationship was likely to end in both career frustration and likely relationship difficulty. Rightfully, they believed there were too many core differences to overcome.

The subsequent phone call was difficult.

"You know Buddy, I love you very much. I can't believe we can't see each other anymore. I'm feeling better now. Can we just meet at the carwash one more time? Tell your parents you are going down to get some windshield washer fluid. Please, please, please, don't do this to me!"

"I don't think lying to my parents would be wise."

"Why are we breaking up then? Is it because you don't like my swearing? I know you think I have a temper. Is it because I go to St. Vincent's?" Raising her voice, "Tell me! What's the matter, are you a coward?"

"Please don't scream at me Cory, you just don't understand."

"By the way, what does 'equally yoked' mean anyway? It sounds like you expect us to be a pair of oxen!"

With that I heard her sobbing as she pulled the phone away. Someone had come in the back door. I heard her mumble, "He's dumping me! Can you believe it? I ought to give him what he deserves for this! Little Biddy Bible Buddy...Oops!" The rest of the conversation was muted.

Quickly rousing into another fit of rage, she took her hand off the mouthpiece and yelled, "You can just go to...", catching herself mid sentence, she changed and concluded her tirade: "I hate you Buddy Olsen!" With that the headset slammed to the cradle. All I heard was the dial tone.

Fortunately, I didn't need to worry about background snickering anymore; we now had a private line.

I didn't go to the New Bergen car wash again. The Providence car wash required a little more elbow grease but that was fine with me.

⌂

Later that month, I became interested in the youth activities at First Apostles. Over a period of time, St. Bart's hadn't encouraged its youth to remain in the church. First Apostles constructed a new youth building and large gymnasium while St. Bart's was focusing on global social causes. Sleepover retreats at church camps were organized, however, I limited myself to the sporting activities. Persistent as ever, Mae Lynne continued to show an interest in maintaining our friendship despite my having let her down so many times.

One early spring weekend, First Apostles rented the high school gymnasium for a youth game night while the church's gymnasium floor was being re-sanded and varnished. Desiring to keep its momentum alive, the church decided the school facility would help it meet its goal.

Two weeks had passed since I purchased new wrestling shoes. I was very disappointed when I discovered on that Saturday night that they were not in my steel locker, the ones specifically assigned to those participating in a winter sport. I went to Coach Frantz's office, but he said he had not seen them. Fortunately, my regular gym shoes were still in my PE basket. I would have used them for this night's activities anyway, but I wanted to at least be seen with the new ones!

Later that evening, and much to my ire, I spotted my shoes on Pat Davis' feet.

"Take them off or I'll take them off for you! Now, you little pipsqueak!"

After the brief confrontation, I decided it was time for action! After a few more choice words, I physically overpowered him and pulled my shoes from his small feet, socks and all. Getting what I wanted, I hoped the whole issue was behind me until I saw Mae Lynne and her father peering disgustedly over my left shoulder.

Trying to excuse my behavior, I blurted: "I was just getting what was mine! This piece of trash stole them!"

Placing his large weathered hands on my shoulder, and with a wrenching squeeze, the physically strong, Ed Davis replied, "My, my, you have quite the temper! I know for a fact that you didn't inherit that trait from your parents."

Then looking at me with his strong clear eyes he patiently explained, "Buddy, God doesn't make junk. Now apologize so we can forget this ever happened." The inflicted pain was excruciating; I knew I was not going to cry in front of him or his children.

"Come on Pat, let's see if we can find your shoes." Calmly, father, daughter, and son walked away.

⌂

The Spring Prom was not to be taken lightly at Providence High. No way would I repeat last fall's Homecoming escapade!

I approached the large, wooden porch wrapped around the front elevation toward the welcoming front door. On this occasion the back door was not appropriate; only the front would suit. Gingerly walking around Bouncer, so as not to soil my rented long tails tuxedo, I climbed the steps leading to the front doors. The canine bolted up the wooden stairs, repositioning himself at the entrance.

Looking at my reflection in the parlor window one last time, I didn't expect to look so much like a penguin!

Baseball uniforms or the new rage, Levis blue jeans, were more my style. "You clean up pretty good!" Mrs. Davis joked with me as she opened the screen door. She didn't feel the perspiration trickling down my armpits as I nervously stood on one foot then the other.

With Easter past, the spring weather was turning beautiful and perfect. When Mrs. Davis later saw a bead of sweat running down my forehead she offered, "Maybe these will help." She knew candied orange slices were my favorite.

"Can you come here Mom?" Always timely, I knew Mae Lynne was almost ready for our Prom date. Hearing her sweet voice made the sweat come even faster. With that Mrs. Davis proceeded up the wood staircase. In the front room, Mr. Davis quietly sipped a cup of coffee while nibbling on a windmill cookie.

A princess-like aura surrounded Mae Lynne as she appeared at the top of the staircase. I know she could hear my heart beating loudly; I nearly fainted. Dressed in a glowing orange dress with matching purse and shoes, she walked down the elegant staircase looking simply angelic. I caught Mr. Davis' twinkling eye as Mae Lynne said, "Yes Buddy, we can go out the front door."

Smoothly, I opened the passenger door and held her hand as she gracefully stepped into the car. I hadn't noticed, until I got behind the steering wheel, how she discreetly slid toward the middle of the sedan's bench seat.

"Wait a minute before you take off. Let's pray for God's protection."

I knew Mae Lynne was religious, but I didn't know how to react. What could a God who was light years away, and by some reports dead, do to protect us? Besides, if he was still around, he had other work to do! After all, we were only going to the Providence High School Prom!

"Bow your head and close your eyes." Demanding little thing she was!

Mae Lynne grabbed my hand, saying: "Lord Jesus, I ask you to put a hedge of protection around Buddy and me. Please watch over us as he drives. Please give us joy and friendship. Please give us a good time together; may we laugh and enjoy the evening, embraced in your protection. Also, please protect all who attend this prom and do not allow Satan to enter our school's hallways. I pray this prayer in Jesus' name, Amen. Did you want to pray?"

"Oh no, I just want to get going. You did the job for both of us. You said that so naturally. It was like you were talking to someone in the back seat. Oh yeah, what did you mean when you said, 'Please watch over us as he drives'?"

"I didn't mean anything derogatory; the Lord just put it on my heart to pray for us as we drove. Just the same, I am glad you were listening!"

Quickly, I learned this dance was going to be different than my experience at last year's Homecoming. Mae Lynne possessed an unequalled talent as a graceful dancer – something I had never known nor seen before; so much for my assumption about dancing and being a Christian.

⌂

Although eighteen-year-old David Fox's blood alcohol level, as determined by an autopsy, was barely below the legal limit, the county sheriff's report, described in the *Providence Purveyor*, reported that his speed was well above the limit. Estimated at over 105 mph, the bright red Dodge Charger was completely flattened after David apparently lost control and flipped into the freeway median at about 11:20 p.m. on Saturday night. The reality of the lost lives was clear in the newspaper photos showing the car being delivered to Norm's Auto Wrecking yard, just southeast of town. Fresh blood and fur were evident on the passenger side windshield and hood. The newspaper also reported the remains of three deer had been strewn along a 1/2 mile portion of the rain saturated median.

Killed in the wreck along with David, were Jill Benedict, Larry Dreger, and Jackie Pullman. Although the Sheriff, because of the ages of the younger victims, could not confirm if the passengers had been drinking, the newspaper noted "it was reliably reported that the officers removed both empty and full bottles of alcohol from the vehicle, once it had been winched out of the ditch and onto the shoulder." Adding to the grief, the spring rains made the recovery of the automobile's passengers impossible until the car was secure on higher ground. The delay dashed any hopes of survivors. There were unconfirmed reports around school that illegal drugs were found in the purses of both girls.

Having left the Prom at approximately 9:00 p.m., the foursome was believed to have been racing back to Providence in order to be at the Prom by 11:30 p.m., the post prom party curfew. Along with Mrs. Ziegler and Mrs. Rosen, several parents had organized an all night, on-site post prom party complete with food, games, cards, tournaments, music, and a teacher run dunking tank. Each student brought a change of street and gym clothes. Cots had been set up in the library, locker rooms, and home economics room. Following a buffet breakfast scheduled promptly for 7:00 a.m. Sunday morning, the attendees were free to leave the locked down school.

Both the Providence police and school authorities elected to keep the tragic news from the sequestered students attending the post prom party. They decided the post prom party offered an important change from the past. They decided it was best for the students' parents to speak with the students individually. They believed the school's responsibility was solely "book learned" education.

A school assembly was hastily scheduled on Monday morning. Lined up at the front of the hall, one faculty chair was noticeably empty. A quick review confirmed the absence of Miss Grainger.

A large screen had been set up on the stage. Without introduction, Superintendent Archer stood and asked to have the lights dimmed. The windows had been darkened with black construction paper. Immediately the movie began: *Teen Age Drinking and Driving–The Grave Consequences.* Following the movie, fully uniformed State Police officers gave personal testimonies of their experiences and observations as they investigate such tragedies. Although he was not a speaker, Mortician Mel Mattson's presence as the lone representative member of the School Board, was both subtle and explicit.

Charlene Nicole Grainger was later charged by the State's attorney with possessing and dealing in illegal drugs. A substitute teacher completed the remaining portion of the academic year.

⌂

In early summer, Providence was brought into the real world. Chicago continued to be the site of destructive war protests, held in conjunction with the Democratic National Convention. Chicago had become off limits for most family oriented activities, even Mom determined Cubs games would not be part of the summer's entertainment.

It was early morning on June 25th that a U.S. Army Jeep accompanied Mattson's hearse for Bill Schmidt's final ride through town. In his younger days, Bill, always known to "bomp" through town just to see what was going on, was now taking his last ride through town. Many believed that his recklessness would be his end; little could they know he would die a decorated hero.

Bill's funeral was heavily attended. The whitewashed, wood frame Catholic church had seen others of its parishioners tragically fall. Anger was everywhere. It was not until sometime later that I was able to forgive Bill for his youthful misbehavior. I was guilty of unforgiveness. For many years I had held him prisoner in my unforgiving mind – after all he was a big bully, likely something Pat Davis now thought of me!

Late in June, Providence was shocked when former Mayor Earl Finch was arrested and charged with eight counts of selling alcohol to a minor and four counts of involuntary manslaughter in the deaths of the four Providence High School students, the night of the Prom. Found to be acting as supply conduits, both of his children, David and Monica, were placed on civic probation and ordered to perform extensive community service.

Most in the community had pre-judged Vaughn Dreger as a guilty contributor. Vaughn, grieving his son's death and visibly shaken by the accusations, razed his Railroad Tavern and had it hauled away to the nearby landfill.

Unknown to most, Vaughn became a born again Christian, when he accepted Christ just six short weeks after the loss of his youngest son. He later became an elder at the Providence Church of the Nazarene. Despite the havoc Vaughn's tavern wreaked in his brothers' lives, Dad, in a show of his own integrity, became the first to personally congratulate Vaughn on his newfound life. Dad, along with hundreds of others, also anonymously, each gave Vaughn $500 in seed money to support his community effort to support Providence area families with alcohol-induced social, family, and economic problems.

⌂

That summer, Mae Lynne and I had an on-again/off-again dating relationship. I was struggling with my faith and

148

she was having trouble sustaining hers. Neither of us was bold enough to take the next step in our relationships between both ourselves and our Savior. We believed we were sitting comfortably on an elevated plateau believing Satan could not find or see us.

It was good in that Mae Lynne was given an opportunity to take classes at Northern State University. Three nights per week she attended college preparatory classes that would help her test out of general undergraduate work. Reciprocity agreements were in place between NSU and the University of Wisconsin – Mae Lynne's ultimate collegiate goal; she was also encouraged by Mr. and Mrs. Hendricks. Her flexible work schedule allowed her time to work, study, and attend night classes.

⌂

The morning chores were complete and the skies were clear except for a few cirrus clouds low in the eastern horizon. Humidity levels steadily increased and heavier clouds began to form by late morning. The day became unbearably hot. By then, I had drunk two gallons of water and sweated three. When the foreman called "lunch break", I was more than ready.

"Big game tonight Buddy?"

"Yes. It should be a good ending to a long baseball season." Only a Friday game was scheduled.

During the spring I played on the high school baseball team. During the summer I played American Legion games on Friday and Saturday nights both – good entertainment for the residents. On both teams, I remained the starting catcher. My batting average continued to be in the low .300s and my extra base hits and home runs led both the high school and American Legion leagues. I played 28 straight games without a pass ball or error. Both teams were competitive; both earned state competition playoff berths.

The afternoon hurried by. Two truckloads of gypsum wall board had been scheduled for Friday afternoon delivery. Since I completed the insulation and vapor barrier installation in the morning, the hangers would be able to start first thing Monday morning. With the wallboard distributed and the humidity and heat becoming unbearable, it was beer time for the older workers. Since I was underage, getting done early gave me extra time to race home, shower and dress for the game. During the summer, the Legion League was able to use the school district fields, but we were not able to use the locker rooms.

After completing my shower, I was most surprised to see the dark clouds towering in the southwestern sky. They appeared to be a long way away but they looked ominous; I judged the distance to be 20 miles. I put on everything but my spikes...and cup. After throwing the remainder of my equipment in the car, I drove the six short miles to the ball field. The radio crackled with the telltale sound of static generated by the approaching thunderstorms.

Both teams were on the field warming up when the first cooling breeze arrived. A change was imminent. As the sky darkened further, the smell of rain was in the air. A powerful lightning bolt drilled the water tower a mere two miles away. Deafening thunder was heard within seconds. Counting to myself how long it took between seeing the lightning and hearing the thunder, I figured the storm would arrive in a matter of minutes.

Quickly, the coaches ordered everyone off the field. As the weather deteriorated and the hard clayey surface flooded, it became apparent the game would be called off. "We will try again tomorrow night. Be here and ready at 5:30 for a 6:30 game," Coach Ziegler announced over the public address loudspeaker.

Since I had parked the sedan near the dugout, I quickly ran to it, closed the windows, and decided that rather than drive through a deluge, I would just sit it out. I hadn't seen the beige Ford Galaxy 500 parked under the large maple tree. A light tap on the passenger window was immediately followed by the opening of the passenger door.

"Mind if I join you?"

"Of course not."

"I saw you get into your car just after the lightning started. Mr. Hendricks said if I wanted to come watch your last regular season game, I could leave work early."

"That was nice of him. Did you hear? They have re-scheduled. Maybe tomorrow night the weather will be better."

After a few minutes of total silence, she gathered her thoughts and said, "It's real stuffy in here. Now that the lightning has subsided, let's go sit in the dugout."

"Are you sure? You may get wet."

"Remember, you're talking to a farmer's daughter. I've been caught in a lot worse storms than this!"

Volunteers had constructed the new dugout just four months earlier. The front bench had been shortened to accommodate the bat rack and an equipment storage cube was built into the rear corner. The home dugout was neatly painted and trimmed in the Providence colors of black, white, and grey. Appropriately, the visitor's dugout was painted the ugliest hot pink ever produced, trimmed in white, with large black polka dots.

Like a deer bounding through a cornfield, Mae Lynne quickly picked the equipment cube as her seat of choice. Feeling somewhat awkward by her forthrightness, my eyes were suddenly opened; her wet look enhanced her incredible natural beauty.

Continuing the small talk, I said, "You know, farmers call this timely, steady precipitation, *a million dollar rain.* Its timing will bring this year's crop to full maturity before the killing frost."

Still on His mission, she responded: "I've been praying for you. Buddy, I'm concerned you haven't found what you are looking for. You seem so moody. Partying doesn't seem to satisfy you. You've been frustrated with your baseball performance. You complain that because you're a southpaw, opportunities haven't been given to you as they have the other boys, and Coach has been looking at others who may have more natural talent. No wonder you say you are so exhausted when you come home from work and that all you want to do is escape into a deep sleep. Frankly, I'm exhausted from your pessimism!"

"It sounds as if the rain is letting up. Why did you wait in the car? After all, the game had been cancelled and everyone had gone." After a brief pause, I said, "I didn't see that you were here. Do you want to go for ice cream?"

"Later Buddy. We need to talk, just like the last time we had a serious talk. I would like to know what your plans are for next year."

"I don't know. I'm afraid of leaving Providence. For that matter, I'm afraid to leave this dugout! Don't tell anyone about this, OK? I'd like to play professional baseball..."

"...as a left-handed catcher? Are you sure that is God's plan?"

Gaining more confidence, she then said, "First, remember, as your friend, I will never violate your confidentiality. Secondly, you've been very rough on the underclassmen. We never talked about this before, but you were very heavy handed with my little brother last winter. I don't know whether you know it or not, but he didn't steal your shoes! Pat forgot his gym shoes in the car and yours apparently had been left out. He found yours in the lost and found barrel. They were way oversized, but he needed something!"

I thought about it...she was probably right. I didn't remember putting them back into my locker after the meet the night before, since I remembered clearing out all my dirty laundry. I also remembered they weren't in my laundry bag when I got home.

Staying focused, she asked, "Is it something I said or did that made you turn on him like that? He said he was sorry. You know he is slightly retarded. We don't always understand what goes on in his mind. It's almost like you were Saul on a mission to destroy." Slightly raising her voice, she firmly pointed out, "And, like my dad said... he is not a piece of junk!"

"But Paul killed Christians didn't he? Your brother survived."

"No, Saul killed Christians – until he saw the light in both body and spirit. Do you remember the story of his conversion?"

Caught flatfooted, I said, "Yeah, but I guess I don't remember it that well."

"I have my Bible in the car. I'll go get it."

"No, it's muddy and drizzling! We can do it some other time, besides it's dark in here."

"Do you have any other excuses? Maybe we should read Jesus' parable about excuses."

With that the young doe quickly bound to the Galaxy only to return just as quickly with a pen, one Bible, a small box, and a large flashlight. I readily recognized the small box probably contained a new Bible. The second Bible was tattered and loose at the binding. Asking me sarcastically, but in good humor, she continued, "You do carry your Bible wherever you go, don't you? Maybe I can change that!"

Mae Lynne's flashlight was capable of sitting on its base, flooding its beam onto the white roof boards above. Catching her breath, she said, "Here, this one's for you." In addition to the new Bible, she gave me the pen in her hand. As she opened her tattered Bible I could see handwritten notes in the margins. She easily found Acts Chapter 9.

"Open yours to Acts, Chapter 9... you know Matthew, Mark, Luke ... just kidding."

"I know my books; I had to recite them for my Confirmation test! Acts would be after Habakkuk, right? By the way, why do you write in your Bible? Isn't it a holy book? We don't do that at St. Bart's. Besides, we don't need Bibles anymore since we have the inserts in our bulletins." Thinking and talking at the same time, I added, "Apparently, Sunday School kids don't need Bibles either since we have several hundred unused copies on the basement book shelves, in case they would ever need one."

After reading the conversion story together, Mae Lynne announced, "You know Buddy, when we get done here, I want to have accomplished four things."

"Four? Sometimes I don't know who is more determined, you or my Mom." Adding, "Why so many? What are they?"

"God's timing will be perfect, you don't need to fret. First, I want to write something in your Bible. Next, I want you to publicly profess your belief in Jesus Christ as your Savior by asking Him into your heart. The other two, you'll have to wait to find out."

At first, I was uncomfortable marking and writing in a Holy Bible. Although Dad had always carried the large black Bible with his name engraved, as the years went by, even that one stayed home. Mom carried a small red hardcover Bible that she used for teaching Sunday School. When she quit teaching, using the inserts became more convenient.

"Are you ready for the first? Give me your Bible."

With another pen in hand, Mae Lynne opened to the partially lined, cover page. With beautiful penmanship she wrote: *To Willis, Your friend in Christ, all ways, and always. Mae Lynne.* She then dated it 08/16/68. I could see deep sincerity in her twinkling eyes. The flashlight gave her an amber tone of warmth. Her hazel eyes were true and clear.

"Buddy, I would now like you to publicly state your faith."

"I did that."

"When?"

"At my Confirmation."

"With your head or your heart?"

"Have you been talking to Coach Ziegler?"

"What?"

"Nothing; he always says that to me."

I then affirmed my belief in Jesus Christ as my personal Savior, the one and only Savior, the Messiah, God in the flesh. I confessed my sinful nature and I asked Him to live in my heart.

With that my eyes were opened further. I saw the inward beauty Mae Lynne possessed. We both knew it was the right time for number three. I leaned over and we both celebrated our very first long kiss – in a rain soaked baseball dugout!

Leaning away, she softly said, "I guess I didn't need to tell you number three! I don't think that kiss will cause either of us to go to hell either."

"God's timing was perfect! So what is number four?"

"How 'bout splittin' a split?" With that we got into my car and headed downtown toward Hendricks' Drug Store and Fountain. Entering the double doors, she yelled like she owned the place, "Two large, banana splits with double hot fudge on the chocolate scoop, please!"

"I thought we were sharing."

Teasing she said, "Better not, I wouldn't want to spread any germs – could get mononucleosis you know!"

I sensed the wind had changed. Approaching 7:00 p.m., the store would close shortly. Precisely at 7:01 p.m., Mr. Hendricks told Mae Lynne, as he headed for the back door, "Be sure and lock up when you leave. Eat more ice cream if you want! Leave your dishes in the sink. I'll wash them in the morning."

⌂

Finally! After eleven long years it was finally here! I believed senior status at school would be just my ticket. With George off to Clinton's East Iowa University, I believed Providence High and the Olsen household were now my domain.

⌂

First Apostles planned an early Fall Festival the following weekend. In conjunction with the start of the harvest, bake sales and family activities were planned beneath the big top. Mae Lynne approached me in the school cafeteria on Monday and asked me to join her for the Saturday night revival. Before I could answer, she said, "I'll pick you up at 6:30." Never did I think she was not iron-willed.

I was surprised to see such a large crowd. Mae Lynne promptly walked me, her arm in mine, toward the front rows. There I recognized several local business people along with a few friends from school. Among them were Mark Farmer and Don Longly together with Marilyn Rosen and Karen Rae Armstrong. Sitting next to Karen Rae was her father and Mr.

and Mrs. Hendricks. An empty chair separated Mr. Armstrong from Mr. Hendricks.

I sensed the cohesiveness of the assembly as the participants individually called upon the Lord. In a somewhat different manner than I was accustomed, verbal responses were freely spoken as several speakers called for the Lord's presence within this place. Arms and hands were waving. Did they expect Jesus to show up? Or, did He show up and I couldn't see Him amongst the crowd?

The revival had also been held on the previous three nights. As was the case for the previous nights, Reverend Daniel Talton, from Louisville, Kentucky, was tonight's guest preacher. His sermon tonight, based on Acts 9:8, was titled: ...*Led by the hand along Damascus Road.*

Like the music and scripture, which preceded the sermon, Rev. Talton's sermon intensified towards an altar call. I remember his closing statement well: "You don't need to worry about your earthly neighbor or the person sitting next to you; this is between you and the Lord." He then led the assembly in the Sinner's Prayer for salvation with an invitation to come to the front of the tent "if you had indeed prayed the prayer in your heart".

Rev. Talton closed the service by singing the Doxology in his strong baritone voice. I will always remember the words that resonated following his benediction: "My fellow Believers, preach Christ. Use words if necessary! Now may the Peace of God which passeth all understanding, keep your hearts and minds in Christ Jesus!"

To which the entire body, including me, shouted, "Amen!"

1969

"Grab a towel Willis." I was somewhat shocked by hearing my given name; I had always been "Buddy" to her in the past. "So what are your plans after this spring's graduation?"

The time after the Holidays was the famine after the feast – so I thought. Since I had gone to first service, I had no commitments except to be home for Sunday dinner, served precisely at 12:00 noon. Since there were now only three of us, Mom resumed cooking Sunday Dinner at home.

Also beginning with the New Year, St. Bart's instituted a coffee fellowship time between services. Proceeds of the free will offering went to youth programs. Students were expected to set up the refreshments and clean up the area afterwards. I was not a coffee drinker, but I liked to grab a caramel glazed donut and orange juice. It was nearing time for second service to begin when Mrs. Ziegler and I discovered we were the only ones remaining to wash the used dishes.

I had always believed Mrs. Ziegler to be bold, but this time she shot me with both barrels! I explained that I had taken general studies, but as I spoke, it quickly became evident that I had no clear path of study. I had a strong math aptitude and I did well in science. I did not like Chemistry, I decided to forego it in favor of the Biology plus Physics option. This meant an additional class but I didn't think I could successfully pass Chemistry.

She badgered, "That all sounded good but you really didn't say anything. You need to be specific. What do you want to be – an engineer, or maybe, since you have so much experience, an allergy doctor? Let's try again, what are your career goals? You realize you don't have a whole lot of time before graduation!"

"I like history but I don't have a clue how to apply it. I love looking at the pictures in *National Geographic*. I love maps with accompanying photographs, especially those that indicate archeological sites – like the ones in Dad's big black Bible." I could see she was beginning to lose patience. "I guess I want to be a world famous, rich, photographer/ cartographer/archeologist – living near Providence of course."

Not missing a beat she inquired, "...exploring, mapping, and photographing archeological digs in Providence? Trust me; there is more to the world than Providence. And, do you think you could provide for a family traipsing around Illinois looking for world changing archeological digs anyway? You would go broke!"

Attempting to take off some of the pressure, I countered, "Tell me about you and Coach Ziegler."

Seeing right through my feeble attempt at changing tracks, she played along and asked, "What do you want to know?"

"How did you decide on your career? How did you get such an important bank job? Working for Uncle Marvin must be tough! Where did Coach Ziegler learn to be so easy going? I have teachers who are impatient when I need help, but Coach always offers encouragement. I can tell that you have that same spirit. Whenever I come into the bank, you have that same servant's attitude."

I saw by the clock, second service was well underway. Seeing we were going to be here a while, she offered, "I suppose Coach won't miss me up there. He knew I wanted to talk with you and when I saw him earlier, I told him I just might have a good chance this morning.

"Would it surprise you if I told you I believe the Lord led Coach Ziegler and me to Providence and St. Bart's to fulfill His purpose? Do you believe He also has a master plan for your life? You told me a lot of things just now but I never heard you even remotely say anything about God's plan. Do you think you have it all under control or are you going to put it in His hands? After all, he knitted you in your mother's womb."

"Are you saying I can just sit back..."

Cutting me off mid-sentence, she countered, "... and become complacent? Not in the least!" I began to understand – she was speaking from a much higher level of faith. "Where is that faith you witnessed last fall at the Revival? You did profess the Sinner's Prayer, didn't you? I saw you go forward with Mae Lynne. Were you up there for show? Buddy, you need to start seeking the Lord's guidance. The Biblical verses that say, 'He who has ears to hear let him hear' aren't necessarily only talking about a physical part of your body. Has your *heart* heard His message or, as I suggested, were you going through the motions?"

"Have you been talking to Mae Lynne and Coach Ziegler?"

"What?"

"They say that a lot too... about my heart." How stupid, I thought, of course she talks to Coach Ziegler.

Turning her face toward me and looking me squarely in my eyes, she said, "I have been specifically praying for you for the last six years."

"You've been praying for me? Directly to Jesus?" A tear began to roll down my cheek.

"Willis, you need to listen to those around you who love you and want you to listen to His calling."

After a short pause, I broke the silence: "There, the last one is put away. We're done. It looks like it is exactly 11:30. Second service is over." The kitchen was spotless.

We heard Coach Ziegler coming down the stairs, turning back towards me, she asked, "How are you going to get home by noon?"

"I'll just call and have someone come pick me up."

"No, we can take you. I know how good a cook your mother is. I wouldn't miss one of her Sunday dinners for anything!"

When we got to the farm, Coach Ziegler shut the car off and started to open his door. At the same time Mrs. Ziegler opened hers and began to get out. From the back I said, "No need for both of you to help me out; I can make it on my own."

Overlooking my ignorance, Mrs. Ziegler said, "I told you I wouldn't miss your mom's cooking for anything. She invited us over for Sunday dinner when she and your dad were in the bank last week."

With that I knew the relationship established over six years ago was going to last a lifetime. Mom prepared her favorite dinner: roast beef, with cooked in peeled red potatoes, carrots, and onions – all smothered in rich, dark brown gravy. To top it, off she served rhubarb pie ala mode. Graciously pardoning Mrs. Ziegler, Mom, and me, Coach and Dad cleaned up. When the dishes were done, we leisurely sat and talked the remainder of the early afternoon. However, shortly thereafter, droopy eyes soon took over. The Zieglers knew it was time for them to return home and do the same – nap.

Walking out onto the front porch to say goodbye, Mrs. Ziegler suddenly gave me a hug. This time, a small tear was running down her cheek. Wiping it away she said, "Buddy, it's time to start that walk. There are spring lambs everywhere. Preach Christ. Use words if necessary."

Realizing where I had heard that before, I began to see how the Lord had truly provided the Zieglers as strength and support. They were indeed chosen role models who were there to keep me on God's straight and narrow path. "You went to the revival? I guess you told me that earlier and it didn't sink in. Sorry, I guess my head is still spinning from our conversation this morning."

Kindly responding, Mrs. Ziegler said, "I hope you take our conversation seriously. It was all in God's perfect time. Besides, like I said about your mother's cooking, I wouldn't have missed that conversation for anything."

◠

No longer playing organized baseball, as I remember, Ben Armstrong was putting on a navy blue beret when I rounded the corner heading for a mid-week baseball game with Big Stone. Feeling a bit mischievous, I ripped the beret from his head and ran toward the locker room. I was running a little late for batting practice so I told Marty Polanski to return it to Ben. I quickly dressed and headed for the ball field, not realizing Marty was already on his way toward the awaiting school bus.

During the top half of the second inning, while waiting for the ball to be put in play, I suddenly saw the Coronet 440 fastback racing down the hill towards the ball field parking lot. Jumping out of the car, Dad marched a straight line toward the team bench and Coach Ziegler.

I thought this was unusual. After work, it was usually Mom who picked me up following a game. Calling time out, and motioning with a telltale finger command, Coach Ziegler decisively pulled me out of the game. "Take off your chest protector, mask, and shin pads!" In front of all, like a cat carrying its young, Dad grabbed me by my collar and immediately whisked me to the family car.

"Bill Armstrong called me at work right before I punched out!" Right then I knew I was in trouble. Never was anyone to call Dad or Mom at work unless it was a dire emergency. "He claims you stole Ben's hat! We are to meet Ben and him at Rosen's Men's Wear, where you will buy Ben a new hat!"

Driving almost as fast as when he pulled in, I had very little time to interject my side of the story of how I relied on Marty to return the hat. Hearing the story, Dad calmed from boiling to simmer. "Relying on Marty? What were you thinking? Here, I will lend you the money until you get home, at which time you will pay me double the cost of the hat as a fine. Call it extortion if you want, Buddy, but you need to start using that noggin for more than a hat rack!"

Totally humiliated, I had no choice but to wear my uniform and cleats into the store. Ben selected a replacement hat; I gave the money to Mr. Rosen. Dad then drove me back to the diamond where I sat by myself, in the bleachers, for the remainder of the game. We lost, or should I say I lost the game 5–4 when, in the top of the seventh, our substitute, junior varsity catcher failed to tag out a runner streaking toward home.

⌂

It was well after dusk; the sky was moonless. Lightening bugs and the first visible stars were the only source of light when I recognized the lone car as it crested the hill above the diamond.

"Do you need a ride home?"

"Boy am I glad to see you. Yes, thanks! I've never seen Dad so mad. Needless to say, I think I let him down."

"When I called for you from work, surprisingly George answered; he told me what had happened. He said as far as he knew you were still at the diamond. Were you supposed to have called home when the game was over?"

"They chain locked the hallway doors before I could get to the pay phone – and, I didn't have a dime. Coach left right after the game so his office door was locked. It seemed everyone left before I even had a chance to find help."

"Mr. Hendricks overheard the conversation and told me he saw your dad leaving town at about six o'clock." Dropping me off at the end of our drive, she said, "Good night Buddy. Remember, I am going to Madison this upcoming weekend."

⌂

"What do you think are your chances of success?"

I was chosen again for the American Legion ball team in 1969. Because of a large need, the military lottery quickly made several ballplayers' decisions inconsequential. Older boys enlisting for the four year hitch could not adequately provide the numbers needed. America committed its resources, but not necessarily its heart, to halting what was perceived as the Communism domino effect in Southeast Asia.

Deferments were based on the quota needed by the local draft board and the presumed goals of the individual. A low number was exempted only by a claim of hardship or academic pursuit. Colleges were bursting at the seams. In addition to the normal scholastic achievers, a certain number of others were seeking the draft protection offered by the college campus. Men who had not chosen a career were hastily picking something, even if it meant they changed majors three or four more times, extending their educational stay beyond the normal four years. Still others used academia as their own pulpit to stir unrest and globally change institutional thinking. Some chose to go north to Canada.

My draft number would not be determined until the summer of 1970. Not yet eighteen, I held the false hope that another year would buttress my plans. The Itasca County Board had become known as a no-nonsense group of veterans. Although rare, individuals were sometimes called to appear face to face in front of the previously anonymous Board. These behind closed door sessions made a significant impact on many a life.

Coach Ziegler asked, "Once you have registered and become 19, do you think your special talent as a left-handed catcher is going to give you a deferment?" I realized aspirations of becoming a professional ball player would not likely persuade the local board that playing baseball was a profession of national urgency. Furthermore, I believed I would flunk the physical because of my chronic asthma. "That might not be a guarantee if the military needs stateside staff. Did you ever consider a four-year enlistment? That may give you additional educational opportunities. You know, entering one of the military academies is no longer an option, since scholastic achievement and political appointments are not in your favor. Besides, the graduating Class of 1973 candidates have already been chosen nationwide."

⌂

By the end of spring, Providence High School's baseball team had repeated as the Big Valley Conference and District champions. Several small college recruiters and town league scouts had been in attendance during the championship games. Because of the size of schools participating and their remoteness from urban areas, no large university or professional team scouts attended the championship tournaments.

Disappointed but thinking ahead, Coach Ziegler invited several regional teams to compete in a late spring exhibition tournament to bolster Providence's Memorial Day activities. Fulfilling Dad's prediction, in less than a decade the significance of the military contributions had indeed gone away.

Coach Ziegler hoped to showcase some of the best area talent. He was pleasantly surprised when assistants and coaches from Illinois, Wisconsin, Indiana, Iowa, and Minnesota came to watch the three day tournament. Coach Ziegler conducted personal tours to display Providence's renovated ball field improvements including new lighting, fencing, grounds, and the latest electronic scoreboard. Even the elevated press box became part of his all inclusive tour.

Since these baseball programs extended beyond school activities, the school district had formed a joint partnership with the newly formed Providence Athletic Commission to share the use of, and manage the facilities. The old name, Pilgrim Field, was changed to Fox Field. The recreational park, also newly developed, was now appropriately named Schmidt Memorial Park. Dad was noticeably pleased when he learned that an area within the recreational park would be set aside as a memorial to Providence's veterans. Almost overnight, the entire complex had become the best facility within a two hundred mile radius of rural communities.

Graciously attended to by a large group of volunteers, several small interview tents were raised for the visiting scouts and coaches. Conferences within the interview tents were conducted by invitation and appointment only. Area coaches lobbied feverishly to present their individual players in the best light.

I received only one interview. I knew I had to make the best of it since this would likely be my only passport to the future. Prairie Ridge Technical College was a two-year college located approximately 150 miles downstate in the medium-sized farming town of the same name: Prairie Ridge, Illinois.

Seeing me after coming away from one of the tents, Coach Ziegler asked me, "Well, how did it go?"

"Honestly Coach, I thought it went well. He was very easy to talk to. It was almost like he knew everything about me even before I entered the tent."

"What did you expect – that he interviewed you on a whim without checking your credentials? Coach Ziegler then surprised me as he announced, "I graduated from PRTC."

"You did? I didn't know that."

"From there I continued my studies at the University of Rockford; that is where I received my teaching degree." He went on to speak highly of the baseball program. I was honored he saw my potential for success both athletically and academically. "Coach Morse has led the program for almost 50 years. Well-known as a coach in areas such as skill enhancement and career guidance, Coach Morse is also known for two other strengths – his walk with God and his genuine compassion. Just to let you know, often his Christian walk is challenged by the more liberal thinking staff who perceives his decisions as outright discrimination. You will soon learn that Coach Morse's foundation is set on the Rock."

⌂

"Coach Ziegler tells me you ran the 100 yard dash in 10.3 seconds."

"No sir, I don't run track, I only play baseball."

"No, he said you ran some sprints during a game where he had taken you out of the game because of some errand you had to run with your father. You ran it in your baseball spikes, right?"

"Yes sir, I did."

"Well I won't ask you what was so important that you had to be pulled out of the game. I guess that is between you and your dad." Pausing briefly to clear his throat, he continued, "Willis, this is the first time I've taken such a risky notion, but, I think I can help you with both your talents and your career. Coach and Mrs. Ziegler have spoken highly of you. They said you are a young man of character, specifically they said, 'like your dad'. I trust it is the right kind of character."

I will never forget the follow-up phone call. Just two short weeks earlier, I had been turned down for so much as an interview by the University of Minnesota and several others. Coach Morse had offered me both a work program scholarship and a guaranteed position on his Soarin' Eagles baseball team! "Your acceptance to the college will include a room assignment in the campus's best dorm and a part-time campus job with the Prairie Ridge Police Department as a security guard at school and athletic events. The job should include enough hours to pay for your books, tuition, and room and board."

"Furthermore, I am pleased to tell you this work scholarship will be automatically renewed for the second year provided you letter your first year, maintain a 3.0 or above grade point average, and have no social demerits. We will provide you with talent and career counseling and provide up to three letters of recommendation if you satisfactorily fulfill this two year agreement."

"This is my kind of enlistment!" I thanked him profusely. At the time, I didn't know which was going to be the hardest to achieve – the 3.0 grade point average or no social demerits.

168

The upcoming American Legion season would be my last. I hoped that becoming a Soarin' Eagle starter would place me on a semi-pro team by the summer of 1971.

⌂

The garage door always sounded an alarm. Whenever I needed to quietly sneak home, unfortunately the stretching springs loudly announced my arrival. Any sleeper was soon rousted from the depths.

When I came in the back door, Mom sleepily asked, "What time is it?"

My curfew was at midnight and it was now almost 12:30 a.m. "It's just after midnight," I said, justifying in my mind why it was all right to stretch the truth.

Rolling over, she mumbled, "We'll see you in the morning. We love you Buddy."

It was about 7:45 a.m. when panic set in. Thinking I could never get ready fast enough to catch the car leaving the garage for the eight o'clock worship service, I covered my tracks by yelling out the back door, "I'll go to late service and be home in time for dinner." Only the garage mice heard me since I neither heard nor saw an acknowledgement. Realizing I could slip in another 2 hours of sleep, I fell back into my bed.

The sound of stretching springs again sounded the alarm. I knew I could now get up and have enough time to make it to late service – on time. To my surprise, the alarm hand was positioned for 9:45, however, the hands read 1:30. What had happened? I then realized I had forgotten to pull out the alarm clock stem.

Coming in the back door, Mom spoke first, "Didn't make it to the second service either, we see. That's too bad. Coach Ziegler was looking for you. He wanted to ask you to usher at second service next week. We told him you would. Leif, maybe you and I can go see the Cubs next Sunday."

Foolishly ignoring the real issue, I said, "Gosh, I'm hungry, what's for dinner?"

"Oh, we already ate. I'm about ready for a nap; how about you Leif?"

I suddenly discovered my dilemma. No Sunday dinner meant nothing had been set out to thaw, no one to fix it, and no one even interested in my empty stomach.

Arrogantly I said, "That's OK. I'll just take the sedan into town and pick up something at the Dairy Del."

⌂

The tractor was outside so I knew someone was at home. Seeing the open sliding door, I quickly ran towards the machine shed. "Mr. Davis, can I buy some gas? I ran out about a quarter of a mile past your drive." Coming to the realization I only had a sixteenth of a tank when I pulled the car into the garage, I calculated one gallon was what it would have taken Dad and Mom to drive to church, make a trip to The Food Basket, and return home. My inconsideration had just totally backfired on me.

"Doesn't your dad have any?" He knew I couldn't ask Dad. "Sorry Buddy, all we have now are those new diesel tanks over there."

Disgusted, I figured my only other choice was to walk home and face the music. I couldn't bother Dad and Mom. I also couldn't figure out a way of getting two cars down the same road. Having sold the tractor, nowadays, our only gas can was an oil/gas mixture for the lawn mower. I knew better than to use that in the car.

When I got home, I was surprised to see neither the fastback nor Dad and Mom. I then realized my only remaining option was Mom's old bicycle. A large wire basket was fastened over the front tire fender. It had only one speed, with large balloon tires and a back tire coaster brake. I knew my image as a cool almost-18-year-old would be badly tarnished if I was seen in town riding Mom's bicycle.

My plan was to take all of the side streets, stay off Main Street, and hide the bicycle out of anyone's view behind the hedges that screened an adjacent warehouse wall.

Off I went, pedaling away. Fortunately, the Sunday clerk at Ronnie's 66 Service Station knew Dad was Ronnie's cousin; he lent me the station's sole five-gallon gas can. Pumping it full, he did not offer the same generosity as he had with the can. He took my ten-dollar bill; he offered no change. One thing I fortunately discovered, the large front wire basket was still in good order.

"Be sure and bring it back this afternoon. We need to put it back on the wrecker."

Gasoline quickly covered my hands; as the fuel began to slosh, noxious fumes rose out the relief valve. The heavy, oversized can severely impaired my ability to steer. I hadn't thought of only purchasing 2 gallons or of bringing along a rope to tie it down. It was almost 4:30 when I got back to the disabled car. I emptied the can, put it into the trunk, and rode the bike home. Walking back to the car, it was almost 5:00 p.m. and I still needed to get the can back to the service station.

To my disappointment, a sign had been posted on Ronnie's door: *Closed Early – Service Call.* I hoped they had grabbed a new replacement can off the shelf before they left to make the call. Maybe that was the idea behind the clerk's "insurance premium". Then, looking in the service bay overhead doors, I saw the wrecker parked next to the open bay.

With 4 gallons to spare, I calculated I easily had enough to get back into town fill it up the rest of the way and have the tank full for use Monday morning. My other idea–I would ask Dad for some gas money when they got home.

Coming in the back door, I heard Mom ask," Leif, wasn't that a great time? Everyone kept asking where Buddy was."

Seeing me moping in a living room chair, Dad chimed in: "We figured you would be the last to miss an all-church potluck and ice cream social. They even brought out the ice cream social string of lights. Mom won a German Chocolate cake in the cakewalk. Anna, mind if I take it to work tomorrow? It's John Sullivan's 15 year anniversary with the company. I need to drive tomorrow morning. What a beautiful night. Too bad you missed it Buddy."

Standing, I humbly asked, "Dad I need gas money."

Quickly turning around, laughingly he said, "Gas money? Mom gave you a full tank when you left last night, and now you're out? Where did you go... Iowa?"

All I'd eaten all day was a peanut butter sandwich on the stale, half-frozen ends of the loaf. I had been further humiliated when I realized we were out of milk and eggs. "Buddy, how about making tomorrow's lunches before you go to bed. From her living room chair, Mom peered over the top of her glasses and added, "Check the refrigerator in the garage." In the old refrigerator, I discovered Dad and Mom had purchased a smoked ham, along with cheese, lettuce, bread, juice, fresh fruit, icebox cookies and milk before returning home from church earlier that day. My favorite, a quart mason jar of Mom's homemade applesauce was thawing on the top shelf. Mom said, "I'm defrosting the kitchen refrigerator; please put everything back in it before you go to bed. Thanks."

"Buddy, you forgot to put Mom's bike back in the garage after your trip to town. I put Ronnie's gas can outside the garage door so it wouldn't stink up the car. He said you had borrowed it from the station. We saw him and his clerk at the ice cream social. They looked like they hadn't done a lick of work all day. Good night, we'll see you in the morning."

I knew no matter what else happened on this Sunday, I didn't care if it ever came again. When I got in the car on Monday morning, I saw the bike had been neatly put away. It had a new dent and Dad's car had telltale blue bicycle paint on the front chrome bumper. As I loaded the gas can back into the car, I realized my parents were always there for me, especially now during these times of national unrest. In a single day, they helped me realize I was leaving my teen age years and rapidly becoming a young adult.

⌂

Our senior prom did not have the tragedy of the previous year. The post prom party was well-received. Most students, still in shock from the previous year, individually determined fun and games were better than newspaper coverage. Mae Lynne and I enjoyed the entire evening.

Greeting me at the church's front door, Coach Ziegler said, "I didn't realize I had assigned you to usher this month at the 8:00 a.m. service. I'm glad you're here but didn't you take Mae Lynne to the prom and post-prom party?"

"Yes to all of the above. Mark Farmer and I had so much fun with the girls we decided to play nine holes of golf before he dropped me off here. Suddenly remembering Coach's strict dress code and that I was not dressed in a suit and tie, I asked, "This golf shirt and slacks isn't too informal for church is it?"

Not letting him negatively answer, I quickly said "Mae Lynne and Karen Rae were too tired to join us. How's that for getting in a full day before sunrise!"

"I'll have to tell Sam. I think you kids wore her out, too. She said something like 'See you Monday morning', as she slipped into bed this morning about 7:30."

⌂

In 1969, our Baccalaureate was held the Sunday night before graduation. A Christian ceremony blessing the graduates, by the mid 70s it had been banished from Providence Public Schools after various organizations convinced the School Board it violated the Constitution's right to separation of church and state. Among our classmates however, it remained a well-received, patriotic and virtuous tradition. Junior Class President, Karen Rae Armstrong, gave the invocation scripture as she symbolically took the spiritual reins from our Senior Class President, Mark Farmer.

⌂

While gathering in the terrazzo floored hallway, each soon-to-be graduate began to realize this was the end of one era and the commencement of another. Although each of us had dressed formally beneath our rented, paper thin gowns, we realized this dress code may become a practice of the past.

Superintendent of Schools, Herman Archer, welcomed all of the guests to the Providence Area School District Spring Graduation Ceremony of 1969. Little did we know at the time that changing times would further come to lowly Providence.

Some of us would go on to college; some of us would resume farming or marry sons who would inherit the farm;

some of us walked down that gymnasium aisle on our way to serve our country in Vietnam. America was in a troubled time of transition when core values were being severely challenged, exposed, or in some cases, diluted and destroyed.

As friend and family alike entered the gymnasium, programs became cooling fans to dissipate the early season heat. Suits, ties, and dresses, already becoming disposable to this generation, were giving way to blue jeans and paisley or tie dyed shirts. Each family was given four tickets for the floor seats. The processional had been rehearsed several times so students could tell their parents on which side of the aisle to sit. With only 22 rows of chairs, half of the parents were forced to the less desirable inside seats.

Awards for attendance, science and mathematics merit, and sports were presented during the ceremony. Valedictorian Marilyn Rosen told the crowd that we were at one of life's crossroads. She said we would never return as this whole body again, stating nervously, "Remember, tonight's sunset will never be repeated and tomorrow will be a brand new beginning."

⌂

It was common practice in those days to exchange small name cards amongst the graduates during the preceding week and to formally announce the full names of the graduates during the ceremony. Though common throughout the South, middle names were rarely used in the Midwest, except by parents during a time of anger. School Board Chairman Fitzgerald was to present the diploma portfolio and shake hands as each student walked across the elevated stage.

It started to grow with just a few students, but it quickly spread across the body. As names were announced, nicknames were spontaneously chanted in response to Chairman Fitzgerald's announcement. Despite becoming very embarrassing for both, neither the Chairman nor the School Superintendent did anything to stop it.

Some already had readily recognizable nicknames such as: Legs, Woody, Toothpick, Clark, Lumber Woman, Soupee, and Hawaii Five O. Throughout my childhood, my nickname had been Buddy. Most people in town didn't know my real name; they too just called me Buddy, the affectionate name my Dad gave me as a child.

When my classmates heard "Willis Harold Olsen", some who had never heard my full name, responded by questioning, "WHO?" However, just as spontaneously, as if it had become an echo, embarrassingly, the whole class began chanting, "WHO. WHO. WHO. WHO."

With all diplomas handed out, little did we know that the formality of graduation would soon be a thing of the past. As Superintendent Archer completed his final announcements and before the band had a chance to start playing *Pomp and Circumstance,* from the right hand side of the stage, from a door leading to the boy's locker room, a young man dressed only in his birthday suit and a hood over his head, streaked in front of the podium. Making a right turn, and disappearing as quickly as he entered, he then exited to the outdoors through the door next to the girls' locker room.

Embarrassing laughter moved throughout the crowd. With nothing more to say, panic-struck Superintendent Archer waved a sign to the band director to begin the recessional music. It had been a long year for Superintendent Archer. The woes of this seasoned administrator were likely to become even greater in years to come, as child discipline was removed from the schools and teachers' duties became more important than education. Yes indeed! This day's sunset would never be repeated and tomorrow's dawn would be a brand new beginning.

It was later discovered that underclassman, Marty Polanski, was the graduation ceremony prankster. Marty, in true form, would never fess up to the incident. From descriptions, I soon concluded Tina Polanski was the driver of the getaway car. Fortunately for her and Marty, her family's 1965 Impala was not easily recognized around Providence.

◻

I kept my job as a laborer for the same contractor I worked for the previous summer. Arriving early one Saturday morning, to my surprise, I discovered my good friend Buster Mazzocco had been hired too. As a young father, he worked hard to continue his education. Remaining in school he graduated with the Class of 1969. He had worked the second shift in a foundry in an effort to support both Kitty and their 1½ year old child. Buster had lost a lot of weight and looked haggard as he began this additional job. Just as we completed the workday, he asked to talk with me.

I could see Buster was in great distress as he shared his story:

"As you know, the Davis farm, on its south, borders a two tire, dirt, section road. The township has not improved Wright Road, electing to keep it as a farm road connecting the two main north-south blacktopped roads." The roadway remained pretty much as it was during the early days of the automobile. Without improvement, it had the reputation of being a lover's lane.

"Ed Davis received the phone call one night last spring at about 11 p.m. The sheriff's deputy told him: 'Some of your cattle have broken through the south fence.' Ed, choosing his new Oliver as his best means of transportation, drove a short mile down Wright Road. Just after driving over a short rise, Ed thought he recognized the blue Mustang in the grassy ditch along the side of the road. Inside, a woman, dressed in a loose fitting bowling shirt, was behind the steering wheel while a man was desperately trying to push the car free before the tractor arrived. From his high vantage point, Ed quickly recognized the young man as his nephew Ben Armstrong. Seeing the approaching tractor, the woman flipped the visor to hide her reddened face, but not quick enough to prevent Ed from seeing who she was. Ed saw heavy grass stains on their clothing; both were covered with mud. Ed stopped the tractor short of the rear bumper and methodically hooked chains to the frame of the car. With the gentlest of pulls, Ed freed the car from its mooring. Without even so much as a thank you, Ben jumped into the passenger side as quickly as the car sped away."

Since the car damaged several of Ed's fence posts, Ed thought it best to meet his brother-in-law and Ben at the Armstrong home early the next morning. Standing in his tattered pajamas, Ben flatly denied any wrong-doing in front of his father. Ben knew his grass and rubbing compound stained jeans, still hanging from a basement door hook, were enough evidence to convict him. Ed had seen the barbed wire scratches left on the Mustang's steel hood before he rapped on the side door. Later, when leaving the house, Ed reminded Ben that he recalled that his car was driven by a woman. "I hope Kitty wasn't hurt. I understand she later stopped at the hospital emergency room with significant bruises." Turning as he walked out the door, his Uncle Ed said directly: "Ben, hopefully, you didn't do something you might regret later."

Only later did we learn the rest of the story. Arnold and Victoria wisely brought Kitty and her son home to live with them. Kitty was later served with divorce papers. According to Buster, Mr. Armstrong willingly paid all legal costs.

With the incident still on his conscience, it seemed appropriate that Ben enroll in a military high school in Indiana. Up until now, nobody knew why Ben had not been in school the last six weeks of the school year.

Buster's tears were heavy. He regained his composure after this great burden appeared to have been lifted from his shoulders.

Suddenly I verbalized the idea in my conscience, "How 'bout joining me at First Apostles Sunday? Right now, I suspect you probably have a pretty big void down in that heart." Despite his anguish, Buster agreed it would probably be a good idea for both of us.

◯

"What a surprise!"

I am not sure who was more surprised, the Zieglers or us. Entering First Apostles, Buster and I were overwhelmed by the hugs and sincere greetings of brotherhood and fellowship given to us by the two door greeters. Memories of my grandmother's pre-church affection raced through my brain.

Mrs. Ziegler excitedly bubbled, "I am so glad to see you Buddy. Coach and I have joined First Apostles. We believe we have completed our mission at St. Bart's. You will really enjoy our pastor. We call him 'Pastor Chuck'. Come on in and sit with us. I'm glad to see you both brought your Bibles. We don't have a liturgy, however, you will be using your Bible extensively! Here's a pen; I'm sure you'll want to write notes in your Bible." From a nearby table she grabbed her own well-used Bible. Unlike our first meeting at St. Bart's, Mrs. Ziegler and Coach walked directly to a row of open chairs. Like sheep, Buster and I followed. We both knew we had come to the right place.

Opening my Bible for the first time in quite awhile, I discovered a new signature and verse had been placed below Mae Lynne's. Recognizing her hand writing, Mom had written: *"I Peter 4:8"* – along with her initials.

⌂

Sunday, July 20, 1969, was not only an historical day for America, it was also my first day of college orientation as a future Prairie Ridge Soarin' Eagle. Gathering in the basement of PRTC's Alice Hall at 9:56 p.m., a large contingent of new students, along with their parents, witnessed the landing of *Eagle* onto the lunar surface and Neil Armstrong's famous quote, "...one small step for man, one giant leap for mankind". Television did have some benefits. Both Dad and Mom had taken time off in order to see that my next step went perfectly as well.

After visiting Coach Morse early in the day, it was visibly apparent that Dad and Mom were now more at ease.

"You know I have always thought highly of my daughter's intuition," Coach Morse commented. It had not dawned on me until that very moment that the picture in his office was that of a young Sara Amber Morse Ziegler. It began to make sense now why the Zieglers were able to give me such good directions to Prairie Ridge and why Coach sometimes affectionately called his wife "SAM".

⌂

Other than occasionally passing each other on the road into town, Mae Lynne and I didn't see much of each other that summer. I stopped by the drug store to pick up a few personal toiletries late one August afternoon. Since I also needed to have a prescription filled, I brought my items to the back pharmacy counter. Mae Lynne was bubbly and her smile was as beautiful as ever. Busily she said, "This will take a minute."

Sadly, no other customers were in the store. A new white box chain store had opened on the outskirts of town.

This lull did however give us a chance for some much needed catch up conversation.

From behind the tall counter, she began, "I read in the *First Apostles Letter* that you and Buster joined First Apostles. Isn't Pastor Chuck great? I like the way he has taken our congregation from the Law to the New Covenant. That follows what Paul did when the Word was preached to the Gentiles after the Jews rejected the Messiah. I'm not sure what becoming an "Evangelical" church means but since First Apostles has been around since 1833, I'm confident it will find its way into the '70s."

Leaning against an adjacent column, I offered, "Did you know Buster walked up last week and publicly acknowledged answering Christ's call in his heart?"

Almost dropping the brown medicine bottle she was holding, Mae Lynne sprinted around the desk corner where she pushed me back into the column and gave me a strong farm girl hug. "You planted that seed! I know you've had so much influence on Buster and I am so proud you helped him come to Christ. You are a good man, Willis Olsen. Some young woman will be proud to be your wife some day. At one time, I thought that was going to be me."

Looking up from his pill counting, Pharmacist Hendricks did everything he could to maintain his professionalism, finally murmuring, "Pesky, isn't she?"

Mae Lynne appeared anxious and excited about her upcoming move to the University of Wisconsin; however, it was a long way from Prairie Ridge. As I prepared for my evening shower, I was very surprised by the extra contents in the bag of toiletries. Somehow, it seemed, the cashier had slipped in a small bag of candied orange slices, with a handwritten note. It said only, "When will I see you again?"

⌂

Although we won the sub-district with a bases loaded walk-in, in the bottom of the seventh, we were eliminated in the first round of district play by a strong Effingham Legion team. As my baseball years progressed, several players continued to reappear in year-end tournaments. Just after Labor Day, I was pleasantly surprised to see an Effingham alum, Erik Malander, when I moved into Room 204 of Hetland Hall. Also residing on second floor was my former opponent now roommate and teammate, Louie Peltier of New Bergen.

⌂

I had ridden with a second year student back to Prairie Ridge on Labor Day. After a tiring, weather slowed drive, unpacking quickly, I fell asleep the second I hit my dormitory bed.

Rap...rap rap...rap rap rap.

"Just a minute, I'm coming".

"Willis, it's your dad on the phone. I think it's an emergency. Its past eleven, the switchboard has already shut down for the night, but the long distance operator was able to get through."

"Buddy, your mother has died."

His phone call was devastating. Saying his beloved Anna Rose Carson Olsen died suddenly, but peacefully, in her sleep a few hours before, I heard the grief in his voice. Somehow I knew he was strong – knowing she was on her way to heaven. Like a lightning bolt, I suddenly remembered the time I kissed Mom and told her I would tell her *why* some day. *Some day* never came. I realized how much of a procrastinator I had become.

Awakened by the commotion, Louie asked, "Will you need me to drive you to the bus station in the morning?"

"Probably so. That would be very helpful."

Dropping to my knees at my bedside, I remembered how Mom loved baseball. How focused and caring she was. How she loved each of us unconditionally. A physically strong woman, the daughter of a highly successful farmer, she possessed an inward and outward beauty that became more evident as she aged. Truly a Proverbs 31 woman, she offered her unending love even when times were tough.

Oh, how I wished I had been mature enough back in 1966 to tell her how much I loved her!

"Buddy Olsen?...telephone." I could hear Erik Malander's still sleepy shout down the dormitory hallway. "Oh Buddy, I heard the awful news." Mae Lynne sobbed," I don't have classes on Thursdays or Fridays; I'll leave Madison tomorrow night. I thought so much of your mother. She was always so kind to me. If I only had her faith!"

The Lord called his servant home when her purpose had been fulfilled. At the age of 57, she had worked as a registered nurse until and including the evening of her death. Many a trumpet sounded that day as the chariot carried this Godly woman's soul home.

Later, more often than not, Dad became a guest at the Davis home. Mrs. Davis enjoyed listening to Dad and Ed's politically inspired conversations over her freshly baked pies. Although not good for his chronically high cholesterol and triglycerides, Mrs. Davis thought it perfectly healthy that he be given this "home remedy" every Sunday.

Retirement was still too far off for Dad. He was the only member of his immediate, Norwegian immigrant family to graduate from high school. He was determined to help each of us earn college educations. I believe, in hindsight, he never wanted George or me to go through the hell he saw as an infantry soldier in the European Theater. Secretly, I believe, he sensed America had developed a cavalier attitude and gotten itself into an unwise predicament. He knew God would always provide a way out, even for an entire country.

⌂

I prayed, "Lord, if only there was someone who was just like her; someone who would fill this new void in my heart."

It was a lonesome holiday season. We ate together Thanksgiving Day. Susanna then took Dad to O'Hare airport where he flew to Tennessee to visit Barney Collins. Susanna, George, and I returned to college, acknowledging that the farmhouse may soon be for rent.

Following tradition, George and I cut a small Scotch Pine tree the first weekend in December. In Dad's absence, but anticipating his eventual return, we decorated the house with some, but not all of Mom's large assortment of decorations. Mom's golden angel was placed on top of the tree. Each of us came home from college on Christmas Eve. Holding back a flood of tears, Dad gathered us in the living room on New Year's Eve saying, "I've decided to sell the few remaining livestock and implements to Ed Davis. I've decided to lease our 120 acres to Ed. He will be given the first option to buy the land, if as a family we decide to sell."

That occurred just six months later when Ed and his son Pat purchased both the house and land. Dad graciously divided the windfall between our individual savings accounts. Much to Dad's surprise, Ed had an addendum included in the sale documents that allowed Dad to live rent free in the house until his death or he decided to move on, whichever came first.

With Pat's social and mental abilities somewhat impaired, Dad quickly got a glimpse of the loneliness that was being experienced by both men. With no worldly obligations, Dad recognized Pat's future world would likely be limited to farming our 120 acres and living in our modest, former home – hopefully, Dad prayed, Pat would not be alone.

Dad purchased a home in Providence near Uncle Marvin and Aunt Ella. Even residing six miles away, Darlene Davis made sure he was always well stocked with home canned food and desserts.

1970

The two public hall telephones had been replaced over the Holidays. It was a cold, snowy afternoon when our newly installed dorm room telephone rang. Louie was studying at the Library; I was expecting Mae Lynne's call, so confidently I answered, "How are you babe?"

Stunned at first, the caller quickly recovered and said, "I sure didn't expect that greeting, but I'll take it! Buddy, it's been a long time since I've seen you. The last time I saw you I told you I would see you again someday."

Realizing I did not recognize the voice, she taunted, "Do you know who this is?"

"...Well, ah, I guess not!"

"This is Tina. You know, Marty's cousin. How are you? I'm here in Prairie Ridge on business. I hoped we could get together tonight and then go out for ice cream."

"Ice cream? It's January!"

Remembering our last encounter, I hoped she wouldn't be around more than just tonight.

Coincidently, both Prairie Ridge and Wisconsin would be off for mid-term grading on Thursday and Friday. At PRTC, the dorms were remaining open, giving us the option of staying on campus through the long weekend. I had been expecting Mae Lynne to call with an arrival time. She was scheduled to come in on the bus from Madison Thursday afternoon. Friday was her birthday. I had arranged a room for her in the all-girls dorm.

Considering the offer, I remembered I had a large test on Wednesday night. But this was only Tuesday afternoon. I reasoned I would have most of the day on Wednesday to study. Tina's invitation seemed harmless.

I could hear the excitement in her voice: "Great! I'll pick you up at six o'clock sharp."

Retuning to my nap, a short time later the phone rang again. Learning from my first mistake, I answered, "Willis Olsen."

"Willis, I tried you earlier but your line has been busy for almost an hour. Is everything OK? This is Coach Morse. Can we get together tomorrow afternoon? I need to go over a few things with you about this spring's program."

"Yes sir, I can meet you."

"I know you don't have any afternoon classes this quarter so I'll meet you at the Commons for lunch, let's say one o'clock. Are you staying the long weekend? Maybe you can come over and join Mrs. Morse and me for Sunday dinner, after church of course. We were hoping Mae Lynne would be in town. She's such a nice girl."

"That sounds like a great idea. Thanks. We'll plan on it. Mae Lynne'll be here tonight, no, I mean on Thursday. She will be staying in Tina Hall the entire weekend."

"I'll tell Edna to plan on Sunday. Don't you mean Alice Hall? We don't have a Tina Hall."

"Oh yeah, you're right. I must be studying too much. Thanks again for the invitation. I'll see you tomorrow. Goodbye, Coach."

"Goodbye. It sounds like you need some rest! With mid-term tests and all, tomorrow could be a long day for you."

⌂

"What did you say you were doing in town?"

"After finishing vocational school, I took a job with a Chicago based cleaning equipment manufacturer as an on-the-road saleswoman. Suggestively motioning her head towards the back seat, she said, "Check out my parts!"

Still astounded, I was speechless. Approaching 22 and more than three years older than me, and, having not seen her in over four years, I was awestruck by the beautiful woman she had become. Her jet-black hair was long and thick. She had inserted a butterfly barrette to hold it up. Dressed in a tailored black business suit with red accents and a white sheer blouse, the outfit modestly showed the slightest hint of her femininity. Black stockings added to her splendor.

Navigating her way through Prairie Ridge quite well, Tina made several unexpected turns. I was confused. Eventually heading out of town I said, "There aren't any ice cream shops south of town. Where are we going?"

"Remember, you said it was January. You made it sound like it was too cold for ice cream, so I'm heading for a supper club about 7 miles outside of town, along the river. I made reservations there. It's BYOB."

We were escorted to a small, secluded, candlelit table over near a river-facing window. A placard noted the table had been reserved for: Tina P and Guest. I thought it was odd when she told the maitre d' that we didn't need menus.

Quickly breaking the ice she cooed, "It is so good to see you. Let me get a closer look at those baby blue eyes again." With that she brought her face forward from across the table. "Like I told you the first time I met you – you are a handsome one!" Clearing his throat, the server tried to interrupt her mesmerized stare. Turning, she told him, "We would like 10 ounce ribeye steaks with two large baked potatoes, loaded. Grill the steaks to medium well. We would also like two iced glasses. Thank you."

The server hastily returned with two, colored, dinner glasses. Tina slowly pulled a small bottle of wine from her large purse.

"Care for some?" Again, without waiting for a reply, she put a small amount in both glasses, pushing the blue colored glass toward me. The wine had a foul smell but it warmed my insides all the way down.

A cold front rolled in and it soon became an icy night; the alcohol warmed the conversation. After eating our steaks, the server brought fresh glasses to be refilled. Handing the server the dinner tab and a large bill, she told the server to keep the change, likely her way of rewarding the server for his discretion.

About nine o'clock, a local band started playing soft music. The daughter of Polish immigrants, I learned she had been taught to waltz and polka at a very young age. Warmly clasping my hand, the relaxing music magnetically drew us to the dance floor. She sang along softly, in Polish, as we gracefully floated across the floor. I couldn't understand a word she whispered. A light dusting of sand made the floor a dancer's dream. Fortunately for this wallflower, Tina's experience and elegance completely masked my inexperience.

"I am amazed how many people are out on a Tuesday night." Then it hit me! "I need to be in the dorm by 10:30 sharp!" Sensing my panic, Tina speedily arrived at the dorm's front doors with two minutes to spare.

Remaining behind the wheel, she confirmed my feelings: "What a great time!" Pausing briefly, she daringly added, "Like we talked, let's do it again tomorrow night. However, tomorrow night sign out like you are leaving for the long weekend. That will give us more time. Tomorrow night, I'll pick you up at eight o'clock in front of Black Earth Hall."

Although I was very groggy when I first awoke, the hot shower seemed to help. I went to my morning classes. Fortunately, both consisted of going over last week's laboratory tests. I met Coach Morse from 1:00 to 3:00 p.m. From the Commons, I hurried to the Library where I studied right up until my Economics exam, which started at 6:30 p.m.

Amazingly, I was able to concentrate on the test problems. I was relieved to see that some of the more difficult theories, which the professor recently introduced, had not been included.

The bright red Firebird's engine purred softly as I approached the passenger side door. I soon saw that Tina had relocated to the passenger's side. Walking around the front of the car, opening the driver's door, I was greeted by warm air and the smell of expensive perfume.

Tina had let her hair down and was made up to perfection. She wore a beautiful black wrap dress that was cut low; it landed high above her knees. Her charcoal fish net hosiery and tall boots complemented her dress. Getting situated in the driver's seat, I was promptly awarded a welcome kiss. Her lips were warm and soft. I decided I should have more. She whispered, "I didn't want you to forget anything from last night!" She remained close as we drove off.

"Look, no more gadgets in the back." Peering over my shoulder, I could see all that remained was a small suitcase.

She asked, "Same place OK?" With that I followed her directions as we drove to White Pines Inn and Supper Club.

"Good evening Mr. Jefferson."

"Good evening Ms. Polanski. You look stunning!"

After an enjoyable evening of prime rib, dancing, and flirting, Tina asked if I was ready to go.

190

"Yes," I said. "I need to get back to the dorm by midnight. I took my first curfew extension. I only get four per semester."

"You signed out for the long weekend, didn't you?"

Nervously I said, "Yes, I did."

"Then that means you don't need to be back until Sunday, correct? I checked out of my corporate room in Prairie Ridge since I was to drive back tonight anyway. We have a room here instead." With the same suggestive motion of her head, she instructed: "Go down the hall like you are going toward the restroom; proceed up the stairway, around the corner and down the hallway to Room 208. I'll pull the car around the side and be up shortly. I hope you're not too tired. You'll find the door is already unlocked."

The drapes were drawn and only the desk and nightstand light remained lit. A chocolate had been placed on the turned down bed. The suite contained a desk and couch in one room and a bed in the other. The bathroom had doors leading to both the bedroom and front room. I noticed a large suitcase, matching the one I had seen in the backseat earlier, had already been placed in the bedroom. Naively, I suddenly realized I hadn't brought a thing.

Tina's beauty radiated as she entered the door. Hanging her winter coat on a wall mounted rod, she kissed me softly and immediately entered the bathroom.

⌂

Early Thursday morning, I was awakened by her beautiful singing. Tina was fully dressed by the time she came out of the bathroom. A walking princess, she returned to the front room of the suite. Her hair had been pulled back into a bun; her makeup perfect. Pulling the drapes open, she offered, "Do you want to use these?" grabbing one of the motel's complimentary toothbrushes and a tube of toothpaste. She looked as fresh as the winter morning's newly fallen snow.

"May I use your comb?" I must have looked and smelled awful. She was ready for a new day. Still wearing my same clothes, I wasn't so sure about myself.

Having an 8:30 a.m. appointment in Rock Island, Tina gave herself just enough time to make the two and a half hour trip. The only way she could drive the 100 miles and make her appointment on time, was if the roads were plowed and clear. After dropping me off, the last thing I heard as she sped away was, "I'll call you the next time I'm in town."

Fortunately the back service door was slightly ajar when I returned to the dorm early Thursday morning. Maintenance crews were out salting sidewalks. A frozen door latch held the door slightly ajar. Walking quietly to the front desk, I quickly found the sign in sheet and a pencil. I erased my weekend return entry and inserted a false Wednesday night "In" time. I went straight to bed. Since everyone except two other men were gone from the floor, I concluded a Wednesday night bed check had not been conducted. Only too soon did I learn that that was not the case!

"I need to talk with you Olsen. Meet me in my room!" Resident Advisor Erik Malander looked very stern as he barked out the orders. Now going on seven o'clock, his loud hammering on my door sounded similar to a Mack truck using its engine brake.

Entering his room, he immediately yelled, "Sit down! Gosh you stink! Did you fall asleep with your clothes on?" Waving the doctored form in front of my face, he bellowed, "You know we have a reason for these sign in sheets. If something happened to you last night, this sign in sheet would have at least given us an idea of your truthful intentions and where to start. Under the strictest policies, I should have called the police, who in turn would have called your dad in the middle of the night. Is that how you want to be treated? I thought you were a man, not some child.

"We saw you with a black-haired woman at the White Pines Supper Club. My girlfriend and I were celebrating our one month dating anniversary but we at least made it back to our individual dorms before curfew. I saw that you were being served setups; I know you did not return to the dorm last night! The ice storm is a flimsy excuse, but I may need to use it! You religious guys are all alike; you don't walk your talk!"

After his anger finally subsided, he said, "I will not report you to Coach Morse providing you are squeaky clean the next five months. Starting right now you are on my probation list. Got it?"

"Yes, sir!"

"Willis, I must say, she was extremely attractive and quite the dancer; she even made *you* look good! Hopefully you didn't do something you might regret later. Go take a shower and get some sleep before you start studying. That's what you're here for, isn't it?"

◠

"Where have you been? I tried to call you up until eleven o'clock last night! That's when they shut the switchboard down. They didn't reopen it until a couple of minutes ago."

Obviously in a rush, Mae Lynne got right to the point. "I'm calling to tell you I can't come down. Grandma turned gravely ill. I'm sorry. Mother and Dad are picking me up in an hour to drive on to Green Bay. I already checked and I can get a refund for my bus ticket. I'll call you Sunday night."

I barely got in "Happy 19th Birthday!" before I heard the humming of the dial tone.

⌂

Tina called back that evening. We talked at length. We set a time to meet again at White Pines on Saturday night. We agreed, this time we would drive separately. With the regular weekend dorm curfew set at midnight, and my car scheduled to be back from service that afternoon, I calculated I would have ample time to drive out to White Pines to meet her again.

"You're getting to be kind of a regular here aren't you? Let me see your driver's license... just as I suspected. I don't want to see you with any setups, do you understand? She's over at the table nearest the dance floor. "

Tina looked very sad. Mysteriously sensing this would be our last time together, she gently held my hand. Dressed much more conservatively, she spoke first. "You are everything I want in a man and more. In some ways, we are just too much alike. I know you have baseball aspirations. To be honest, I thought I could change your mind. I'm looking for a man who will give me five children – a big family just like my parents had. Even though it might not look like it, I hate this on-the-road job. I'm not really the carefree party girl I've tried to portray this week. All I want is a large home in the suburbs where I can enjoy my children. You know a house with a white picket fence in front and a large backyard with a tire swing hung from a tree, like the one you hung over the creek."

Speechless, I carefully worded my response before I said, "Tina, I really appreciate your sincerity. You are a very beautiful woman and I wish you the best. I'm glad we both agree this infatuation is not what either of us is looking for and we're parting as friends."

"Tonight the band starts earlier. After we eat, can we have just one more dance? I hope it is a long, slow one." The band met her silent wish.

"It's almost nine thirty. I need to head back to the dorm." Only then did I realize I was in an awful dilemma. In my haste, I had not cashed a check at the bank before leaving town. I knew that I surely couldn't pass one at a tavern. As we walked toward the cashier, the maitre d' somehow sensed the awkwardness of my situation. Stepping forward, he said, "We have a special promotion tonight – buy one, get one free." With that Tina coolly took the tab and placed a crisp ten dollar bill on top of it.

"That will be just right. Have a good evening folks. I enjoyed watching you dance. You make such a nice couple."

Tina graciously said nothing about the maitre d's greed as we held hands and walked to her Firebird. "Let's sit inside while it warms up."

Tina's car seemed slow to heat up. With a new found resolve I said, "Tina, I believe the Lord has prepared a path for you to fulfill your dream. In a most unusual way, I know you have helped me find my way."

"Thanks Buddy, I wish you the best too. I know you have helped me. Believe me; I have never done this before with anyone. The other night, I know that couch was terribly uncomfortable for both of us. That is all I wanted – to hold you close to me all night long. Buddy Olsen, I will never forget you!"

"Nor will I ever forget you!"

Tears froze on my cheeks as I got out of her car and watched her car's taillights fade into the distance. I was confident tears were also streaming down the driver's cheeks.

Back in town, approaching the second set of stoplights, I suddenly found myself directly behind the red Firebird. Proceeding through, suddenly Tina turned onto a narrow residential street rather than following the road northeasterly towards Chicago. Driving approximately three blocks, she turned left into St. Edward's Catholic Church's small parking lot. Quickly looking, I could see the church sign indicated the evening mass had been over for several hours.

Seeing her car's heavily frosted windows and believing something might have been wrong with her car's radiator, I veered into the gas station located across the street. Observing from my car I was again in a quandary. Should I go offer help? Maybe she didn't need my help. She sat in the idling car a few more minutes.

Momentarily turning on the dome light, I could see she pulled a string of beads from her purse. She was praying the Rosary. Putting the beads back into her purse, Tina got out of her car and walked to the Rectory where she robustly knocked on the front door. A housekeeper came to the door; the two talked. Although quite dark, I saw the same housekeeper close the door and turn the large cast iron handle back to its locked position. Within a few minutes, a nun opened the church's front door and invited Tina inside. Briskly walking through the large wooden door I could see Tina taking off her overcoat and hat as she entered. She disappeared into the church.

Waiting for the coast to clear, I snuck in through the unlocked door. Silently walking through the Nave, I entered the Sanctuary. From a distance, I saw her sitting on a front pew. I began to walk towards her when a dim light suddenly shown off to our left. Immediately standing, she straightened her dress and began walking toward the light. I saw only her silhouette as she passed behind a full length velvet curtain covering the framed opening leading to the confessional booth hallway. I heard the creaking sound of un-oiled hinges as I imagined a large door opening and closing. I realized her private confession was not for my ears.

"Eeek...Where did you come from? You scared the dickens out of me!"

Appearing from behind a marble column, the house-keeper whispered, "Remember, you told her: 'Tina, I believe the Lord has prepared a path for you to fulfill your dream.' Did you try to interfere with His plan? Don't you believe your own words?"

Whispering softly, I asked, "Who are you?" She appeared to be re-sweeping the same stone in the floor. "How did you know what I said to her? She and I were the only ones in the car!" Suddenly, as the light shone from a flickering candle I could see she was neither the housekeeper nor the nun. In fact, she's not even of this world. Speechless and thunderstruck from the confrontation, I bolted out the door and ran toward my idling car.

I was tucked into my warm bed one and a half hours *before* curfew.

I later learned the Morses had invited Erik Malander and his girlfriend to the evening performance at the Prairie Ridge Playhouse. Sleeping soundly, I was well into dream world by the time the curfew police made their room check.

⌂

After a good night's sleep, I met up with Coach and Mrs. Morse on the steps of Prairie Ridge First Apostles Church. "We're sorry to hear about Mae Lynne's grand-mother's death. Have you had a chance to send a sympathy card?"

Following a delicious lasagna dinner in their formal dining room, Coach and Mrs. Morse invited me into their less formal den. There I soon found out where Mrs. Ziegler got her forthrightness. Coach began, "What are your plans with your relationship with Mae Lynne? Sara tells us she is well-founded, very gritty, and follows her Lord. You know a good relationship and marriage are just like a strong foundation that is built one stone at a time. Remember, it also needs time to let the mortar cure. Trust is uncompromising in a good relationship. Edna and I have been married 40 years."

Mrs. Morse chimed in: "How has your long weekend been? Have you had time to catch up on both your sleep and studies? Coach said you were somewhat discombobulated when he spoke to you the other afternoon."

Before I had a chance to answer, she then asked, "Have you ever gone to White Pines Supper Club? It is such a wholesome place. It might be a great place to go tonight since there's no dorm cafeteria service on Sunday nights. "I hear a lot of the business travelers stay at the resort when they come to town. They say the rooms are as nicely furnished as the restaurant. We usually go out there for the Friday Fish Fry, but for some reason, we forgot it this week. We like the Wednesday night prime rib too, but we can only go during the summer when we don't have Wednesday night church. This past Wednesday night we didn't have church because the pastor was at a fidelity conference in Rock Island. But, because of the ice storm, we decided not to go anywhere. I'll bet they didn't serve much prime rib that night."

What a way to leave me hanging! I hoped they couldn't see the torrent of sweat running down my armpit.

Standing up from the love seat, Coach then walked me to the door, "We're so glad you could come over."

"Joe, wait a minute…," we heard from the kitchen.

"Here Willis, take these three $5 gift certificates for White Pines Supper Club. Most everyone knows how to get there. Use two of them next time Mae Lynne is in town. Take the other one to use tonight. Just ignore the BYOB signs. Just ask for Mr. Jefferson; he's the Owner. He is sometimes the maitre d'. We know him well. "

⌂

Late in the season, Coach Morse called me aside and said, "Tim told me he relegated you to the right side before you showed him your real strength was behind the plate. I need you behind the plate, but with Moises Cortez in the hospital with a tonsillectomy, I need your leadership and defensive skills on the infield even more. I'm going to start you at first base tonight. If we want to advance to the championship tournament we need to eliminate Bettendorf College in just two games. That should give us enough days off to bring our team back to health. I can put you back with Erik and Louie if we make it to Omaha."

With that said, Coach Morse announced the lineups to the other members of the team. "One more thing Willis, since Lindy hasn't memorized the signs, and Louie can't see me when in his pitching stance, I'll flash you the signs and you convey them to Louie. I'll just tell Lindy we will be going with all fastballs. With his limited defensive zone you may need to cover the plate if he lets one sail to the backstop."

The Soarin' Eagles had secured a five run lead going into the top of the eighth inning. Our #3 through #6 batters kept the ball in play as we continued our small ball strategy to success. If Louie could remain strong, we felt he could go the full distance.

In the eighth, however, Bettendorf had put men on first and third when a pass ball allowed the first base runner to advance to second. Following a sacrifice fly, Louie gave up a four-pitch walk to Bettendorf's #3 batter. I looked for the sign from Coach Morse. He was nowhere to be seen! Like an eagle soaring for prey, Louie kept staring at me from his forward looking, stretch position. Both assistant coaches were oblivious to our dilemma. I knew I had to make an immediate decision. I flashed in "curve ball, inside, at the letters". I remembered that Bettendorf's cleanup hitter couldn't resist that same pitch earlier in the game, having struck out on it twice already.

Louie let it fly. This time the batter swung with what appeared to be a lighter, shorter bat. His line drive was hard hit as it soared approximately three feet inside the first base bag. Easier for a right handed first baseman, especially with the man running, I instinctively back handed the liner as it soared just below my knees. With the first base runner well on his way to second, the inning walk off was very rewarding.

"What happened?" Coach Morse questioned as the last player jumped over the base line and entered the dugout.

"Where were you? I needed a sign!"

Coach Morse put his strong arm around me and whispered, "Edna's leftover Lasagna. I couldn't resist. I guess its after effects came at a most inopportune time."

"We got him again coach! He showed us his weakness and we capitalized on it."

Exhibiting new vigor, Louie pitched the required nine strikes to Bettendorf's #5, #6, and #7 batters in the top of the ninth. The home team fans rose to their feet as the Prairie Ridge Technical College Soarin' Eagles were on their way to their first post season national tournament ever.

Two days later, Coach Morse joined Moises in the hospital, where Coach had emergency surgery to remove his gall bladder.

Many of the players had developed superstitions as our success continued. Some players genuflected, some didn't change part of their uniform as long as we were winning, and some even insisted it was the number on their uniform that gave them luck. While other teams might not shave while on a winning streak, Coach Morse did not allow facial hair, even though it would have been a struggle for some. To some the baselines were sacred – "Thou shalt not step on the baselines either going onto or coming off the field" – was their eleventh commandment.

"You know if you're going to win the National Technical College Baseball Championship, it will be for God's purpose, not by your plays. Willis, you do know that, don't you?" With that Mae Lynne gave me a kiss and a pat on the rear as I boarded the charter bus heading west on Interstate 80 across Iowa to bordering Omaha, Nebraska, site of this year's NTCB Championship Series. "I wish I was riding with you but I just don't have the time right now. Do you have any money with you?"

"I forgot to go to the bank to cash a check."

"Here's $10 to get something to eat. Be sure and call me every night, OK? You can call collect."

Earlier in the week, Assistant Coach Ethel led a grueling series of practices. Collectively, we were relieved to see Coach Morse returning for the last practice before our trip west. Coach Morse decided flying would be more comfortable for him. It would give him additional days to recover. Eight regional champions gathered for the double elimination tournament. We were seeded 7th because we had no tournament experience. Also, our schedule difficulty and regional ranking were lower than all but Region 5. Any team with two losses was eliminated.

Our first pairing was second seed Palm Area Technical College from California. The only team seeded lower than us was Foley Tech of Minnesota. Foley Tech's tenacity and depth eventually earned them two wins over what appeared to be an overrated, number one seed, Massachusetts Bay Tech.

Early in the game, it became evident that our cross-country opponent, Palm Area Tech, was not going to be a pushover. Against the odds, we defeated the number two seed in just two games. Games at the other field, between the third and sixth seeds and fourth and fifth seeds, were decidedly much closer. Both sets ended 2–1 as number three seed, Athens, Texas, earned the right to play winner Foley. We were to play number four seed, Hamilton, Alabama.

Athens quickly handed Foley two straight shutout games. Hamilton put up a good fight but we eventually eliminated them in just two games. The week-long tournament was nearing the weekend, with the Championship series slated for Friday night and Saturday afternoon.

If a deciding game was to be played, the Championship game would be scheduled for Sunday afternoon following an early morning third place finale. Early in my career, Sunday games would be sparsely attended and many players were not even allowed to play on Sunday. That had all changed now.

"Men, we have come this far and I don't expect to go home empty-handed." Although not fully recovered from his emergency surgery, Coach Morse knew this may be an accomplishment never to be repeated in his tenure. "We are going to start Erik tonight with Louie tomorrow afternoon. If I see trouble they may both pitch in both games. I plan on taking Sunday as a day of rest. Let's go!"

Pitching strongly, Erik Malander carried us well into the sixth inning. Athens typically relied heavily on their long ball power to overwhelm their opponents. A new strategy had been implemented in the bottom of the ninth. Several key substitutes were called off the bench. Following a lead-off strike out, the Athens Cowboys put together three straight singles. Needing two runs to tie, Erik hurled a wild pitch; the man on third streaked for home. The ball ricocheted toward the third base side of the diamond. I was able to gun down the second runner foolishly sprinting from second. With this decision, I conceded the run. With first base now open the fourth batter was intentionally walked. The fifth batter in the lineup hit a powerful shot through the left side of the infield. Playing left field, Moises Cortez's quick reflexes and strong arm threw the man out trying to stretch it into a double. However, Moises didn't need that call. Running recklessly, the man from second had been hit by the ball deflecting it oh so slightly away from Moises. The umpire immediately called, "runner out". He was right on top of the play. PRTC had won the first game of the Championship series.

Athens appeared to have lost their drive when they hit the field on Saturday afternoon. Now the home team, PRTC posted six runs in bottom of the 1st. Louie got stronger with each passing inning. Giving up only three hits, he walked no one and tallied nine strikeouts. I subsequently picked off all three runners. Athens soon realized they were unlikely to overcome this battery on this particular night. Just as Coach Morse had hoped, the National Championship was decided in just 2 games, leaving Sunday as a day of rest. The Soarin' Eagles were now the 1970 NTCB National Champions!

In the locker room, Coach Morse gathered his champions around him and said, "I'll see you all in the motel lobby tomorrow at one o'clock sharp for the bus ride back to Prairie Ridge. As I told you after last night's victory, an alumnus has graciously given each of you a gift certificate for dinner at Omaha's finest steak house, the Black Steer Inn. You're free to spend the rest of the night enjoying yourselves. For you who are returning next year, there will be no organized practice until after the first of the year.

203

Thanks for a great memory. For those of you joining me at Shiloh Road Apostles Church, be in the motel lobby by 8:30 a.m. See you tomorrow."

After taking my shower and dressing, I confidently told coach as we walked out of the locker room, "Mae Lynne and I will be joining you tomorrow morning. I haven't seen her yet but she told me her flight was scheduled to get in just before the start of the game. I don't remember where she's staying but I should be able to find her shortly. A bunch of us are going to meet and eat at the Black Angus Inn."

"No Willis, it's not the Black Angus Inn. You need to start listening; I said the Black Steer Inn! Yes, if I see her, I'll tell her where you are. Did you tell her where we're staying?"

⌂

Visibly exhausted after the long game, Louie said, "Willis, I've changed my mind. I'm tired; I think I'll go back to the room and sleep. If Mae Lynne calls, I'll tell her where you are headed. I guess that leaves just you and Erik going to the steak house. Enjoy yourselves." With that, Louie got out of the cab and walked in the motel's entrance gate.

Speeding off, I rolled the window down and yelled back to Louie, "Be sure she has the directions to the Black Angus Inn, OK?"

The driver's English was somewhat broken as he confirmed, "You really want to go on to the Black Steer Inn, right? It is expensive but it's not far from here. There is no Black Angus Inn."

"Yes sir, we can afford it; we have gift certificates!"

Heading westerly, the cabby dropped Erik and me off ten minutes later at the restaurant's front entrance. "That will be $3.50." Handing him a $5 bill, I told him to keep the change. "Here's our phone number. Call dispatch and I'll come get you when you've finished eating. Thanks for the tip."

After ordering the dinner special, a 22 ounce porterhouse, our waitress served a glass of wine to both of us. "It comes with the dinner." Neither of us blinked. Nor did we tell her we were underage. I kept my eye on the front door. I wasn't sure what Mae Lynne's reaction would be if she saw me drinking wine. The glasses kept coming throughout the meal.

Pushing himself away from the table, his speech somewhat slurred, Erik said, "I'm gonna go to the toilet, call that cabby, and head back to the motel. You sure you gave Louie the right name of this place? Remember, Coach Morse had to set you straight earlier this evening."

After settling the bill, the waitress suggested I sit at the bar and wait for my girlfriend there. She assured me that I would be well taken care of. "Tony, give this young man a glass of sherry. I put my remaining $5 bill on the bar. The bartender proceeded to spend the money like it was his. Finally, at 1:00 a.m., with no sign of Mae Lynne, it was time for the restaurant to close. There was no sign of the friendly waitress either – just me and the bartender talking about all of life's problems.

Walking me to the front door, Tony said, "Just walk towards the street light and turn right, the Midwest Motel is straight down Center Street at 10th Street. Just follow the sidewalk and you will run right into it." The door quickly closed and locked behind me.

⌂

Not knowing it was already late Sunday morning, I was surprised to see Mae Lynne when I awoke on the couch.

Disoriented and with a splitting headache, I blurted, "Where am I?" The taste in my mouth was awful.

Showing no compassion for her boyfriend, Mae Lynne scolded me saying: "You must have made a complete fool of yourself last night! I finally found you passed out on a park bench just west of 13th Street. At least I got to you before you wandered into some stranger's car! I eventually found someone who told me where some of the baseball teams were staying; at least that limited my search. I never did find the Black Angus Inn!"

"Black Angus Inn? Oh no! Did you talk to Louie?"

"Yes, I think I woke him up. Whatever the name," sarcastically she continued, "it looks like you were well taken care of without me there to help!"

Sitting up, I gasped, "What's that terrible smell?" At that same moment, peering around, I realized that I had no clothes on other than my briefs. My slacks, tee shirt, white shirt, tie, and sport coat were nowhere to be seen.

Angrily Mae Lynne added: "Don't like it? Trust me; it was a whole lot worse about eight hours ago. Trash cans, waste baskets, even the bathtub for crying out loud! Kind of like wine, do you? Where in the world did you acquire a taste for such awful stuff? I hope this is not the way you care for God's Temple, or is this an indication of your future conduct? By the way, the reason you have only your underwear on is that they were the only thing that was clean! Your slacks and sport coat are hanging out on the deck; the rest of your clothes are down in the apartment's laundry. Because of quiet time, I had to wait until this morning before I could use the washing machine. I'm glad you had your room key on you. I woke Louie early this morning. I was able to get your suitcase out of the motel room."

Walking to an end table to retrieve something, Mae Lynne returned saying, "Here, this fell out of your billfold when I pulled it from your pants pocket. In your condition, you must have had trouble putting it in its secret compartment. So, you're 22 and from Winnetka – in your dreams! Where did you get this anyway? Your baby face picture gives away your true age. Did you have to show it at the bar, or did they just take the money?"

Having turned as red as a beet, she finished: "This is Karen Rae's apartment. Remember, she let me use her car and her apartment as a place to stay last night. My original flight was cancelled, so they let me take a later flight. I missed the entire game! When I got to the stadium, everyone was gone. The only thing there was a brood of pigeons! I spent all night walking and driving up and down the main streets looking for you or your motel. What I wasn't expecting was to find you bombed! So much for my ten dollars!"

"I got lucky and they never carded me, but as you saw, I was prepared. Oh, oh, I think I'm getting sick!" Since it was a one-room efficiency, I made a mad dash towards the lone door.

"Lucky, huh. I guess I never considered barfing my guts out as being lucky."

⌂

"What did you do, sleep in your clothes again?" Erik Malander was giddy with laughter when Mae Lynne dropped me off at the motel precisely at one o'clock. Louie looked like he had gotten some sleep at least, since he hadn't had a roommate. It was obvious to all that I did not have a good night; my damp and wrinkled clothes were telltale. Needless to say, the bus ride across Iowa was verbally and physically torturous.

⌂

While running errands one Saturday afternoon in Providence during semester break, I saw Cory Sullivan over by the cigarette counter in Myrt's Grocery. Her tie-dyed smock and beads were quite unappealing. What appeared to be an unlit joint hung from the side of her mouth. Her beautiful strawberry blonde hair was streaked with yellow highlights. I estimated her weight to be a mere 100 pounds stretched over her five foot seven inch frame.

With a glazed over look, she was stoned, floating in an area well beyond this earth. I know she saw me; I'm just not sure she recognized me – I was now over six feet tall. Sadly, we didn't speak.

Dad told me later that Cory was kicked out of her home by her unforgiving father. Her return flight back to her new home, San Francisco, late in 1970 was her last. Previously busted for drug possession at both Chicago's O'Hare Field and San Francisco International Airport, she now carried an undesirable notoriety – the first drug overdose casualty of tiny New Bergen.

Her body was flown back from California to New Bergen, where she was cremated. Attending her memorial service at St. Vincent's Church, I did all I could to keep my composure. My good friend Buster sat by my side.

As we walked away from the church, Buster wrapped his arm around me and said, "Cory's death has really made you think, hasn't it? In this case, be sure it is your heart that is doing the thinking! As your mother used to say, 'Buddy, I can see through you like a glass.' You have your heart out there right now. I can clearly see it."

"Cory let herself be wasted by Satan!"

"So tell me, how are you any different? What have you done to trample Satan under your feet? What are you looking for in life? Do you really think baseball will get you to Heaven?"

"It's funny you bring up my Mom. I've been thinking a lot about her lately. Dad seems so broken-hearted. It's been over a year now. Through marriage, they truly became one."

Cory's ashes were thrown to the drifting wind from a small rise just outside of New Bergen. How ironic! She died on Christmas Day while some of her fellow high school classmates were serving America 10,000 miles away, attempting to win freedom for others – a viewpoint she so vigorously challenged.

Turning around, we re-entered the now empty sanctuary. Buster suggested we sit down and talk. The New Bergen church seemed so cold and bleak – it also seemed the right time and place.

"I look at the strong traits of my mother and wish that I too could have a woman who would support me like she did Dad. I met a girl from Chicago, who I really liked, but we were different in ways that make a difference to me. It took me awhile to see, but she taught me more about myself than anyone. I thought I loved Cory, but we were too different in some of our core values. Did I ever tell you that Dad and Mom insisted that I break up with her? They could see what I couldn't. It surprised me then, but now that I look back, her life was so unlike mine – hers became so filled with tragedy. That is what I probably miss most about Mom – her wisdom and support, especially in a time of need. Did God make any wise women after Mom?"

Ignoring my silliness, Buster said, "Buddy, I'm sure he has. Now don't go messing up a true gift God has given you."

Acknowledging his wisdom, I responded, "I think I know what you are talking about. I can see through you too."

1971

"Yes, yes, yes, yes, yes! Thank you Jesus!

"Willis Olsen, there were so many times I wanted to shake some sense into you in order to help you make this decision, but I knew it would be in God's time, not mine. I was so happy when you took me to our prom three years ago. You were so handsome that night! Did you ever wonder why I was wearing an orange dress? I knew if you loved me even one-tenth the amount you love candied orange slices, then that love would be sufficient to carry us through a long and happy life. Right then I knew you were God's blessing for my life. I now know that your love for me is infinite.

"Willis, I love you very much and as I said two years ago: 'Some young woman will be proud to be your wife some day.' I'm so glad that woman will be me. I so look forward to it."

Quickly I inquired, "Why were you so standoffish to me when we were younger?"

Looking deeply into my eyes, Mae Lynne said, "I knew where my head was, I just needed God to show it to my heart. It's hard to explain, I just needed to trust His wisdom."

"You are so sensible. I would like to have just one-tenth of your understanding."

"Don't kid yourself. You do! You just need to trust it in your heart."

We embraced...and kissed.

◻

Coach Morse was able to begin the baseball season early by scheduling a late winter tournament in Hawaii. A gift from an alumnus enabled each player to fly free; spouses or girlfriends could fly at a prearranged reduced fare on a sparkling new 747. Other competing teams represented Pennsylvania, California, Oregon, New Jersey, Ohio, Minnesota, and Colorado.

"Specifically," Mrs. Morse reminded the players, "married women will share rooms with your girlfriends or fiancés. No men will be allowed in the women's area and vice versa. Absolutely no cohabitation will be allowed."

◻

Originally Coach Morse shrugged "It's just heartburn. I think I had some bad food last night."

Having trouble breathing the second morning of our trip, Mrs. Morse told us she thought it would be best if he rested in the hotel room. The team had eaten late the night before. Most of us agreed the restaurant's food was not good. We accepted her reasoning.

Assistant Coach Ethel was in his early 30s. Handpicked from a large group of alumni players, he had the respect of Coach Morse and the entire team. Assistant Coach Ethel earned this respect through his broad knowledge of the game and his innate ability to field a winning team. An alumnus of PRTC, he was a professor of small ball.

PRTC ended the Hawaiian tournament with a 7–1 record. Our only loss was to the much improved Palm Area Technical College team. Their championship was well deserved. Our small ball strategy worked well, but in the long run it boiled down to the natural skip of the ball. Several times we left the bases loaded; good defense and good pitching stymied our bats. Our long ball bats were mysteriously gone and our clean up hitters were consistently off their game. Looking back, maybe we had too much to eat – like our head coach. Or was there another reason?

Coach Ethel coached two of the games entirely and substituted for the ailing Coach Morse mid-game of a third. Fortunately, Coach Morse had gotten over his heartburn just in time for the eighth and final game – it was also just in time for the long twelve-hour flight back home.

⌂

As our spring season came to a successful close, we were once again the league, district, and regional champions. This year, the national tournament was to be held in Cookeville, Tennessee.

Expecting hot weather conditions, Coach Morse wisely ordered new uniforms. The rich golden-colored, lightweight uniforms mysteriously arrived in time for the regional championship pictures taken just prior to the national tournament.

After receiving the news via my weekly phone call, Dad burst out, "Great, that's close to Barney and Colleen! I'll call them and see if they can drive up." Dad was not going to miss this opportunity. With a new car in the garage, Dad asked the Davises to join him for a week's vacation. Ed knew he had nurtured his crops the best he could; all he was waiting for now was maturity and harvest. Since he no longer had livestock, it was an ideal opportunity for him to get away too. He knew Pat could handle the daily chores.

Sitting on all sides of him, the stands were filled with both the Davis and Collins gangs. Dad was glowing with pride as he wore his wool PRTC baseball cap presented to him by Coach Morse. Several scouts were reportedly in the stands; however, their identities remained secret.

As a team, we were not surprised by Cookeville's June heat and humidity; it appeared burdensome for all teams. We retained our number one seed by duplicating 2–0 wins in the first and second rounds. Palm Area Technical College successfully defended their number two seed, despite wearing their traditional heavy cotton uniforms. Without a noticeable breeze, the weather conditions seemed to worsen as the week progressed. We were destined for a rematch with Palm Area.

Palm Area took the first game with a resounding 14–2 victory. With Palm Area up by three late in the second game, our backs were up against the proverbial wall. Coach Morse, suddenly leaving the dugout, ordered Coach Ethel to take the reins. Through strategic substitutions, we gained back two runs in the bottom of the sixth. Assuming we could hold their offense in check, we had three innings remaining to put across the four runs we needed. As leadoff man in the bottom of the seventh, I doubled to right. I was confident about my chances to score. We had worn down the Pirates' starting pitcher and were now facing their game closer, the familiar Peter Swann.

We had seen Peter the day before when their coach foolishly brought him into the game after they had accumulated a virtually insurmountable lead. His overall stamina appeared to be waning in the heat; we were confident we could tie the series. Our #7 batter hit a single straight to the shortstop, who leaped up in time to stop the ball, preventing me from advancing to third base, but not in time to make the out at first base. The #8 batter singles. Bases were loaded with the potential winning run at bat.

"Time!" Coach Ethel called for the umpire's attention. Why would he call time? He had already nearly exhausted the roster. What could he be thinking?

He later confided, "A winning team is one that is also in the game; my only remaining player was yesterday's losing pitcher, Louie Peltier. Louie told me earlier that the team needed a miracle to bring it to the deciding game."

Closing his eyes, Louie was startled out of prayer when he heard a booming voice yell, "Peltier, go in as pinch hitter for Erik Malander."

Louie was no different than most other pitchers. The #9 batter in the lineup, just as in the big leagues, was generally reserved for the pitcher. Pitchers, then as now, are not known for their hitting skills.

A math major, Louie excelled in the classroom, however, his batting average was a mere .125. He had never hit consistently, especially for extra bases. Most pitchers, recognizing his lack of a powerful swing, threw strikes his way; they thought they would just let him defeat himself. I thought a grounder to the right side of the diamond would at least send me safely home. Then, if Louie could just get on base, we would have a better chance of winning because we would have successfully forced the Pirates into the top of our lineup. The outfielders, playing shallow, were at the ready.

We didn't expect, at least from Louie, such a great unleashing of power! I heard the solid crack of the bat – his towering fly ball easily cleared the right field fence! PRTC took game 2 of the Championship series 5 to 4. Greeting him as he navigated the dugout steps, I asked, "Where did that come from?"

"I may have looked like I was out of the game, but I was studying their pitches. The Pirates' catcher has no concept of mixing up pitches. In all situations, he works strictly in repetition. He calls four types of pitches. The first is a fastball, slightly outside to a right-handed batter. The second is a low curve at the knees. The third is another curve ball, this time at the belt. And the fourth goes back to the fast ball, this time in the middle of the plate, at the knees. Once your know this, you've broken their pitch code."

"What are you saying, Peltier?" Coach Ethel joined us behind a row of lockers.

"I am saying they have probably had this plan in effect for both games. I first started to analyze it when we lost to them in Hawaii. It took me awhile tonight to test my theory, but I was able to confirm it when Olsen hit the same pitch our previous two batters missed. Counting where he was in his sequence, I knew the second and third pitches would be inside to me; identical, except the second being eight inches higher. I knew it would be the first pitch that I would be able to lift. The second would have taken more physical strength to carry long, however it likely would have resulted in a catchable line drive."

"What else did you learn?" Coach Morse just returned from the toilet.

"Their catcher has the same sequence with every pitcher in every situation. Their pitchers are good at delivery so they don't necessarily think about anything else; apparently, as long as they keep believing in their catcher, no one rocks the boat."

Fortunately, only Coaches Morse and Ethel, Moises, and I had heard Louie's theory.

Coach Morse whispered, "Ok, this will be our game plan. I'm going to make two changes for tomorrow's game. You'll see them early in the game. Olsen, Peltier, and Cortez, you must not disclose this strategy to anyone, at any cost." With that, the five of us banged fists and solidified our pact.

A cool front had blown through on Friday night. Saturday morning the Morses, Collinses, Davises, Dad and I met at the Executive Inn for the breakfast buffet. To our delight, Mae Lynne and the Zieglers arrived promptly after driving to Cookeville from the Knoxville Airport. With low humidity and temperatures in the low 60s at game time, the sky was ocean blue behind the light cumulus clouds. The host university's ballpark was oriented so the afternoon sun did not blind either the fans or players. The field, located in a heavily wooded park, utilized the park's many maple trees for shade. With a slight breeze blowing, both the fans and players anticipated a great day of baseball.

Arriving in the locker room, I saw Coach Morse had posted a rearranged lineup card. It was his intention to use Moises, Louie, and me as leadoff men in each grouping of three. Coach Morse arranged his batting order so that Moises was the leadoff hitter, I was in the fourth position with Louie as the seventh batter.

With Louie pitching, most right-handed batters would likely pull inside balls to the left side of the diamond. Louie and I were instructed to pitch for action on the left side of the diamond. We were also instructed to mix fastballs and changeups so the batters' swings would be off stride. Coach Morse hoped wide-ranging shortstop, Moises Cortez, would cover a lot of ground in addition to having a busy afternoon. He relied on his battery to eliminate the left-handed batters. If needed as a closing pitcher, Erik Malander was to stay warmed up throughout the game. If Coach needed to replace Louie, Louie would stay in the game and go into right field. As a final instruction, Coach encouraged me to step up the chatter. Recognizing the players had seen me in the two previous games, Coach Morse wanted to improve his chances of success by bringing my unconventional positioning into their heads. He wanted me to be both seen and heard!

With this much at stake, Coach Morse was afraid to disclose any other information to the rest of the team. He returned the reins to Coach Ethel.

⌂

Chatter was an accepted part of the game, although never personal or derogatory; phrases towards a player's mother, ethnicity or heritage are never acceptable. The harmonic chorus of chatter: "Hey, batter, batter, batter" of youth baseball was replaced by: "You swing like a rusty gate", "Choke up before you choke" and its sister phrase, the double entendre: "Don't forget to choke."

As I said, my goal as catcher was to be obvious and sometimes obnoxious. I could single-handedly remove a player's concentration. An innocent question such as "What did you do last night?" could be interpreted as: "<u>During</u> last night's game, or <u>after</u> last night's game?" The one I liked the most was a simple, "You've gained weight since the last time I saw you." Trying to look fit, a batter would unconsciously stiffen his posture – frequently hitting harmlessly to one of our infielders.

⌂

"They've changed their pitch system and added a changeup. They've juggled the sequence around and it looks like it is now: curve, changeup, fastball, higher curve, fastball," Moises whispered to Coach Morse, after scoring our first run. "That is why I took five pitches before coaxing my walk on that curve that veered out of the strike zone."

"Take a good look, Daryl. Let the other two know if he is correct," Coach Morse instructed his assistant from a seated position in the corner of the dugout.

Because I was abreast of the sequence change, I continued Moises' rally. We amassed three runs in the first two innings. By the start of the third inning, Coach Ethel confidently flashed counter signs reflecting this programmed sequence.

We added to our lead with each inning. Down by 10 runs and going into the bottom of the fifth, suddenly the

Pirates' coach called "time". He walked straight to the home plate umpire. On deck for the fourth time, I heard the whole conversation.

"They're stealing our signs! Just watch number eight here, their catcher, or number 12, the pitcher; no matter where they go, they transmit signs to the third base coach who in turn flashes it to the batters. They point to their numbers a lot. They are doing something illegal, but I am not exactly sure what it is."

Apathetically, the umpire said, "Have you made your case?" Then, turning to Coach Morse, who had sauntered toward the gathering, he said, "Coach, I have never known you to steal signs from an opponent. Are you?"

"No, we are not."

"I believe him; case closed. Batter up!" Shocked by the response, Palm's coach mumbled obscenities as he returned to their dugout.

With the final score of 15–2 now officially in the books, we received our trophy at home plate amongst our fans and families. Calling Coach Morse aside, the Tennessee Conference umpire disclosed the following: "I figured out what you were doing after your team came to bat in the second inning. You cracked their catcher's sequential pitch code, didn't you? Throughout the series, I was amazed no other team figured out how their catcher handcuffed a very talented team by methodically using the same sequence of pitches over and over again. I'm surprised their coach never realized his problem. As long as they kept on winning I guess he didn't look beyond."

When the excitement died down, Coach Morse invited only the team back to the locker room. There were not enough crying towels to go around as Coach Morse announced that his heartburn was more serious than originally disclosed. "I am scheduled for open heart surgery in Peoria following our return." New procedures were being tested worldwide – encouragement for stricken patients. "I am hopeful for a full recovery. Regardless of the outcome, I will be retiring. This has been my last game."

Concluding his brief announcement, he went on to say: "By the way, for those who are interested, Sam, Tim, Edna, and I will be attending church here in Cookeville in the morning. The service starts at nine o'clock sharp."

"Mae Lynne and I will join you," I said quietly as he stepped away from center stage.

"Kind of like last year?"

"No. To prove that was just a fluke, I'll even drive for you and Mrs. Morse. Be ready by 8:30."

"With gas approaching 40 cents a gallon, that's a deal I won't pass up!"

⌂

Never one for fanfare, Coach Morse invited the team and their families to a small ceremony at Prairie Ridge Field the following Thursday. After introductions and a brief overview of the past season, he announced: "I will be retiring three numbers as a result of our second championship. Olsen, Cortez, and Peltier, please come forward. It is with great honor and pleasure, that I will be hanging #08, and #6, and #12 on the Prairie Ridge Fence of Fame. You boys, I should say young men, have made me very proud."

As I looked out across the field I saw where three numbers, each with black letters on a rich golden background, had been exposed from behind a hanging tarp. The freshly painted plywood cut outs, sawn into the shape of a player's jersey, found a home amongst the other nine inductees, including: #1 Morse, #22 Ziegler, and #31 Ethel.

Out of Coach Morse's sight, a large, tarp-covered, arched sign remained hidden from view. "Whoa, wait a minute...I think there is something you missed." Interrupting the ceremony, Coach Ethel proudly announced as the tarp was taken down: "By executive order of Provost Ziegler, Prairie Ridge Field will as of this day, July 1st, 1971 be renamed Joe Morse Park – Home of the Soarin' Eagles." Caught totally by surprise, Coach Morse was visibly humbled by the announcement. Coach Ethel went on to announce that a formal dedication ceremony would be held immediately before the first home game of the 1972 Season.

Never one to be outdone, Coach Morse leaped from his seat and said, "Wait a minute; I too have something else to say! Please, Edna, hand me that piece of paper...no the rolled up package next to it". Coach Morse then stepped up to the podium. Purposely gazing into the unexpectedly large crowd he said, "John Hendricks, please come down here." I hadn't seen him in the bleachers. Up until that moment, neither had I known he was a PRTC alumnus.

Continuing, Coach Morse said, "On behalf of Prairie Ridge Technical College, and myself, as your rookie, first year coach, it is my extreme pleasure to inform you that Prairie Ridge Technical College hereby retires your well worn number. This is a well-deserved, albeit delayed, honor." With that, he unwrapped an old jersey with the number 92 on its back. "We don't believe you knew Jayne has kept it all these years alongside your WWI uniform." Laughingly he observed, "It looks to me like you can still fit into either one!"

He then followed, "Some of you may not know this, but after returning from World War I, John Hendricks played on this team for two years. Now do the math; in 1920 and 1921, John Hendricks was the starting catcher for the Screamin' Eagles – at the age of 28 and 29 – more than ten years older than his teammates! While pursuing undergraduate studies in chemistry, he went on to play at the University of Rockford

220

where he lettered for an additional two years at that school. John, our heartfelt thanks go out to you." After John received a well-deserved standing ovation, Coach Morse walked to and reached into the end of the dugout. The large crowd, following his lead, walked across the diamond to left center field where Coach Morse personally hung "#92 Hendricks" alongside the others.

Coach Morse's last words: "Thanks for coming. Now let's go celebrate our country's one hundred ninety fifth birthday and the freedom and rights we have been given! Have a great long weekend."

⌂

"You know, there were pro scouts in Cookeville. That scout from Milwaukee told me that if I found a team that would let you play, he would personally come and assess your ability. He also said he would pass his assessment of last week's game on to his fellow scouts. I told him that I had a pretty good idea who would give you a chance. I said I knew a pretty good shortstop and pitcher, too – kind of a package deal, I thought." I had joined the Morses for Sunday dinner a week later. Mrs. Morse served her supreme lasagna bake.

"You did? How can I thank you?"

"A table prayer will be adequate."

⌂

With my Associate's degree in hand, I made the long trek through northwest Illinois and southwest Wisconsin to my new apartment and job in West Bend, Wisconsin. My '64 Valiant struggled as it pulled its loaded caravan through the glaciated hills. Even though the Interstate had been built between Madison and Chicago, the most direct roads remained the north-northeasterly routes toward the southwest side of Madison.

My small one-bedroom apartment, housed in an old two-story fourplex, was located on a busy street just three blocks from my work. At $90 per month rent, I just knew I would be bringing in an abundance of money – after all my salary was $650 per month. Madison's east side was 60 miles away. We moved Mae Lynne to Columbus in order to make for a shorter drive.

⌂

This was the last Christmas we would call our individual family homes in Providence "home". Returning to Providence together, Mae Lynne and I began planning for next year's wedding. We both knew this Christmas would later be looked at with fond memories as we slowly brought our individual possessions together to make our own home. My employer, Haugrud Construction, went out of their way to accommodate our plans *and* my hopes for a long-lasting baseball career, even if I was considered an oddity in professional baseball circles.

⌂

Just before the New Year, Bjorn Haugrud asked, "Do you know someone who would be interested in our newly expanded position of Restaurant Construction – General Superintendent?"

With America's increasing desire to have fast food restaurants on every corner, Bjorn saw an opportunity to partner with upstart Burger Giant. Remembering my good friend, Buster Mazzocco, was looking for an opportunity outside of Providence, I gave him a call. Bjorn interviewed and hired Buster – on the spot.

Shortly thereafter, Buster moved in with me. I didn't ask for any rent. When Kitty countersued him for "irreconcilable differences", whatever that meant, the lenient judge attacked Buster like a lion pursuing a lamb. He lost most of his possessions and savings. Having been drained of what little he had, Buster was happy to move in, even if it was literally with his entire wardrobe on his back. After about four months, he was able to afford an apartment by himself. Buster became somewhat of a loner and this solitary time gave him an opportunity to relish the peace and quiet he sought.

Buster performed his duties with exemplary skill. Within a short time, he was appointed Vice President of Haugrud's Restaurant Construction division, now located in leased office space in Beaver Dam. Leaving West Bend, he moved what few belongings he had to Beaver Dam.

1972

"Do you want to try out?" Moises Cortez asked when he phoned from his home in Port Washington one night in early February. "A new semi-pro league is being organized around Port Washington by Coach Daryl Ethel!"

"Coach Ethel? I thought they were going to make him Head Coach since Coach Morse retired."

"That's what I thought too. Apparently Coach Ethel saw this as a way to get to the big leagues, especially since this spring, the Milwaukee team will be starting their third season. This could be our chance too."

I realized the Port Washington club could attract scouts from Milwaukee, Chicago, or Minneapolis. Hoping to find a diamond in the rough, scouts would likely venture to these small market games. Ultimately hearing of the favorable outcome of players visiting the club office, I thought it might be a great opportunity for me too.

⌂

Although each player was in competition for a job, each was united in their quest to move to the higher competition only the big league farm clubs could offer. They knew success for the individual was based on the success of the team.

"1, 2, 3, Go!" Coach Ethel yelled above the sound of the springtime wind. Starting on the third base line, our speed was being timed for ninety feet. Groups of five stretched out between home and the edge of the left field grass. Each of the five coaches and assistants timed and recorded one individual's speed between the chalk lines. "From last year, you've made a big improvement Olsen. An average of three point two seconds between the chalk lines is very impressive. Let's see, what you did throwing between home and second." Grabbing another clipboard marked "Position Throwing" he read, "average – one point eight seconds. Congratulations! It looks like you still have your Blazer. Nice job. We'll announce the team early next week."

Fortunately I made the first cut. Moises Cortez joined the Sailors as a shortstop in late April following a second chance tryout. Improving exponentially with each game, his ability to cover a large area and his rapid release soon became well-known throughout the league.

⌂

While playing at Whitewater one Saturday evening, the lives of Moises and me became further entwined. We were up by two runs in the ninth inning, however, the Wildcats had men on second and third with just one out. I picked their runner off at third base when he ventured a little too far down the line. Unaware of my arm strength and accuracy, he became an easy target as the left-handed batter provided me with additional maneuvering room.

The loud crack of the bat made the hard line drive sound even more like a base clearing hit to left center. Like a cat leaping for a caged bird, Moises snared the liner. With its kinetic force he landed literally on top of second base. Brushing himself off, he knew he had just recorded an unassisted, walk off double play.

Frequently, wives and girlfriends were offered the unused seats on the coaches' bus. Along with other team guests and sponsors, Mae Lynne had been able to join the team for this weekend's series. Usually, the guests sat together in the stands, thus creating our own little cheering section.

Although they shared an interest in the team and its players, as individuals, they rarely socialized. Remembering each player was in competition for a job in the big leagues, that competitiveness trickled down to the player's acquaintances.

As we left the locker room together, putting his long arm around me, Moises easily spotted Mae Lynne's five feet ten inch height. Turning his face toward me he said, "I would like to introduce you to my fiancé." Seeing Mae Lynne was standing alongside a petite young Mexican woman, Moises asked, "So have you two already met?" Before either could answer, Moises said, "Honey, I'd like you to meet..."

"...Buddy? Buddy Olsen from Providence; that was you! I never knew your first name was Willis!"

Startled, because no one had called me Buddy in such a long time, I quickly turned my attention from Mae Lynne to Moises' fiancé. Immediately recognizing her voice, I asked, "Are you still sowing those seeds?"

"I believe the last time I saw you ...must have been in the fall of 1963 just before President Kennedy was shot, right? Remember what I said when I got off the bus?"

About that time Mae Lynne recognized Maria too – "I thought you looked and sounded familiar! Gosh, you have a good memory. Tell us what you've been doing and how long you've been here in Wisconsin."

Rushing to speak, I said, "You know, I went over to the railroad cars looking for you the Saturday after the assassination, but you were gone. Do you miss Texas? How about we get a bite to eat? I'm starved and I want to hear everything!"

Seated in a secluded booth, Mae Lynne looked across the table; starting the conversation she asked, "Where did you meet?"

"Go ahead, you tell them."

Moises began, "I first met Maria in 1969, during the summer before I started at PRTC. We were both assigned to several corn fields, pulling tassels for a hybrid seed corn company from Arnzeville. It seemed like we were always on the same crew. At the end of the summer we went our separate ways."

Maria jumped in, "Then, in late winter my older sister and I formed a cleaning service company, partnering with a Chicago-based cleaning equipment manufacturer. We contracted to clean buildings in and around Prairie Ridge, even at the Technical College. I never went to any of the baseball games. I guess I was too busy!"

Mae Lynne turned to me and said: "Are you OK Willis? You seem to be sweating bullets."

Moises explained, "A year later, we met again in the fields. We have written each other ever since, seeing each other only occasionally. I never thought you might have known her as a child. I knew several families from Pharr worked near Providence, but I never made the connection. Moving from Jacksonville to Port Washington, just two days ago, she had never been able to come to our games until tonight."

Mae Lynne became sentimental. "What a love story. I knew it right away, however with us, it took Willis much longer to decide I was the one for him."

What started that early Friday evening ended well into Saturday morning. Moises and I quickly understood intertwined lives were not coincidence. Maria Rodriquez was still on fire for the Lord's work as much as she had been when we first crossed paths as children. She truly was planting one hundred fold.

As Mae Lynne and I returned to the team motel, she predictably asked, "Well, how many seeds have *you* sown?"

With an evening game scheduled for Saturday, both Moises and I, as roommates, agreed to sleep well into the morning.

We met the girls for brunch. Mae Lynne said, "Let us pray...." With that, our meal with Moises and Maria was blessed.

Like we hadn't missed a beat, Maria asked, "Buddy, why don't you ever pray before you eat in public? I remember the time your mom prepared that delicious Thanksgiving supper for my family. I saw how your family prayed before that meal. Are you afraid to witness in public?"

I countered, "You and Mae Lynne always pray from your heart, blessing the immediate need. I've always prayed to myself using the same prayer I was taught as a kid. That..."

Maria cut me off, "No more excuses! I think we need to help you with that!"

⌂

After just a few years in public athletics, I learned that the seasoned player needed to become deaf to both fan encouragement and harassment. Successful players focused on the Coaches' directives and the observations of a few fellow players. Players were instructed to be personable with fans and children before the games; however, once the umpire announced "Play Ball", the professional player needed to focus solely on the task at hand. This was the professional's line between fair and foul. Most players were, therefore, viewed by the general public as self-centered and arrogant. Like I alluded to before, these critical days were a player's opportunity, and livelihood, in some cases.

⌂

"So why did he blow up?" Mae Lynne asked me on the phone.

"I think the prospect that the Sailors would not be playing a second year finally got to him. Prior to tonight, his patience was phenomenal. I know several of us would have exploded a whole lot earlier.

"Several Latino players were jeered when we played in Appleton that Friday night. Since we were leading Oshkosh by two full games in the standings, it appeared several Oaks fans thought they could help their team when we played at nearby Appleton. Since Oshkosh and Appleton are approximately thirty five miles apart, it was an easy drive. Also well known, a fan's pilgrimage might include several planned stops for liquid refreshment.

"During the Appleton game, most of the jeering, unlike player chatter, came from seats along the third base line, just beyond our visitors' dugout. Scattered amongst our small contingent of fans were several young men dressed in Oshkosh orange. Several Sailors' wives and girlfriends complained to field security just before the start of the third inning, but to no avail. We posted an early 5–0 lead. Appleton's fans sitting on their hands seemed to be enjoying the cool early autumn evening. The uninvited Oaks' fans, however, must have decided that this apathy should change. Following most of our plays, one or two individuals began yelling derogatory remarks or slurs either at our players or coaches.

"Fortunately, in the fifth inning, uniformed Appleton police escorted six of the instigators out of the stands, where they were loaded onto a school bus and driven away.

"However, the biggest instigator would not give up. Turning around, as he was escorted from the stands, he yelled an ethnic slur directly at Moises. As team players, it was like a knife to our collective hearts. As you know, Moises is a fifth generation Texan whose ancestors fought for Texas' independence. Each of us thinks of Moises as a gifted player whose heart is as large as the state he came from. Coach Ethel knew the comment would not demoralize this team. Carefully controlling the team's demeanor and power, we added to the lead. The vacant stands told the whole story for us; it was an impressive 9–0 shutout."

"What did Coach Ethel say to the Oshkosh general manager before tonight's game?" Mae Lynne inquired.

"He didn't tell us anything, but he was visibly upset when he saw those same cronies sitting in the seats nearest our dugout. This time their harassment could be amplified since they were surrounded by other fans complacent to their actions.

"The wound didn't take long to fester. Unfortunately, a fly ball in the bottom of the third inning became wind-driven, carrying it beyond the third base line towards the stands. From his shortstop position, Moises called for and unfortunately took the foul fly in front of the thugs. His momentum carried him over the short brick wall. Prior to his well-timed leap at the four foot wall, a fan clearly reached into his closing glove and knocked the ball free.

"The third base umpire called 'no play!' Immediately, Coach Ethel signaled to the home plate umpire, and time was called. 'He caught that ball! Those fans interfered with my player. I want them removed!' Coach yelled. The umpire condescendingly responded, 'Can't handle a little harassment? Go back to your bench. Play ball!' With that he walked back to home plate.

"Turning a routine grounder into a 6-4-3 double play, Moises then assisted in closing out the inning. Returning to the dugout, he immediately stopped in front of Coach Ethel, lifted his shirt, and exposed several large red areas near his kidney, telling Coach how one of the thugs sucker punched him when he fell over the wall. Coach Ethel said he'd lodge another complaint. The jeers continued in the bottom of the fourth. The jeering was instigated by the same group of young punks who, although they were near the same age as the players on the field, had been athletically surpassed by the superior athletes on the field. Alcohol's subtle effects inflated their self esteem, resulting in their own perceived collective bravery.

"Unfortunately, Oaks' management was slow to react. Moises caught the hard line drive just as a half-empty beer can, thrown from the same, close-in stands, rocketed toward his head. Possessing eagle-like peripheral vision Moises saw the missile coming. Its length was strong, but its accuracy was slightly off. Moises easily equaled that same distance, pulling the ball out of his web, he rifled a blistering fastball toward the still standing instigator's chest. Arriving almost as fast as the bullet he threw, Moises quickly grabbed the thug by his shirt, as the instigator fell forward, in pain, over the wall. Throwing him to the ballfield ground, he placed his steel cleats firmly on the thug's sternum. Turning to the home plate umpire, Moises yelled, in perfect English, 'Are you going to get this bum and his cronies out of here before someone gets hurt?'

"You could have heard a pin drop within the 2500 seat stadium. Embarrassed and in a virtual tizzy, the home plate umpire quickly called time. From a nearby corner, three uniformed policemen rapidly moved in to remove all of the remaining cronies. Two plain clothed officers sprinted across the field, into the stands, and arrested the ring leader. The last we saw of him, he was off towards the hospital in the back seat of an unmarked police car. Two Emergency Medical Technicians who were assigned to the game later smirked as they told Coach Ethel, 'We had to apply the four inch wide medical tape directly to the ring leader's hairy body; that is part of the medical procedure.' It seems they were 'unable to find a razor', and besides, they were 'in a hurry'. Assuming he probably had several bruised ribs, they had applied the tape to the entire circumference of his chest, from just below his armpits to just above his navel. The police officers added insult to injury by making him sit upright in the back seat of the squad car. Moises was ejected from the game and a substitute brought in. The rest of the evening was relatively calm, except for our bats!"

For this night only, Coach Ethel broke one of baseball's unwritten rules–never needlessly run up the score. Final score: 22–0.

This was not the last time we would see this deplorable home plate umpire.

After Coach Ethel received several superficial apologies from Oshkosh Oaks management, Coach Ethel cancelled the remainder of our games with the Oaks. Following this game, the Oaks fell into a slump eventually ending the season in fourth place.

We went on to win the league championship. Both Louie Peltier and I were named Co-Rookies of the Year by the league and Louie was runner-up MVP. Fortunately, the League overlooked Moises' incident in Oshkosh, naming him League MVP for 1972.

◊

Neither of us had the desire or the funds for a large wedding. Dad willingly paid cash for his responsibilities. For some reason, he always reimbursed us more than what it cost.

Secretly, he gave me $500 to purchase wedding rings.

Mae Lynne's mother helped her plan the small, church wedding. Mae Lynne was a member of Shepherd's Church of Columbus. Brother Holland readily agreed to perform the ceremony since he had gotten to know us quite well. We limited ourselves to 100 invitations.

That clear fall day was truly God given. It rained all day Thursday and Friday only to clear by five o'clock Friday afternoon. The late afternoon clearing shower moved eastward leaving a full arch rainbow over Columbus. Saturday remained clear.

Dressed in the same, retailored, orange dress she wore on our first prom date, Mae Lynne was attended by Maria Cortez and my sister Susanna. With George as my best man, I chose Buster Mazzocco as my only other groomsman.

Mae Lynne's mother had a light supper catered, including what was now a family favorite: Edna's Lasagna. Of course orange slices were part of the menu. Darlene Davis counted them as our daily serving of fruit.

Although we sent invitations to each, sadly we neither saw nor heard from the Zieglers, Morses, or Hendricks.

Following a short honeymoon in Cornucopia, Wisconsin, we moved into a two-bedroom apartment in Beaver Dam. Upon our return, the mail included our invitations to the Zieglers and Morses, both stamped "*Return to Sender. No forwarding address given.*" The Hendricks' invitation arrived two days later; it had been stamped similarly.

Two weeks later, we were both pleasantly surprised to find out that Buster Mazzocco met one of Mae Lynne's pre-med classmates, Ruth Daily, at our wedding. Their courtship began. Ruth, Buster, and I joined Shepherd's Church in Beaver Dam, a mission church planted by Brother Holland, the Sunday after Thanksgiving. Each of us knew we had a lot to be thankful for – even the steel chairs of our mission church.

⌂

"I have a New Year's resolution. It's time we start praying together. God has put us together for His purpose. We need to profess our prayers together to the One who made us one." With that we knelt alongside our bed as we each, out loud, raised our individual prayers to heaven. "Amen and Amen. That was a great prayer!"

1973

Fortunately we had seen it coming and had wisely decided to relocate out of the area, choosing Beaver Dam as our first home. The Sailors obtained their nickname from Sailor Jack's Smelt Company, a local fishery and cannery that based its sole financial strength on the tiny fish's annual spawning migration. Environmentalists, quickly becoming an all inclusive word in the English lexicon, blamed lake pollution for the previous year's dreadful spring run. Others blamed the early ice melt – part of a general earth warming, they said. Whatever the cause, the cannery folded. The Sailors were unable to meet their January 5th payroll responsibilities, thus leaving Coach Ethel and last year's roster of players without a team.

In late winter, I was invited by the Mitts Baseball Club to join their team for the 1973 season. With Moises moving up to an AA Farm Team, I was determined to make an individual impression on both the fans and coaches in Beaver Dam. As always, I hoped to impress the ever reclusive scouts.

Looking back at PRTC's dismal season under Coach Erik Malander, the Board of Regents unanimously selected Daryl Ethel as the new head coach and athletic director of the PRTC Soarin' Eagles.

Mae Lynne graduated from the University in the spring with a double major in Biology and Pre-Med. She had been accepted into the Medical School but we didn't know where we would find the money for her to continue her studies.

"We need to take this to God in prayer."

"Yes." I began, "Dear Father..."

⌂

It was to be my third game as a Mitt. The stands were expected to be packed as Mt. Horeb had previously showed good support for their home team. It was also rumored that the Mitts had a left-handed catcher with pretty good potential – good enough to make it into the exclusive fraternity of left-handed catchers who played in the Big League.

"You're that catcher for the Mitts aren't you? Your picture was in this morning's paper. We love our Trolls."

"This will be my third game and I'm anxious to make a good impression. I heard there may be scouts from Milwaukee in the stands tonight."

"Here, this marshmallow malt will top off that hamburger and fries just right. I hope it doesn't upset your stomach. Handing her a five dollar bill, she unexpectedly said, "No, it's on the house."

Early in the game, while crouching, my tight fitting pants ripped the entire length of the crotch seam. Suspecting the fans did not want to see that much of me, the game was delayed for approximately five minutes while I returned to the equipment trailer. "No you can't wear those, you need your uniform to match." To me, it appeared my only choice was my white pair of home team pants. The equipment manager then gave me his only unused pair of away pants. I thought they would be four inches too large. "I don't have any more 32's, you'll have to wear 'em." His size 36 fit fine.

Late in the game I got on base with a double, my second of the game. Down by one run in the top of the ninth, I ran to third following a single to right field by our pitcher Louie Peltier. Louie was quickly pinch run by speedster Tyrone Bowman. The top of the lineup was then given a chance to win the game.

The steal sign was flashed to Tyrone. When the first pitch hit the plate careening wildly towards first base, third base coach, Assistant Coach Weibel yelled, "Go Olsen! Go!"

I broke for home. Troll's catcher, Mike Ottsen, fielded the errant ball and lunged back towards home plate. All catchers practice this play many times. With the plate open for just a split second, Ottsen miraculously stretched as far as he could to brush my sliding arm away from the treasure. His inertia carried him so far, his face stopped on the plate, without my arm crossing the plate, I had just slid in the dirt.

Reflecting back, since a second base steal was signaled, a command to the man on third to steal home was even more risky. Assuming the speedster beat the throw, a better strategy would have had men on second and third base. A subsequent base hit would have scored one, possibly two runs.

Coach Rodman angrily pulled me aside, yelling, "What were you thinking Olsen? Assistant Coach Weibel told me that he told you 'No Olsen! No!' Olsen, you need to use your head for more than just a hat rack."

"Willis, I heard him say Go, GO!" In Mt. Horeb, the third base visitor's dugout was within five feet of the coach's box. Louie had perched on the steps closest to the box. Louie said, "That is not the first time I've heard him lie to Coach Rodman. Someday it will come back to haunt him."

As teammates again, Louie Peltier was quickly becoming a lifelong trusted friend. His trust helped me through what I was beginning to perceive was going to be a tough year. As we grew closer, his brotherly kinship became invaluable as a confidant and ally.

Coach Rodman later called me aside, "Olsen, you need to call a better game behind the plate. I've assigned Assistant Coach Weibel to help you strategize the pitches. You know Assistant Coach Weibel was the successful head coach at

Palm Area Technical College before he came to me."
Pausing to spit tobacco laden saliva into his makeshift
spittoon, he continued, "Your arm strength, defense, and
hitting are exemplary, but you just don't know how to plan
out the game. Also, stay away from the shakes, fries, and
hamburgers. You're putting on a few extra pounds. Married
life must be good to you."

⌂

"Why are you calling me at work?"

With the new office completed, I began to work full
time at our branch office in Beaver Dam. My project cost
estimating and accounting position was perfect for me. With
a strong aptitude for numbers, I easily set up systems to track
our firm's costs. This effort paid dividends for the company.
We remained on the cutting edge, always seeking new
estimating technologies. Systems I developed helped our
estimators determine a project's true job cost. We were
awarded, and successfully completed, several large
commercial jobs.

We had been married for almost seven months. "Can
you come home for lunch?" I wasn't sure if Mae Lynne was
in a romantic way or if she wanted to announce something.

Still startled, Mae Lynne, through tears, said, "Read this
letter. It came via registered mail. Their address and phone
number are included."

I read:

Dear Mae Lynne and Willis,

*As you know, Mae Lynne's scholarship offer was
good only until she graduated from the University. You
may also have heard that on June 1st, after nearly half a
century, we had to close the doors of our drugstore
because of the new chain store in town. Through those*

238

fifty years we remained steadfast in the way we conducted our business, but, despite joining a cooperative with other drugstores, we were never able to compete with the chain's mass merchandising and high volume pricing.

For some time, our fountain was not attracting the young people it had in the past. New state rules would have required us to extensively remodel the fountain. If we continued to serve ice cream, everything would have had to be clad in stainless steel; the beautiful wood would be covered up forever.

With that said, God has blessed us through the years. The drugstore was very successful. We have sold the building and it will become Breunig's Floral Shop and Bookstore.

We have prayed and do hereby offer both of you full ride scholarships to further your individual careers. We have contacted Attorney Peter Swann, Sr. who will be in contact with you in order to set up the trust accounts. Through our trust, we will provide funds through the Doctoral level for both of you.

After we sold our home in Providence, we purchased a retirement home on the ocean, near Key West, Florida. We have a small group of relatives and friends in the area. You will be glad to know this group also expects to seed a mission church in one of the new housing areas. All we need are some chairs to get us started.

Again, best wishes to you. We are sorry we could not attend your wedding or give you this gift at that time. We hope you will honor us by accepting this belated offer.

Yours in Christ,

John and Jayne Hendricks

⌂

Trailing 4–2, it was our turn to bat in the top half of the fifth inning. We needed to produce a rally. The summer heat was unbearable for this mid-July double header. The team was anxious to play two and win two. A sweep would bring us back to a .500 record midway through the season.

An all-star game had been slated for the following Wednesday night, giving the team a full six days rest before play resumed next Friday. Because of our rookie year performances as Sailors, both Louie and I were chosen for the All-Star Team. We had been selected as *at-large* players.

During the first half of the season, Louie and I had posted a 2–1 record against today's opponent, the league-leading Baraboo Bears.

Leading off in our half of the inning, our first two hitters sent back to back singles into right center field. Advancing them to second and third, using a surprise double steal, would have enhanced our chances of scoring. "Why not put in Tyrone as a pinch runner?" Assistant Coach Weibel suggested.

Without analysis, Coach Rodman tersely yelled, "No!"

All of us knew what the assistant coach had seen. Assistant Coach Weibel recognized that a left-handed, stout batter, especially one who stood high in the batter's box, would be a large obstacle for a catcher such as Baraboo's. His inability to clearly see second and first could be beneficial to us.

Fortunately, I hit the ball squarely; the resulting double put runners on second and third. We now trailed by one run. Following an intentional base on balls, and with the bases loaded, Baraboo brought in their premier closer, Alex DeVleer. Closing, or should I say slamming the door, is what he did! After a strikeout to the first batter he faced, and with the Bears playing deep, a routine grounder led to an inning ending 6-4-3 double play. Pitcher DeVleer then gave his team an additional four innings of shutout ball. Most of the team recognized we squandered our few chances.

With the summer heat showing no sign of subsiding, the league had wisely scheduled this to be a day-night double header. This gave both teams an opportunity to relax and exchange their sweaty uniforms for clean ones. Baraboo's city-owned park had showerheads in an older portion of a picnic shelter restroom. Hot water was at a premium, but, by the end of the first game, most players didn't consider this a problem.

As the second game began, it soon became noticeable that Assistant Coach Weibel was not in the dugout. Several players remembered seeing Assistant Coach Weibel strolling toward his car after the first game. We all thought it unusual for a coach to have a personal car at an away game.

As the second game progressed, it didn't appear we needed either coach's leadership. The team had put itself on auto-pilot. Louie was pitching strongly. The Bear's pitcher did not have the same desire and stamina he needed to win the second game.

Coincidently, a base stealing opportunity again became available in the bottom half of the sixth inning. With men on first and second, a left-handed batter was again at the plate – me – batting in the eighth position. Remembering the advice Assistant Coach Weibel offered in the first game, I was pleasantly surprised when our third base coach signaled the double steal. It worked to perfection. With men on second and third, Baraboo decided force plays at all bases had a higher likelihood of success than even the rarer grand slam home run. They only needed one out. Since our number nine batter was Louie Peltier, batting average a meager .177, they believed walking me only enhanced their chances of getting the illusive out. I was intentionally thrown four balls and walked to first base.

Watching each pitch closely, Louie swung at a belt high fastball. We'll never know if the sprinting runners would have scored on a routine hit, Louie made sure of that. The resulting line drive easily cleared the right field fence by twelve feet. Louie silently made his point – this group of young men could rise above even the greatest of adversities. Final score Louie 4, Baraboo 0. That evening, he added the two-hit shutout to his portfolio.

"Olsen, thanks for calling a great game. This pitcher/catcher battery is fully charged."

"Thanks. Together, my friend, we are awesome!"

⌂

Due to a rainout earlier in the summer, our final two games that season were a makeup game plus the regular game, both scheduled for Sunday afternoon at home. Immediately following these last games, and with no immediate future, most of the demoralized and unmanaged Mitts were expected to leave their part-time jobs and Beaver Dam, to return to their hometowns.

At the end of the season, league leading Baraboo held a slim one game lead in the standings over Oshkosh. Several Oshkosh fans, seeking to influence the outcome of these two season ending games, approached me and several other players. Money appeared to be no object to these unscrupulous fans.

I remembered my discussions long ago with Mr. Roberts. I knew exactly what to do. Grabbing Louie, together we assembled the team into a small corner of the locker room out of the sight and sound of both coaches. Presenting the facts, each player agreed to rebuff the fans' approaches and play to our best ability.

Each player honored their agreement. Fully focused on the game, the Mitts handily dashed Oshkosh's hopes for the title. With scores of 5–1 and 6–1, the Oaks fell even further, a full two and a half games back. With Baraboo's same day win and wins by both Mt. Horeb and Appleton, the Oaks surprisingly found themselves demoted to a fourth place tie with Stoughton. The Norsemen were awarded the playoff seed because of their regular season record against the Oaks. The Mitts players suffered the same season ending fate as the Oaks. There would be no post-season play for either of them this year.

⌂

We were thankful for the many blessings of 1973. In November, Mae Lynne and I moved into a larger two-bedroom apartment in the upper story of a Cape Cod style house on Beaver Dam's northwest side. Dad and the Davises joined us for our first Christmas in our new home. Not necessarily perceived as a Christmas dish, Mae Lynne baked Edna's Lasagna to absolute perfection. Her dessert? You guessed it: white cake with orange flavored frosting – trimmed with orange slices.

1974

"Will, who do we know in Allouez, Wisconsin? Isn't that near Green Bay?"

Similar to a wedding invitation, the outside envelope had no return address. The inside envelope was addressed: *To: Buddy and Mae Lynne, my Christian friends forever.* Containing a single sheet of elegant penmanship, we quickly learned Tina Polanski answered a higher calling, when she spoke her vows of poverty, temperance, and celibacy, and entered Allouez's Order of the Holy Mary Convent in early 1971. A graduate of Chicago's parochial schools, her roots were well-founded in Catholicism. The convent's affiliation with a local private college assured her that she would soon be a mother to many children; she was enrolled in the Teacher Education program. She accepted the Perfect Bridegroom's proposal – she was now working her way towards Sisterhood. Tears of joy rolled down my cheek when I read her handwritten note of thanksgiving and praise.

Hearing Mae Lynne's inquisitive questioning, I responded, "Come over and sit by me. I need to tell you who she is."

⌂

One afternoon, while sitting quietly in the dugout after an early season practice, I remembered Coach Ziegler's wisdom about bullies. I knew Assistant Coach Weibel possessed a "party animal" reputation.

Already dressed in his street clothes Louie suddenly burst into the dugout, "Assistant Coach Weibel was fired by the team before yesterday's game with the Appleton Reds! Several players have also learned he was arrested and charged with involuntary manslaughter and DWI at 2:00 a.m. this morning."

Although he portrayed himself to be a Christian, Assistant Coach Weibel and his wife never appeared to be equally yoked. "I heard he was having an extramarital affair with one of the team's secretaries, Kitty Thompson Mazzocco. She was fired too."

Kitty's untimely presence in Beaver Dam had become very awkward for Mae Lynne and me. We knew her past. When we saw her, we were cordial, but distant. We believed she initially moved into the area in an effort to reunite with Buster. Unlike Buster, having never remarried, Kitty recklessly and callously placed their child in and out of several foster homes. With her past record, this time we questioned her motives.

I was afraid I was going to lose my cool — always protecting my friend and his new relationship to the hilt. Mae Lynne and I, in what appeared to be a most inopportune moment, literally crossed paths with Kitty as she parked her car one Sunday morning at Shepherd's Church. Mae Lynne's intuition quickly moved into action. Sensing my judgmental attitude, she partially diffused my anger by clutching my hand. Mae Lynne intuitively warned of the confrontation, "The whole thing could blow up if Buster and Ruth arrive at their usual time."

"On no, here they come! It looks like we can't avoid it. They must have seen us; they're heading this way!"

Pitifully, Kitty stood alongside our car. Four against one could easily have become a mob scene. With all five of us now standing awkwardly in the small parking lot, Mae Lynne calmly suggested we pray before we speak.

My thoughts were against the adulteress standing before us. Staring at her coldly, I didn't think we needed her type in this church!

I followed the peacemaker's wishes. While in prayer, I suddenly remembered the day Kitty ran out of St. Bart's. I then realized that even though she had made several ill-advised decisions in her past, we were truly witnessing her bold, repentant step forward.

With heads still bowed, standing in a loose semi-circle, suddenly a voice said: "*Brothers and sisters, why do you persecute her? Are you without sin?*"

Startled, I questioned, "Did you hear that?"

"I did!" Buster quivered. Also hearing the voice, the two women at our sides were visibly shaken.

"What are you talking about? What did you hear?" Kitty naively inquired.

Still trembling, Mae Lynne then spoke up, "We each heard a commanding voice, and it was not one of our own!"

We now fully understood Shepherd's monument sign: "Come as you are. Love will meet you at the door." Ironically, Brother Holland's message that Sunday morning was based on John 8:1–11. Kitty, now viewed in a whole new light, answered that morning's altar call. She later affirmed her baptism, and became a fellow believer. Coincidence? I think not!

Kitty's actions revealed God's true plan when she acknowledged she could no longer raise six year old Anthony, Jr. by herself. Anthony, Jr. desperately needed his father's love. Requesting the Court overturn its custody decree, Kitty, in an emotional scene, asked newlywed Ruth Mazzocco to adopt him into their family. Upon hearing this, Buster and Ruth broke down with joy.

Kitty later moved into a one bedroom apartment in Big Stone. She eventually married law student, and my former teammate, Peter Swann. Listening to and following God's plan, not concocting her own, guaranteed she too was now equally yoked.

$$\bigcirc$$

Coach Rodman likely got wind of his assistant's affair when Assistant Coach Weibel insisted on driving his own car to every out of town game. Although he always had a single motel room, furnished by the team, apparently he only used it to shower in the morning. Coach Rodman later realized Assistant Coach Weibel had been lying not only to him but to his wife Donna as well.

Assistant Coach Weibel never returned to coach baseball. Following his release from prison and Donna's divorce judgment, he slowly drifted across country where Coach Rodman later found him working as a day laborer in San Diego. Coach Rodman attempted to help him many times, but he was never successful.

Coach Rodman kept his managerial position despite the fact that the Mitts were securely, for the second year in a row, in the standings cellar. Needless to say, the likelihood of scouts attending our games was very remote.

Finally reaching a breakpoint one night, Coach Rodman barked, "Who ever tried to make you a catcher must have sure been a dunce! You should have been a right fielder, that way you wouldn't see any action. That pass ball you had tonight, my second grader could have handled it cleanly. We would have won the game if you would have done your job!" Becoming more levelheaded after he sat down, he noted, "I understand you were an awesome pitcher the few times you took the mound. What got you started thinking you could be a catcher, especially being a southpaw? Why did you try to make something out of nothing? Do you think you are invincible? Or, did your bullheadedness get in the way?"

Angrily I said: "Coach, with all due respect, we lost the game by eight runs to the second worst team in the league! I had a dirt speck land on my contact when the ball skipped the chalk line in front of the batter's box."

"Any more excuses?"

Beginning to throw all respect out the door, I screamed, "That's why I turned away in such pain. I know in my mind I can make it in the Big Leagues, if someone would just give me the chance!" I began to cry, "By the way, the person who guided me was a very successful manager. With all due respect Coach, Tim Ziegler gave me something you may never know." With that I flicked the mud off of my baseball cleats I was carrying and walked out the locker room door.

Coach Rodman jumped up, pushed the steel door open, and yelled, "OK, Olsen! Despite my better judgment, I am going to send you to play winter ball with the Key West Kites in the South Florida Winter League. Call the office and they'll make the necessary plane and long-term apartment reservations. You know, you really could make something of your career if it wasn't for your left-handedness, but it is impossible to change that now! I guess it is the way you were born! If nothing else, maybe you could change your stubbornness, or were you born with that too? "

⌂

"Congratulations! I'm glad to see that Coach Rodman finally believes in you." Susan Taylor, secretary in the Mitts' office, handed me my tickets for my flight from Milwaukee to Key West via Memphis, Tennessee.

"I have made a reservation for you on the Sunday morning flight. It's the cheapest fare they have. That way you can get settled in before you report Monday morning. The Kites

248

want you to report by 6:30 a.m. so they can issue the uniform and go over some of their procedures and rules with you."

Busily returning to her desk, dialing with her right index finger, she spoke over her shoulder, "I'm going to phone them with your itinerary. What jersey number would you like?"

In contrast to her kindness, tersely, I bellowed, "Good Lord Almighty! Can't anything go right around here? I want my lucky number 08, just like I've had since grade school. Get it for me!"

Slamming the receiver back onto its cradle, she spun rapidly in her chair, and, with a look that could skin a cat, she said, "Are you speaking vainly to God about your selfish wishes? I sure hope your time in Florida goes better than it has here. I pray that you might even start walking your talk! Mr. Olsen, you need to look for your Damascus Road and I'm not referring to one in Syria either!"

With that she grabbed her winter boots from below her desk, "It's already going on five o'clock; I need to get to church. I'll call them in the morning. You know its Wednesday night, don't you?" Before putting her office shoes in a paper sack, she purposely shook the dust from the heels. Continuing her testimony against me, "May God be merciful to you, son." Quietly praying I could hear her say, "Lord, if he has ears, let him hear!"

⌂

I tried to sleep for awhile; my 6:00 a.m. departure from Milwaukee's Billy Mitchell Field was very early. They first looked like Conestoga wagons racing for Oklahoma. I wasn't sure which way they were blowing as I peered out the small window of the Convair 540. Slowly I realized they were puffing upward and we were flying into the billowing clouds of a mid-south thunderstorm. Having never flown on an airplane, the bumps, rocks and rolls made me nauseous. I heard the collective moaning of my fellow passengers as I discharged my oatmeal breakfast into the small, barf bag.

Dressed smartly in a black suit, Stewardess Adrian quickly grabbed my bag and gave me a glass of ice – all in one fluid motion. Returning to the rear galley, she then quickly flushed the ventilation system with a rose fumigant. I was glad when our tires screeched, signaling our landing onto the hard runway.

Standing on the top landing of the air stair, Stewardess Adrian directed me toward the terminal doors. "Look for the departure information boards when you get inside." She then bid me farewell as I walked down the steps to the tarmac. Once inside the concourse, I began looking for the departure boards and information on my upcoming flight to Key West.

After a quick bathroom stop to cleanup, I reached in my pocket for a stick of Juicy Fruit gum. Passing by me in the wide corridor, Stewardess Adrian politely asked, "Are you feeling better now? I hope we can give you a smoother ride next time."

Walking to a vacant departure gate, a passing agent said to me, "You must be Mr. Olsen. St. Louis headquarters wired us to be on the lookout for you. There has been a mistake on your ticket. Whoever made your reservation scheduled you in here way too early. There's no Sunday morning departure to Key West. It is only on weekdays."

"Stupid woman!"

"You aren't referring to anyone in particular, like your wife or mother, are you? I didn't think so."

Realizing I had my foot and shoe in my mouth, I took a deep breath.

"My ticket says I am to connect at 8:30; isn't that a 30-minute layover? Look, even the departure time here on the board says 8:30!"

Not flinching, Customer Service Agent Zimke explained, "I'm sorry Mr. Olsen, the dark colored numbers mean 8:30 **p.m.** We should have you in Key West by midnight. As you know, there are thunderstorms in the area right now; I hope the skies clear by noon so we can send our originators out on time."

"What can I do for the next twelve hours?"

Agent Zimke suggested, "Do you know anyone in Memphis? There are cabs outside. Just be back here by 6:30 p.m. We'll have an update by then."

"Is Graceland open for tours?"

"Not on Sunday mornings. The cab is the only way to get there and that's $20 for a round trip."

Checking again, I confirmed I had only $25. "I won't have enough money in Key West if I spend it on a Memphis cab."

I resigned to sitting in the airport for 12 hours. Dropping into a nearby chair, I heard a voice over the loudspeaker say, "A Protestant worship service will be held in the airport Chapel beginning at 9:00 a.m. The Chapel is located near Gate 12 in the West Terminal. Come join us."

None of the food counters were open for business. Since my bags had already been checked to Key West, I carried only my introduction papers. Looking around, I realized I was sitting in the West Terminal at Gate 10. I decided to go to the Chapel.

"Mr. Olsen, correct?" gate agent Zimke questioned. "Welcome. Feel free to grab some coffee or orange juice and homemade coffee cake from the table. We won't start for another 20 minutes but you're welcome to go fellowship with the other passengers and airline and airport employees."

I saw the 50 or so chairs were all empty. What I hadn't seen was the 75 or so airline and airport employees fellowshipping around the coffee pots and pastries. It reminded me of my days back at St. Bart's.

At least 60 of the worshipers appeared to be employees of the airlines, all smartly dressed in their different colored uniforms. It suddenly hit me that if a blue law prevented outbound, Sunday morning flights, most of these people came into work early so they could worship together. It was truly a mission church within the airport.

"Welcome to the Memphis Airport Christian Church. We welcome you as fellow travelers. May God show you His path along His Way. Let us open in prayer. Gracious Father we have wandered here from all over this desert, from city and country..."

It was a service I will never forget. During this challenging time in my life, Chaplin and Pilot, Captain Luke Myers, moved the congregation as he spoke from I Corinthians 10:13 and I Peter 4:8. He repeatedly pleaded to the congregation to stand firm and resist Satan during these times of trial and temptation. With affirming responses, it was evident the congregation indeed was seeking forgiveness from their numerous trials and temptations – knowing love covers a multitude of sins.

I was one of only four guests, yet I felt like I had been a member of this body for decades. A tingling warm sensation flowed through my body as we shared the Lord's Supper. I was brought to tears as I realized that this church had successfully broken down all workplace barriers – and my own barriers – to live and fellowship in Christ.

Closing with the invitation, the Spirit suddenly came upon me when it included: "Is there anyone here who would like to be baptized?" Just as Paul heard the invisible voice, I too was answering. Surrounded by fellow believers, none of whom I have ever seen since, I stepped into the water contained within the makeshift baptismal. I came out a new man – having finally affirmed my earlier statement of faith with water baptism!

I spent the remainder of my time in the Chapel. As each member came in and out throughout the early afternoon, I began to understand what a Christian heart really meant. Uniformly, each addressed me, "Willis, my Brother in Christ".

Somewhere around 3:00 p.m. I heard a familiar voice from the loudspeaker: "Brother, I mean, Mr. Willis Olsen, please report to Gate 12."

Seeing Agent Zimke's warm smile behind the podium, I knew things were going to be all right when she said, "We've put you on a one stop through Tampa. Grab your paperwork and jump into my shuttle cart. Your new flight leaves in 20 minutes. They should be boarding shortly. We've already put your bags on board."

As I walked onto the airplane, I received an envelope from the lead stewardess addressed to "Mr. Willis Olsen, Flight 723". Inside, gate agent Zimke's message quoted Acts 22 – Paul's oration of defense given before the Jewish leaders. Agent Zimke had spoken from her heart, being most appreciative of my willingness to step forward, when I could have as easily ignored the original public address system announcement. She applauded that I too had been counted as a fellow Believer in the Body noting: "Following the morning service, the Elders affirmed you as an at-large member of the Memphis Airport Christian Church." She concluded her hand written note: "May your dreams also be His. Yours in Christ, Mrs. Linda Zimke".

Arriving in the hotel lobby at 7:30 p.m., I noticed a small paper bag sitting in the corner of my studio apartment.

The neatly tied paper bag contained two items – an eight ounce bag of Brach's orange slices and the New Testament Mom gave Uncle Harry when he was confirmed fifty three years earlier. The attached note said simply, "I think you forgot these! Love, Pesky".

Almost daily, throughout the winter baseball season, a care package arrived from Beaver Dam via Key West. In addition to being Mae Lynne's on-call delivery service, the Hendrickses attended every Kites game that winter. I had my own personal fan club.

1975

Coach Rodman's phone call took on a whole different significance when he called me at work in late February. "I hope all is going well. We've just signed some new recruits. They appear to have great potential. One, a catcher, we spoke to early last fall as a highly recommended recruit and a graduate of a military prep college baseball program near Chicago. I am confident he'll be in the starting lineup by the end of spring training. If he doesn't work out, I'm going to take another look at that Palm Area Technical College catcher I saw you play against in the national finals. He seemed like a pretty bright player. No team has signed him yet. You know he called all of the pitches for them. Something you should learn to do while you're in Florida."

I had to suppress my real thoughts. "The Palm Area catcher should fit right in. We enjoyed playing against him."

"What's that supposed to mean? You only played them three times."

Never disclosing my secret that this was the same catcher who repetitively called the same signs, I answered honestly, "Yeah, you're right; but we won the two we needed!"

⌂

It didn't hit me until I saw the back of his shirt, *B. Armstrong*. We had both arrived two hours early for the first spring practice. Mae Lynne needed our car; I wasn't sure why he was there early.

Tall with wide shoulders, he had slightly enlarged ears. I will never forget those ears. Ben would humor junior English by methodically tucking each ear into itself. Then, raising each eyebrow, and to the laughter of the class, each ear would pop back out. He was known to do either a double or single ear, depending on his desired impact. Not a disciplinarian, Miss Grainger never did figure out why the classroom burst into sudden fits of laughter – usually when she was about to make an important point.

"Ben, I can't…"

"Buddy," he interrupted, "I've followed your career beyond high school including Prairie Ridge, Port Washington, and now with the Mitts. You've had an impressive career, competing on several championship teams. Your thrown out stealing average has to be astronomical. I'm not sure where that record would be kept, but you must have the highest percentage in all of organized baseball, no matter what level."

"Well, I …"

He interrupted again, "Is it higher than 80%? Higher?"

Humbly I responded, "Yes, I've kept the statistic. It's over 83% since the night I was first called upon by Coach Ziegler: 150 attempts, 138 throw outs, and two unassisted double plays. I think it takes each team a while to figure out my left-handedness is not a hindrance to the team's defense."

Ben, changing the subject, declared: "I've got to tell you…I've been reborn, both from a personal and Christian perspective. What I did in the past, the Lord has forgiven. He died for all my sins, not just some, ignoring others. He has done the same for you!"

Still in shock, I responded, "Wow, what a witness!"

"Remember when you grabbed that blue beret I was wearing? You don't need to ask my forgiveness for that.

Truthfully, I need you to forgive me! You see, my dad didn't know that was not my hat. I found it in the theater department's costume closet; I was planning on using it as a prop for the spring play auditions. I didn't have the guts to stand up to my dad's rage. I just stood by and watched as you became the martyr. I hope you can forgive me for my childish lie of omission. Studying my Bible, I've since learned about the consequences of unforgiveness."

"Of course I forgive you Ben," I grabbed him into brotherly bear hug.

Wiping back tears, he remorsefully said, "Wow, a millstone has been taken from around my neck!"

"I know the feeling."

⌂

All during practice, I stewed over my every move. I was especially worried about the upcoming encounter. I clearly saw Ben's desire to fairly win the starting position, proving that I had pre-judged him unjustly. His throws were accurate. He called good pitches and I could see his poised leadership would surely motivate the team. Ben never missed an opportunity to praise a fellow player, never in an overbearing way, but genuinely with a gift of encouragement.

Blasting in the locker room door, I heard an unmistakably deep voice: "You about ready, Olsen?"

I had regretted hearing this all day. Mae Lynne was unable to pick me up after practice; we asked for Buster's help. Buster stopped dead in his tracks. His eyes bulged and his olive complexion became beet red.

Quickly breaking the ice, Ben spoke up, "Before you say anything, I want to ask you from the bottom of my reborn heart, please forgive me for my selfish actions that ruined your marriage. I have heard you have been reborn in Christ.

So have I! I believe many a foolish way has been forgiven by the risen and living Messiah. I ask you, as a brother, to forgive me too."

There was a long pause. Like me, I saw Buster had been caught totally off guard. Ben had confronted both of us. Now, for the first time in our lives, we learned we needed to walk our talk. Buster strolled slowly around the locker room bench and then abruptly sat on the very end, like he had mounted a horse.

"What can I say?" Holding back tears and turning directly toward Ben, Buster said, "I must be honest and confess to the both of you. I was as guilty as you. At that time, I lusted for any woman that walked, including Kitty. After I conquered Kitty, I looked for several others. Fortunately, I only carried out my lust in my mind. However, I still sinned." Standing, he then said, "When I asked for a personal relationship with my Savior, I began to walk out of that valley. Ben, I have seen my sins, too, and yes, I forgive you. I am equally yoked with Ruth. Together in Christ we have put our pasts behind us. We are looking with hope for our earthly life together and our eternal years in His mansion."

Funny, a locker room is not an unusual place to see three young men cry − although it's usually over a loss. Today, however, it was over something found. Spontaneously, we put our arms around each other and began to pray out loud for each other, our renewed friendship, and newfound brotherhood. We walked three abreast toward the doors, with arms on each other's shoulders.

Ben stopped abruptly, and tearfully responded, "Buddy, after Dad went to the revival, he continued to grow in the Lord. I have never told you this, but I was in the back of the tent that night. It changed my life too − it just took a little longer."

Ben then turned to Buster and said: "Buster, unlike your relationship with Ruth, Mom and Dad were never equally yoked. As Dad grew stronger in Christ, Mom's necklines dropped lower and her skirt hems got higher. She began to spend every evening at the Providence Bowling Alley, drinking her life away. Her tears were heavily concealed behind her made-up mask. About a year and a half after Dad's rebirth, Mom moved out of the house. Eventually, she moved in with a young man fifteen years her junior. Although I can never prove it, I believe their relationship is one of imprudent passion followed by physical and verbal abuse – a constant merry-go-round. Together they live in that twisted muddle."

I believe the Beaver Tail Inn bartender had great expectations for the three jovial men as they entered his door that Tuesday night. With just a few regulars sitting at the bar, he soon saw that we were more interested in talking than drinking. One pitcher of Seven Up, a large batch of onion rings and three bigmouth burgers were to be his only order. With only the four of us still there at 1:00 a.m., it was evident he was surprised with his $5 tip. He never knew how he enabled us.

⌂

Since the start of the season, Louie Peltier's earned run average rose to over 4.73. He was destined to, at best, another mediocre year. His potential to repeat his all-star rookie year and his left-handedness, probably kept him around longer than it should have.

With the Mitts struggling, it was easy to see Coach Rodman had not earned the respect of his players. Louie and I had chalked up two wins early in the season but we too struggled to get the next two wins. We had a 4–4 record going into the July 4th weekend.

It was a particularly hot, humid night. A winning streak could bring us closer to league contention. However, after a series of bad decisions, we were on the brink of the cellar when we played our second game in two days against the Oshkosh Oaks. Coach Rodman's decisions were openly challenged by some of the more senior players.

Louie pitched well through the first seven innings. I noticed he had changed his pitching delivery, his altered motion now favored his left wrist. I asked the umpire for time; he reluctantly agreed to stop play.

Approaching the mound I asked Louie, "You've changed your delivery. What's the matter?"

"I can't grasp the ball tightly. A pain runs right up my arm to my shoulder and then down my butt to my ankle. It started last night. The aspirin I took this morning seemed to have taken care of it until now. It's come back with a vengeance!"

Overhearing only part of the story, Coach Rodman abruptly said, "I think it's all in your head! Go sit on the bench. No better yet...," he motioned to right field towards Tyrone Bowman, "Go out to right field and think about you, I mean *your*, 'pain in the butt'."

Turning to the approaching Tyrone, Coach Rodman said, "You can pitch, right?" With that he slammed the ball into Tyrone's glove. Known as an aggressive fielder and lightening fast base stealer, I knew Tyrone had never pitched before in his life!

"Well I can sure..." Coach Rodman did an awkward pirouette and returned to the dugout. Slamming his fist against the masonry wall, he realized he had called on the wrong player. It was too late by then.

Tyrone asked me, "What are the signs?"

I responded, "They are too complicated for you to learn in 30 seconds; aim where I set my mitt, like you're in an arcade."

With that change, Oshkosh began rally after rally. A gritty team, we did everything possible to get back into the game. Even though Coach Rodman believed big bats would keep us in the game, secretly we players ignored his signs and looked back toward our small ball strategy for success.

What an opportunity! Our hitters had successfully loaded the bases. Two outs were a hindrance, but it would take three to extinguish our comeback. Having a three run base clearing triple earlier in the game, the likelihood of a grand slam was well beyond my dreams. Following Louie's earlier example, I closed my eyes for prayer. The umpire yelled, "Batter up! – Hey, stop your praying. I said, Batter up!"

I fouled the first ball high over the first base stands. The second pitch was a marshmallow. Getting all of it, I sent it sailing well beyond the right center field wall.

"Batter's out!"

Half way down the first base line, I spun around and yelled: "What?"

"Jesus Christ! That's the second time you've thrown your bat at me." I could see the bat lying behind him. Unlike most umpires, he consistently moved to his right for a left-handed batter putting him in the direct line of either the swung bat or hitter.

Getting nose to nose, I started screaming, "What did you say? Are you calling in help from my Savior and Friend? You're going to need it! I can't believe you don't have enough experience to realize you need to get out of the direct line of the released bat. Your responsibility is to judge the play from a safe distance!"

"Why you Bible thumping punk!" With that he shoved me to the ground. Coach Rodman flew out of the dugout along with the rest of the team. Both adults engaged in verbiage you would have only heard in a barroom brawl. Looking at Coach Rodman, he accused, "He tried to hit me with his bat. When he took a swing at me I shoved him to the ground! He's just too big for his Bible thumping britches! I had heard before he was *Mr. Religious*." Then, throwing his arm into the air, he yelled, "Coach, he is out of here!"

Coach Rodman was livid. Pulling me aside in the dugout, he scolded me saying, "Olsen, you're probably thinking you should have stayed in bed when you had the chance! Not only did you assault the umpire you got yourself thrown out of the game! I won't let you play catcher anymore. If you're lucky I'll play you in right field – providing I ever let you play again. At least you'll be less of a problem out there."

Antagonistically, he continued his lecture saying: "You know what your problem is Olsen? You are a goody two shoes. It was good to see you be a little more aggressive, but tonight you took it too far. You don't have a balanced disposition. Besides being thrown out, it will likely cost me $100. Unlike you players, we coaches sign a code of conduct letter. Any breaches result in additional fines."

He probably was right: I should have stayed in bed when I had the chance. My heart was telling me I was in the wrong place at the wrong time.

We lost the game by four runs – the team was unable to get anyone on base in the ninth.

Since the league initially believed the altercation had been instigated by the player, I was ejected from the game and my statistics for the night were voided. I was ordered to sit out two games without pay. The Club paid the league a $100 fine which in turn came directly out of my paycheck. Coach Rodman was also fined $100. He, however, received an anonymous check for $100.

Later, several fans from Oshkosh independently confirmed that the umpire rolled the bat behind him when everyone else was focused on the long ball. Three Oaks fans sent the league office affidavits of the proceedings. Oaks third baseman Steve Gregston testified before a closed door hearing of the League directors. He spoke the truth. The umpire's contract was immediately terminated.

Both Louie and I began to see Coach Rodman would call this "another building year". So it was on Friday morning, August 1, 1975, my baseball career ended when the Beaver Dam Mitts released me from the team. Baseball's ongoing experiment with left-handed catchers, and my attempt at joining that exclusive fraternity, abruptly ended.

⌂

Old family friend, Bethany Collins, phoned us when she entered Wisconsin as a transfer student from Middle Tennessee Junior College where she had attended the two prior years. Although a beautiful girl, at first it seemed she just couldn't overcome her strong Mid-South accent and tomboy appearance. As a result, she didn't have much of a social life. Instead, she had diligently concentrated on her studies.

Providentially crossing paths on campus one spring afternoon, Mae Lynne decided it was time to set Bethany and Ben Armstrong up on a blind date. Shepherd's Young Christians Club had organized a bus trip to the Southern Gospel Music Festival held in a church auditorium on Milwaukee's south side. Bethany readily accepted the invitation. We expected her to feel right at home. What we didn't know was how well she would fit in. It was apparent to all of us who surrounded them, Bethany and Ben were truly meant for each other as God's providence and timing began to work upon them at this beginning of their courtship.

Epilogue

Mae Lynne surprised Bethany by presenting her with a $500 gift certificate to the finest bridal dress boutique in Madison. The ever-prudent Mae Lynne had saved all of her grandmother's large inheritance for discretionary outlays such as this. The two women then went on an all-day shopping spree, much to the amazement of Ben and me.

After a year and a half of dating, Ben, who was no longer in baseball, and Bethany were married in Beaver Dam on Friday evening, September 3, 1976. Mae Lynne's orange prom dress that had become her wedding dress now became her matron of honor dress.

Following the small ceremony, the new Mr. and Mrs. Ben Armstrong moved to the mountains of Tennessee where Bethany took a job as an engineer in a chemical plant. Through a family inheritance, Barney Collins had received a large land tract adjacent to their original farm – perfect for long-term leasing to the newlyweds, both of whom were ready to begin their tranquil futures in the Smokey Mountains.

Never missing an opportunity, Bethany soon became a champion rodeo barrel racer, fulfilling her lifelong dream. Because of his military prep school and ROTC, Ben was called into the Army but did not serve overseas. With the Vietnam conflict in the past, Ben exchanged active duty for a long-term commitment in the Tennessee National Guard.

Mom, before her own death, was instrumental in bringing her sister-in law to Christ. Although Aunt Amanda remained in the City, she drove to Providence on Sunday afternoons the first few years following Uncle Harry's death. The last time I saw Aunt Amanda alive was in her tiny room in a rundown, smelly, Chicago nursing home. Despite all of Uncle Harry's accumulated wealth, including their prestigious lakefront home, her only remaining possessions were an undersized dresser containing a few sets of clothes, her heavily worn Bible, and a framed picture of her Savior, Jesus Christ. The nursing staff reported she was all alone when she died, just after sunset, in her room on Thanksgiving Day. She lived on this earth 82 years.

Aunt Amanda's funeral, that following Monday morning, turned out to be the last beautiful fall day of the year. The magnificent colors of the maple, hickory, and ash leaves became only a memory as a strong northwesterly cold front came thundering into town late in the afternoon. Aunt Amanda was laid to rest beside Uncle Harry on a wooded knoll in Peace Gardens Cemetery, just outside of Providence. As I watched her casket lowered into the grave, I knew only her body remained on earth, her soul had already checked into her mansion in Heaven.

KNOWLEDGE

"You hadn't told me until now that you affirmed your faith through believer's baptism; I had no idea. I knew you'd become a changed man. I am so proud of you! I wish I could have been there, but I guess it was between you and the Spirit that day."

Slowly we walked from the ice cream parlor back towards our upstairs apartment. We were both very discouraged about the fact that I had been cut from the Mitts. On the upside, we knew there would be no more summers of bus rides and sharing cheap, stinky motel rooms with four other players.

Mae Lynne spoke again: "You know we've come a long way since you took me to the Spring Prom in 1968."

Reminiscing I said, "Do you remember our first date? I was shaking in my boots when your dad met me at the front door. I swear he had a shotgun behind his leg."

Laughing hysterically, she said, "He did! It was only a .410 – just enough to knock down a pigeon. He said you looked so nervous; he wanted to see how you would react – if you saw it. He knew you like a son. I guess that is what you were to become."

We had walked this route several times before, but something was different this time. Normally the sidewalk was well-lit. We discovered, for some strange reason, the twelve streetlights that normally lit the winding path, were totally darkened. The air was brisk; a northwest headwind seemed to pick up velocity as we made the gentle climb. Pulling the hood up on my jacket, I tugged the front zipper upward to my chin. The air smelled of rain. Always prepared for the worst, I pulled a small flashlight from my front pocket.

Concentrating on our every step, Mae Lynne broke the silence, "You amaze me. You're always so prepared for the little things, but being cut has really devastated you. I have prayed for you every night. I just want to see you with a joyful heart."

"You're right. God, I pray that I'll find some direction to my life… and soon!"

HIS WILL

As the sidewalk rounded a curve we began to climb the steeper grade. A small monument sign remained illuminated amidst the surrounding darkness. What appeared to be new was a well lit bronze ENTRANCE sign that caught both of our eyes. We had seen the winding paved drive in daylight before but had not seen its entrance glowing under the cover of total darkness. We did not know where it led. Since we had no urgent plans at home, I heard that impish voice I first heard so long ago: "Wanna look?"

Tightly grasping each other's hand, we detected a small, brick and stone building through the leaf barren oaks and maples. Approaching the top of the drive, a street sign contained an arrow that pointed to the right. It read: Damascus Road.

Just beyond, bronze letters on a stone monument wall read:

Damascus Road College and Seminary

A Christian Assembly

Founded 1975

We continued our darkened journey toward the building – Administration Hall and Chapel. On its cast bronze plaque, we read the names of the Board of Directors. Most notably, in large block letters was:

CHAIRMAN OF THE BOARD – JESUS CHRIST

As we glanced down the names, we soon realized we were truly in the midst of a miracle. There, in the middle, without title, was the name:

Mrs. Sara Ann Morse Ziegler

Prairie Ridge, IL.

We were sure the landlord thought we were drunk with alcohol, not in the Spirit as we truly were, when we burst into the side door leading to the stairway to our apartment.

Hovering over the phone, I quickly dialed and asked the directory assistance operator for Prairie Ridge, Illinois. We were visibly disappointed as she told us there was no number listed for Tim Ziegler.

Inspired again, Mae Lynne deafly shouted, "Quick, ask her for Joe Morse!"

Again we heard, "I'm sorry, no listing. No more please, phone company policy".

After a brief pause, in what was a distinctively different voice, we heard: "I do however have a listing for S A M Ziegler. Do you want me to dial it? "

We clutched the single headset as the connection was made. After the fourth ring we heard the familiar voice: "Hello, the Lord's Blessings to You."

Feeling a bit awkward I mumbled, "Mrs. Ziegler? This is…"

"Halleluiah Jesus! …I have prayed for this call for the past three years!"

Mrs. Ziegler went on to tell us of Coach's mid-winter tragic death in 1972 at the hands of a drunk driver who was leaving White Pines Inn and Supper Club. The driver, Erik Malander according to Mrs. Ziegler, was paralyzed and confined to a wheel chair. She recalled his latest girlfriend, a young Latin woman named Rodriquez, was killed when she catapulted out of the car's bucket seat. "I can't remember the woman's first name. Mom said she was Moises Cortez's sister-in-law." Mrs. Ziegler told us the police report said a seat belt may have prevented her death, had she been wearing one. "The State has since closed the Inn because it had been caught several times serving setups to underage patrons."

She went on to tell us about her father's fatal heart attack that same year. He died at the age of 71. With her Provost appointment becoming permanent on January 1, 1972, she and Coach had just purchased a home in Prairie Ridge when Coach was tragically killed. She went on to say: "Coach and I thought we were returning in order to take care of my ailing parents." Sobbing loudly and heartbroken, she said: "Tragically, both Tim and Dad died before the dedication of the baseball field!" She told us how she had lost our address when she moved into her parent's home with her mother after both men had died.

Gaining strength, she told us, "Then following God's purpose, a few others and I received God's call to start the college and seminary on land entrusted to the newly formed school by Daryl Ethel's father." She again shared how she believed all things were intertwined for God's holy purpose.

Sobbing loudly, but speaking distinctly, she said, "Willis, you know you are another part of that purpose. My assistant has been trying to locate your Dad or your Uncle Marvin so I could offer you the newly created position of baseball coach and athletic director. Before we are able to start our athletic programs however, I want you to be the Project Manager for the construction of our new campus buildings and athletic facilities. Since you said you received the Lord's call to ministry, you can enroll in the Seminary when you complete your undergraduate studies. We have an undergraduate agreement with Stephen the Martyr College in Madison. We can meet next week to finalize your studies and contract."

"What? Are you on staff here? But you live in Prairie Ridge. Are you offering me a position on the college staff without having me at least fill out an application or send in a resume?"

"I'll see you on Monday afternoon if you want to go through the paperwork formalities. Willis, this is the Will of God; He lives in a paperless society. Remember, He also writes in stone so you need not worry."

Clearing up my questions, she continued, "Besides assuming the newly created position of Dean of Staff, I am to become the Interim Chancellor. I will be moving to Beaver Dam next month. Let's see, you'll need an assistant coach; I have one budgeted. Louie Peltier and his Godly wife Sue still live in town, correct?" I suddenly recalled her forthrightness.

"Mae Lynne, there is also an opening for a medical intern at East Central Hospital and Clinics. I know the Chief of Staff. Does the name, Dr. Joe Morse, Jr., sound like he could be someone you can count on?"

Without waiting for an answer, Mrs. Ziegler affirmed: "Yes, he is my brother. You met him a long time ago. He remembers you from Hendrick's Drug Store. He told me you once lent him the only money you had in your purse, a ten dollar bill. He realized he had misplaced his billfold just as he was leaving Providence to go to the airport. He said you told him you didn't ask to be repaid. You said you knew his sister well and you were overjoyed he had come to visit. That impression has stayed with him all these years."

Covering the mouthpiece, Mae Lynne turned to me and said, "Will Olsen, you sure know how to pray! When you place the call, God listens!" Drawing the phone call to a close, the three of us agreed to meet Mrs. Ziegler at noon on Monday.

Mrs. Ziegler asked, "Maybe you know a place that serves good homemade lasagna?"

Like it had been planned all along, Mae Lynne offered, "I know just the place! It's cozy up here but we would love to have you and you don't need to help Will with dishes. How do orange slices sound for dessert?"

"One last thing Willis, I am no longer Mrs. or Doctor Ziegler to you. My friends call me Sara."

We hung up the phone, humbly falling to our knees, we began to pray. I opened my eyes and asked Mae Lynne, "Do you have a tingling sensation all over your body?"

Keeping focus she replied, "I sure do, now close your eyes again!"

"…amen and amen!" Rising to her feet, Mae Lynne shouted, "My Will is His Will! Thank you Jesus!" As I too arose, she repeated, "My Will is His Will! Kind of catchy isn't it? Oops, sorry about the baseball reference."

Realizing she had likely awoken the landlord, Mae Lynne softly grasped my right hand as we began to *"walk in a manner worthy of the Lord, to please Him in all respects, bearing fruit in every good work and increasing in the knowledge of God"; Colossians 1:10.*